INDISCRETIONS

Gail Ranstrom

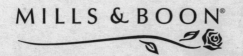

MILLS & BOON®

First published in Great Britain 2007
Harlequin Mills & Boon Limited,
Eton House, 18-24 Paradise Road, Richmond, Surrey TW9 1SR

© Gail Ranstrom 2006

ISBN-13: 978 0 263 85174 8
ISBN-10:   0 263 85174 5

Set in Times Roman 10½ on 12¼ pt.
04-0507-84629

Printed and bound in Spain
by Litografia Rosés S.A., Barcelona

Gail Ranstrom was born and raised in Missoula, Montana, and grew up spending the long winters lost in the pages of books that took her to exotic locales and interesting times. That love of the 'inner voyage' eventually led to her writing. She has three children, Natalie, Jay and Katie, who are her proudest accomplishments. Part of a truly bi-coastal family, she resides in Southern California with her two terriers, Piper and Ally, and has family spread from Alaska to Florida.

Recent novels by the same author:

A WILD JUSTICE
SAVING SARAH
A CHRISTMAS SECRET
  (in *The Christmas Visit* anthology)
THE RAKE'S REVENGE
THE MISSING HEIR
THE COURTESAN'S COURTSHIP

For Shirley, Fritzie, Winnie and Sadie,
who taught me all I needed to know about being a
lady. And for Cheryl, Tanya, Christine and Sandi, who
taught me all I needed to know about being a woman.

And with everlasting gratitude
to Lisa, Suzi, Eileen and Tracy.

Prologue

London
August 11, 1815

The second blow sent sudden pain racing along Elise's nerves to explode in her brain. She cringed and raised her arms to protect her head. Striking back only angered him further. Oh, but the last little shred of pride and self-respect she still possessed demanded that she defend herself, no matter what the cost. No matter what the consequences.

She skittered backward until she cleared his reach and then staggered to her feet. "No, my lord! Back away now, before I call for help."

Her husband laughed at her hollow threat. "The servants won't come, madam. They'd lose their living, and they know it. And you, pathetic cow that you are, will not leave me because you'd have to leave your brat behind."

"Your heir," she corrected.

"*Heir,*" Barrett snarled. "You gave me a puny, sickly squalling little brat. That's what I get for marrying a chit barely out of the schoolroom. But you're going to remedy that now, aren't you, Elise? Spread your legs and I might not hit you again."

He unfastened his trousers and bile rose in her stomach. His eyes were wild and his breath stank of whiskey. If he touched her, she would vomit. She'd had enough of his brutal lovemaking. She shook her head. "Go back to your mistress, Barrett. There is no comfort for you here."

He launched at her with a strangled cry. "By God, your brother did not warn me of your stupidity when I bought you. Give me value for my money. Do your duty!"

Her back hit the wall, trapping her. A thin wail drifted from the adjacent room. Their voices had woken William. She turned toward the sound. The governess had quit after Barrett's last fit of temper, and she hadn't been able to find a replacement. "Let me go to him, my lord. He needs me."

"Your duty is to *me,* Elise, and 'tis time you learned it." He turned and headed for the adjoining door.

Terrified, she followed. "Wait, my lord. Let him cry. I…I will give you what you want."

"Aye, you will. When I'm done here." He threw the door open and crossed to the bed. Seizing the three-year-old, he held him aloft. "Is this what you love best, madam?"

"Barrett, *please,*" she choked, fear clogging her throat. She tore off her wrapper, exposing herself in her thin nightdress. "Put him back and…and I…"

"I'll have it anyway, madam. It's mine to take as I please." He tucked little William under one arm and headed to the window. "But first I'll rid us of this useless appendage."

Oh, dear God! He meant to throw William out the window and he was drunk enough to do it! He had his back to her and, without thinking, she seized a brass candlestick and hit him over the head. He dropped to his knees and William tumbled onto the woven rug, still crying and hiccupping.

Barrett turned toward her, hatred in his eyes and a trickle of blood oozing down his cheek from his temple. "You will pay for that!" He staggered to his feet, the child forgotten in his fury.

It was hopeless. Barrett was insane and he knew her weakness. William would never be safe. His lips drew back in a snarl and his hands stretched out for her. He no longer meant to claim his marital rights—he meant to kill her. She fled back to her room and he tackled her, bringing her down with a breathless thud. Her forehead hit the marble hearth and her head swam as blood streamed from the gash in her skin.

Frantic, knowing that if he killed her there would be no one left to protect William from his father, she groped above her head, seeking anything she could use to stop him.

She gripped the fire poker and rolled faceup.

Barrett's expression was a study in madness. Spittle formed at the corners of his mouth as he ripped her nightdress away from her breasts. Sobbing, she brought the poker down on his shoulder and again on his head. And again. And again.

He collapsed on her and was still, his weight compressing the air from her lungs. Still weeping and panting, she dropped the poker and pushed his weight to the side. She wriggled free, clutching the gaping sides of her nightdress together and using a shred to wipe the blood from her forehead.

William's cry was frenzied now, almost a scream. She half crawled, half stumbled back to the other room, gathered him up from the floor and held him close. Still in a daze, she crooned and rocked back and forth, murmuring reassurances.

"Hush, William. Hush. I won't let anything happen to you."

When she'd soothed the toddler, she put him back in his bed and returned to her room. Barrett still lay facedown and unmoving in front of the fireplace. There was a wide split on the back of his head and his skull showed through a gap in his hair. A widening puddle of blood had formed on the hearth. A clock in a distant part of the house struck midnight.

Her stomach convulsed. She had killed her husband! She groped for the chamber pot, emptied her stomach and then wiped the cold sweat from her forehead. There would be hell to pay! Barrett's younger brother, Alfred, would take William away, then see that she was arrested and hanged. Alfred had always been ambitious for his own sons. Elise would not put it past the man to eliminate William so his own son could inherit the title and wealth.

No. No, she wouldn't let that happen. She staggered to her dressing room and donned a dark blue dress, then pulled her valise down from an upper shelf. With no particular plan, she threw a few serviceable gowns and the contents of her jewel chest into the case, then carried it to William's room and packed the necessary items for him. There would be a ship leaving the docks. Any ship. It didn't matter where it was going. She'd go to hell if she had to.

Chapter One

London
September 1, 1820

Reginald Hunter, sixth Earl of Lockwood, regarded the undersecretary of the Foreign Office with doubt. "I don't know, Lord Eastman. I'm with the Home Office. How can I help you?"

"The lines between the Home and Foreign Offices have blurred recently, especially in the West Indies. St. Claire is a British colony, which would put it under the auspices of the Home Office, but since we are dealing with other nationalities and subjects, the Foreign Office has taken charge."

Hunt settled into the deep overstuffed chair across from Lord Eastman and accepted a small goblet of brandy from the footman. What could the man be about to say that required them to meet at their club instead of the government offices? Either Eastman wanted him drunk, or he had a concern with security at the office.

He cupped the goblet in his right hand and warmed the deep red liquid. "Did Castlereagh inform you that I've tendered my resignation to the Home Office?" The last thing he wanted on the eve of his retirement from public service was to become embroiled in someone else's problem. He'd paid his dues, and an extra measure besides. What more could they ask than his soul?

"Yes, your resignation." Eastman nodded. "That's why we were hoping to persuade you to join us."

"Thank you for the confidence, but why would I trade one dangerous job for another? I'm weary of risking my life at the turn of a corner. And now that we've finally dealt with—"

"The white slaver. Yes, heard about that. Just a week or so ago, wasn't it?"

"That was the last loose end. I can quit in good conscience now, take my seat in the Lords and settle down."

Eastman sipped his own brandy. "You've barely reached your apex, Lockwood," he said, using Hunt's title. "This assignment is a little plum. Easy as pie and something you could do in your sleep. Think of it as a holiday."

In his experience, nothing the government asked of him was that simple. "Then have someone else go on holiday."

"Has to be done on the hush. Very sensitive, as it is a part of an ongoing investigation. You're known for your discretion."

Discreet? Is that what they were calling assassins now? Would discretion reclaim the soul he'd forfeited to do the dirty but necessary jobs that other men refused?

Ah, but he was intrigued in spite of himself. And now he was sure the Foreign Office had a traitor. Why else would they need a man of his "talents"? "Is your leak here or in St. Claire?"

Eastman frowned and lowered his voice. "We don't know. We need an outsider for this, and your name came up since you have holdings in St. Claire. Only natural that you'd want to visit and check on your investments, eh?"

Hunt sighed. "Tell me about this 'little plum' you want me to look into."

"Pirates."

The answer so surprised him that he coughed, drawing the attention of a few quiet occupants of the club library. He cleared his throat and whispered, "Easy? What the hell is easy about pirates?"

"The Caribbean is rife with them. These are a particularly ruthless and bloodthirsty lot and we need to put them down like the rabid vermin they are."

And there it was. They wanted him to "put down" the rabid vermin. *Need someone without a conscience? Bring Lockwood in.* "I'm out of that business, Eastman."

"We're only asking you to gather intelligence, Lockwood. See if you can find out where the pirates are based and who is feeding them information and ship movements. Find our leak. And plug it."

"They aren't likely to be based at a single point. And you must know who their informants are by now."

"Only that they are British."

Hunt digested this information for a moment. "Why St. Claire and not Jamaica or Barbados?"

"We already have operatives there, but they are making no headway. We need someone with a perfect right and reason to be on St. Claire. Ask questions. Cozy up to the locals. The officials. Find out what they're hiding. Only contact us if you have an emergency or urgent news, and go through me or my clerk, Langford."

Hunt sat back in his chair and sighed. He hadn't visited the plantation on St. Claire in ten years. Maybe it was time.

Eastman leaned forward. "It won't inconvenience you too long, Lockwood. Present yourself to Governor Bascombe and his chargé, Mr. Doyle, for introductions. Poke around a fortnight. A month at most. If the opportunity presents itself, handle the problem. Then back to England and on with your life."

Handle the problem? God, he wanted out. Out of the ugly underbelly of government intrigues and foreign machinations.

Apparently reading Hunt's hesitation, Eastman tried a new appeal. "Every time a ship is taken or sunk, we hear the groans all over London. We wouldn't ask if there weren't so many underwriters losing their drawers over this and if prices for imported goods weren't rising even as we speak."

With a sinking feeling that he'd just been sucked into another vortex, Hunt nodded.

St. Claire Island, West Indies
October 9, 1820

Though the journey had been quick and uneventful, Hunt was glad to set foot on solid ground again. He had a full list of things to do today—buy a horse, call on Governor Bascombe, rent a room at the local inn and meet his contact— but first he needed to take the lay of the land.

He shrugged out of his woolen jacket and draped it over his arm. The first thing that struck him as he walked the streets of San Marco was how truly international the town had become. A mixture of languages and accents buzzed around him as he strolled the cobbled streets.

He found an inn, several taverns, chandlers, locksmiths, haberdashers and greengrocers. Midway down Broad Street, he spied a tidy stone building with a divided door—the top half open to admit the morning breeze—and a wide front window with *Pâtisserie* lettered in black script. At the bottom of the window, in smaller letters, was the information, *Mrs. Hobbs, Proprietress*. A baker's rack stood in the window to display a stunning array of pastries and breads.

This would be a good place to start. Bakeries, as much as taverns, were often the hub of gossip and news. He'd once uncovered a pickpocket operation being run out of a bakery in Cheapside. He opened the lower half of the door and entered, setting the shop bell a-jingle. A mouthwatering smell wafted from the back and, along with the sound of feminine laughter, enticed him.

A woman, using a towel to protect her hands from burning, carried a tray of biscuits from the back room. The task had her complete attention as she slid the pan onto the counter, and Hunt used the moment to study her.

Mouthwatering. Yes. Exactly. Sleek brown hair that fell halfway down her back and glinted streaks of sun was tied at her nape with a green ribbon. Her figure was neither thin nor stout, but definitely voluptuous, and a soft smile lifted the corners of those full rose-tinted lips. She was somewhere in her midtwenties, a head shorter than he and, when she turned toward him, he was stunned by the deep green eyes that rivaled her hair ribbon. Her features were a study in perfect symmetry. Greek sculptors would have done mayhem to carve her likeness.

A blush stole up her cheeks, a sure sign she had noticed his interest. "Is there something I can do for you?" she asked as she wiped her hands on a crisp apron. "I'm Mrs. Hobbs."

Yes. Dear God, at least a dozen things she could do for him, and several she was doing at this very moment without even trying. Even her voice raised the fine hairs on his arms.

"Sir?"

"Oh, sorry," he said. "I've come for something sweet."

She smiled again, but this time his heart bumped. Then she glanced away, almost as if she were afraid to look at him too long. "Sweet? Well, then, we have cherry and blueberry tarts, buns with cinnamon and raisins, sweet biscuits, lemon and ginger biscuits and, if you care to wait, biscuits with a wee bit of chocolate. Oh, and pineapple cakes."

While he was still mulling over his choices, another woman

peeked out from the back room. Shorter, plumper and younger than Mrs. Hobbs, this woman was almost as lovely. He had the sudden notion that the wares at *Pâtisserie* could taste like chalk and the bakery would still do a brisk business.

As if sensing his thoughts, Mrs. Hobbs lifted a biscuit off the tray with a spatula and held it out to him. "Compliments of Pâtisserie, sir." She turned her attention to the woman in the back room. "Do you need something, Mrs. Breton?" she asked.

"I just came to see if we have shelf space up front." She glanced at the baker's rack in the window and nodded. With a shy glance in Hunt's direction, she disappeared again.

He took the offered biscuit, still warm from the oven, and shifted it from one hand to the other until it cooled enough to eat. The first bite convinced him that he was in heaven. He watched Mrs. Hobbs's reaction as he ate the delicacy. Her lips parted ever so slightly and her chin lifted a fraction of an inch as if tilting upward to receive a kiss. Oh, would that he could! But, no. She was waiting for his verdict.

"Delectable," he pronounced. "Make that a dozen biscuits, Mrs. Hobbs."

She blinked and nodded, the spell broken. Turning again, she ripped a length of brown paper off a roll, placed the biscuits in the center and tied the package with a length of French blue ribbon.

Mrs. Hobbs took his crown and opened a drawer beneath the counter. "I fear my change is limited. Do you have anything smaller, sir?"

Actually, to his embarrassment, he had something growing larger by the minute. "Sorry, Mrs. Hobbs. Keep the change."

"Oh, no. That is excessive, sir."

The gleam of a gold band on her left hand caught his attention as she withdrew every coin in her till. Of course. *Mrs.*

Hobbs. Damn the luck. The most charming shopgirl he'd ever seen, and she was unavailable.

She held her hand out with the change from the till. "Is there anything else I can get you?"

"Not at the moment, Mrs. Hobbs."

When her eyes met his, she shivered, dropped the coins in his palm and broke the contact. "I shall get change, sir. If you will come back later, I will have it for you."

Chains and an anchor wouldn't keep him away. "Count on it, Mrs. Hobbs."

Hannah Breton elbowed Daphne in the ribs as they craned their heads out the half door to watch the tall stranger walk back down Broad Street. "You've brought another visitor low with your charms, Daphne."

She'd brought *him* low? She rather thought it was the other way around. It was a rare occurrence, indeed, when a man could so take her by surprise that she could not think. She must have looked an absolute fool.

"You should have mentioned you are a widow," Hannah continued.

"Even if I were interested—which I am not—he did not even bother to introduce himself. Besides, I do not want a man."

"And a crying shame, if you ask me," Hannah teased. "You use that gold ring to keep them away. When are you going to take it off? There's certainly no shortage of men for a woman like you." Hannah sighed, then glanced back down the street. "But not many with eyes that blue."

Not blue. Deep, deep periwinkle. Almost violet. And it should be a crime for a man to have lashes so dark and long.

But his eyes hadn't been his best feature. No, that would be his smile. Sensual lips drew back to reveal straight, even teeth and a tiny dimple in his left cheek. Almost boyish, and

completely charming. Daphne always noted a man's smile—
or the lack of it. Men who did not smile made her very
nervous. She always suspected them of an ill nature.

Hannah chuckled and nudged her with an elbow. "There,
that little sigh gave you away. And if you do not want a
husband, who's to say you cannot take a lover? You're alone,
after all."

She shivered. Impossible! For so many reasons. And
she'd never even been tempted before looking into those
amazing eyes.

When she'd seen the *Gulf Stream* in the harbor this
morning, she knew there would be strangers in San Marco—
and she knew they'd be gone soon. The dark, compelling
stranger was no exception. No one ever came to stay on St.
Claire. And that was exactly why she *did*.

A knock on the kitchen door interrupted Daphne's
thoughts. The egg delivery, no doubt. Hannah put her spoon
down and went to open the door.

"Here they are!" their visitor exclaimed. "The treasure of
St. Claire."

"My goodness! Captain Gilbert! Where have you been?"
Hannah asked, an expression of pleasure curving her lips.

"Around the world and back again," he teased. "But I came
to see you all the moment I could."

"How long will you be here this time?"

"A week. Perhaps a fortnight. Need to take on cargo and
make a few repairs before I return to England."

"Then we'd best stock up on pineapple cakes." Hannah
smoothed her apron as she went back to her kettle.

Daphne faced the captain. He was graying and tall, had a
warm smile and clear blue eyes with creases at the corners
from squinting into the sun. "Hello, Captain Gilbert. Nice to
see you again."

"*How* nice?" he asked, tilting his head to one side.

She laughed. He knew she was always happy to see him, and not just because he always brought her an issue or two of the London *Times*. He was the kindest man she knew. "Hannah, would you fetch the captain a pineapple cake?"

Hannah nodded. "Why don't you take Mrs. Hobbs out back for a little catch up, Captain? I'll bring you a nice cup of tea."

Daphne lifted her apron over her head and slapped a puff of flour from her patterned skirt before following Captain Gilbert to the small courtyard outside the back door.

He took a seat at the little wrought iron table and laid the newspapers on his lap. She knew he wanted conversation. He had once confided that he missed female conversation since he was always at sea and his wife had died many years ago.

"Tell me, Captain, how was your voyage and what have you been doing?"

He fell silent as Hannah brought a tray with a teapot, cups, sugar, milk and lemon, and a small pineapple cake on a delicate china plate. She raised her eyebrows at their silence and left as quickly as she could. Hannah would want an accounting of the conversation later.

Knowing his preferences by now, Daphne poured the tea and added a bit of sugar and a squeeze of lemon. He took the cup and sipped, then nodded his approval.

"Working hard, Mrs. Hobbs. It is becoming more and more difficult for an honest man to make a living. But I get by. Made enough last trip to carry me through another voyage. My underwriters are charging an absurd price to insure my cargo. Damn pirates." He sighed and shrugged. "But what else can I do?"

"Not much, I suppose," she agreed. "I fear goods from home are costing me dearly, too. You wouldn't believe what I pay for tea, cloth, paper and ribbon."

"Aye, it hurts on both sides, Mrs. Hobbs. Here *and* there.

Wish there were a way around it. For now I'm just trying to carry the items most in demand in London. Pineapples, this trip. And parakeets and mahogany."

"Have you considered applying for a patent to carry government documents? They wouldn't clutter your cargo space and would provide a nice little bonus at the end of the voyage."

"I did, in fact, apply in London, Mrs. Hobbs, but with so many naval vessels in the Caribbean, they have been providing that service."

Daphne frowned. The Royal Navy did not provide that service for St. Claire. It was a rare occurrence when one of His Majesty's ships put in at San Marco. Perhaps she could ask Governor Bascombe. Yes, she'd speak to the governor, and then tell the captain if the result was favorable.

The captain finished his pineapple cake and set his fork aside. He returned his teacup to the saucer and stood. "Now I'm off to arrange the repairs. I want everything in readiness for the arrival of the pineapples. They don't keep well in a warm hold, you know. The ton pays a pretty price to have them on their tables, and I don't want to dock with a hold of rotten fruit."

She stood with him. "The repairs will require a week or two, will they not?"

"Aye."

Good. She'd have time to talk to the governor.

"Oh, by the way, I've brought a *Times* or two." He dropped the papers on the table and grinned.

Daphne affected surprise. "Oh! You shouldn't have, Captain. But thank you for your thoughtfulness."

He patted her shoulder as he passed her on his way down the alley. He never said goodbye. She wondered if that was a sailor's superstition.

She gazed at the newspapers. There was no time to linger now. The chores of closing lay ahead. But tonight, at home, she would sit and read every word, savoring the little nuggets of gossip and the latest scandal to occupy wagging tongues—any news at all of her family or friends.

Chapter Two

The sun was nearly setting and Daphne wanted to get home before dark. The trade had been very good today and all that remained was a loaf of plain bread, a few buns and three pineapple cakes. She would place them on the table in back, and the poor children from the wharves would take them away in the night.

Hannah was washing up in the back and called to her. "You go on, Daphne. Timmy will be bringing your gig any minute. I can handle the last of the customers."

Her home was five miles from town, sufficient to provide isolation without desolation. She was hanging her apron on a peg as the shop bell rang, and she spoke without turning. "Sorry. We're closed."

"Just my luck."

She turned at the sound of the rich baritone. The stranger had come for his change. Before she could think better of it, she smiled. "I'm glad you made it back." She went behind the counter, opened the till and counted out his change. When she looked up, he was watching her in a most peculiar way. "Is there something you need, sir?"

"I am wondering what other delicious things you might have besides biscuits and tarts, Mrs. Hobbs. I'm thinking I'd like my change in goods."

She laughed. "That would be enough to give you a toothache. And I fear we've sold out of sweets but for a few pineapple cakes."

"Then I shall have to come back. Keep the change on account," he said.

She dropped his change back in the till. "Are you staying aboard the *Gulf Stream*, sir?"

He gave her that slow grin and shook his head. "I have business on St. Claire."

She schooled her curiosity. "Then I hope you find our island to your liking, sir."

"Hunt," he said.

"Mr. Hunt." The name suited him. He had the watchfulness of a predator. He seemed about to say something and then shrugged. "I already find St. Claire to my liking. I doubt I'll be in town every day, but you may be sure I will come here when I am."

Hannah appeared around the corner, making it apparent that she'd been eavesdropping. "Well, then, the widow Hobbs and I will be looking forward to seeing you," she said.

Mr. Hunt grinned widely and bowed his head to Hannah. "Thank you, Mrs. Breton. For everything."

"My pleasure," Hannah said. She turned to Daphne and said, "Timmy is in back with your gig, Daphne. I'll tell him you'll only be a minute."

The heat of a blush crept into her cheeks. She'd scold Hannah later, but the damage was done. And she marveled that Mr. Hunt had remembered Hannah's name from this morning, though he did not look like the sort of man who would miss much.

He raised an eyebrow and said, "You're young to be a widow, Mrs. Hobbs. I am sorry for your loss."

He didn't look sorry as he glanced down at her wedding ring. "Thank you," she told him after a moment's hesitation.

He cleared his throat and stepped back. "Good evening, Mrs. Hobbs."

She stood there for a long minute, staring at Mr. Hunt's back as he left the shop and mounted his horse. Oh, such strong calves, long legs and wide shoulders. There was something very…compelling about the man. Something that piqued her interest and caused a yearning she hadn't felt before. She would have to be very careful around Mr. Hunt. Any careless involvement would have her at the end of a hangman's noose in short order.

Even near midnight, the air was balmy and humid. The soft breeze was a sultry caress on his skin and the scent of exotic flowers overlay the tang of sea air. In the past ten years, Hunt had forgotten the night heat, warmer than a summer day in England. Even the tavern door stood open to catch an errant breeze. He took a deep breath and entered.

Like taverns everywhere, the Blue Fin was dimly lit and smelled of stale ale. The square barroom had a long counter at one side and two dozen tables scattered throughout. Hunt sat in one corner facing the door with his back to the wall, a habit he'd acquired after being knifed in the back by a French agent in a Marseille public house. He ordered a tankard of ale and placed it on the small wooden table in front of him. Half past eleven. Right on time.

A man of average height entered and glanced around. He was dressed in rough brown trousers and a stained blue work shirt. His long sandy hair was pulled back and tied with a black string at his nape. He was the very picture of a longshoreman. When his gaze met Hunt's, he nodded. Hunt nodded back.

The man went to the bar and bought a tankard of ale. After exchanging pleasantries with the barkeeper, the man slammed his tankard down on the counter and headed for the back door with an excuse that he had to use the privy.

Hunt did a slow count to ten, finished his ale and stood. He dropped a small coin on the table, exited to the street and then rounded the building to the rear courtyard of the tavern. And there, waiting for him in the shadow of an ancient oak, stood Oliver Layton, clandestine operations, Foreign Office.

Layton glanced at the rear door to the tavern. "We've got about five minutes, Lockwood."

"Good to see you, too, Layton. Have you found a more private meeting place for us?"

The man nodded. "West of town, just before your plantation, there's a brick mile-marker. Off the road about one hundred yards you'll find an abandoned hut. The track is overgrown, but there's still a trace of it. Behind the center stone above the lintel is a pocket. Leave messages there. I will check for them and leave my own every midnight. If you need to talk to me, meet me there."

Hunt nodded. "Bring me up-to-date."

"Not much to tell. I've been in place a month. The locals are just beginning to trust me. I've hinted that I'd like to make more money and don't care how. We'll see if someone takes the bait. Do you have a plan?"

"Nothing firm beyond a reception to be given tomorrow night by Governor Bascombe and his chargé d'affaires, Gavin Doyle. I met with them this evening. They don't know why I'm here. I gather Eastman fears the problem may have reached the highest levels. In the morning I'll go to New

Albion. I haven't been to my plantation for ten years." Hunt closed his eyes to remember. "Then…if I recall correctly, there is a mountain range that runs down the south end of the island. The mountains come down to the sea, and since it is the windward side of the island, the currents are fairly treacherous. Not much land over there."

"What has that to do with us?"

"There's a small town built on the cliffs. Blackpool. I hear they don't like strangers. Something is wrong there. The captain of the ship I sailed on pretended ignorance of the town. I find that interesting," Hunt told him. "Most shippers want to make the most of a port. If Blackpool has any goods to trade or any need of supplies, it would be a logical stop. That it isn't on anyone's itinerary is suspicious. I intend to pay them a little visit. Have you heard any gossip regarding the village?"

"The townspeople are strangely silent about the other side. It's almost as if it doesn't exist. I asked the harbormaster about ships from Blackpool, and he told me they don't come here, and that our ships don't go there. Then he made a cryptic remark about ill fortune to those who tried."

Hunt laughed. "Good God, what an opening! And you haven't gone to the other side after that tempting remark?"

Layton rubbed the stubble on his chin and shook his head. "The pack of sea rats we're looking for are bloodthirsty barbarians. I'm just a poor longshoreman. I don't go looking for trouble and I don't make any."

"Or so they believe."

Layton gave him a lopsided grin. "So far, at least on St. Claire, that's the truth. My orders are to collect intelligence and stay out of trouble."

Hunt nodded. Those were Layton's orders, not his. The Foreign Office expected him to "handle" any problem on

St. Claire. "Any word, any mention at all, of Captains Sieyes or Rodrigo?"

"None. It is as if no one in San Marco has ever heard of pirates."

"They cannot be blind, deaf and dumb."

Chapter Three

The next morning, Hunt threw his coat across his saddle and left for New Albion, his plantation just west. Lush growth crowded the sides of the road while overhanging trees canopied the track, blocking the sun but not the early morning heat. The road ran parallel to the ocean and he could hear the soft hiss of waves through the heavy growth of mangrove and cypress. Distant screeches reminded him of the brightly colored birds in cages on the wharves destined for London drawing rooms.

That thought brought him back to the most exotic creature he'd seen yet: the tempting Widow Hobbs. Widow. Not married. Fair game. She'd have no illusions of a future together. She was self-sufficient and did not need him—a good thing, since he had nothing to give. They'd be free to enjoy whatever comfort the other could offer without impossible expectations.

When Governor Bascombe had insisted upon holding a reception for Lockwood, Hunt had requested that an invitation be sent to Mrs. Daphne Hobbs. The governor had merely smiled and warned that she never attended public affairs.

Too bad. She had made her own way in the world instead of catching another husband—which would have been an easy task for a woman of her looks and manner. She had a backbone. He liked that in a woman. But if she could not be enticed to attend soirées, he would just have to become Pâtisserie's best customer.

A pair of wrought-iron gates, open to the road, bore the words *New Albion*. He turned his recently acquired gelding through the gate and proceeded down the track a quarter of a mile.

His first sight of the house surprised him anew. He hadn't remembered it looking so typically like a British manor. Two stories, with tall windows open to the breeze, it was constructed of stone and covered with a verdant growth of flowering tropical vines. A row of small well-kept cottages formed a semicircle behind the house, and off to one side across a clearing were the barn and stables. The drive made a loop in front and he dismounted at the wide steps.

A short man with dark, slicked-back hair and a luxuriant mustache came down the steps to greet him. "Lord Lockwood? Good to meet you. I'm Jack Prichard, your factor. You had a pleasant voyage, I hope?"

He nodded and shook the man's hand. "Uneventful, which I hear is a good thing."

Prichard laughed. "Never know when you'll encounter a hurricane this time of year."

Hunt looked toward the cottages. "The staff?"

"And the workers. They are out on the plantation this time of day. Your trunks arrived and I've left them in the foyer until you decide where you want to stay. There is a room upstairs with a crossbreeze or, if you prefer privacy, the guesthouse."

He would prefer privacy. In fact, he would require it. "Where is the guesthouse?"

Prichard pointed to a trail through the garden toward the sound of waves breaking on a beach. "Not far down the path."

The factor signaled a waiting servant who entered the front hall, hoisted Hunt's trunk to his shoulder and followed them. The path took them several hundred yards toward the ocean, but the destination was well worth the walk. Single story, long and low, the guesthouse was built on stilts with a porch surrounding the entire structure. When he opened the door, he was enchanted. Though the house was beneath the tree canopy, the ocean was visible through a wall of windows lining the front.

Prichard slid one window to the side, and then another, and fresh sea air swept through the house, making it feel almost a part of the outdoors. Polished native mahogany floors were interrupted only by rich Persian carpets and low rattan chairs with deep cushions that faced the water.

Hunt dropped his jacket over one chair and went to the other room. A wide bed made up in crisp linen sheets was partially shrouded by transparent netting draped from the ceiling. More floor-to-ceiling windows were open to the breeze. The only concession to cooler months was a fireplace in the wall between the outer room and the bedroom, open on both sides. The privacy would suit him well.

"Shall I assign you a personal servant, Lord Lockwood?"

"No servants," Hunt said. No interference, and no witnesses to his comings and goings.

Daphne smoothed the rich plum silk in her lap. After trying the gown on, she'd only had to take in the seams a fraction beneath her bosom. She'd had the gown remade in Charleston, along with a few others, when she'd gone to visit William at school last year.

And now, with Governor Bascombe's invitation to a reception honoring a Lord Lockwood tomorrow night sitting on her foyer table, she'd have the perfect opportunity to repay

Captain Gilbert for all his thoughtfulness. She'd steal a private moment with the governor, request a patent for the captain to carry official documents and then count her debt to him paid.

The errant notion that she might encounter Mr. Hunt passed through her mind and sped her heartbeat. The mere thought of him was like an opiate—seductive, promising unknown delight, addictive. Dangerous. Every sensible thing in her warned her to stay away from the man. That anything else could bring disaster. That, should he have the faintest suspicion of who she was and what she'd done, all she had worked to build and all she loved would be forfeited.

No, the risk was too great to give in to the temptation that was Mr. Hunt. Nevertheless, and illogically, she twisted the wedding band off her finger, dropped it in her sewing basket and returned to her task.

Taking one final stitch and knotting the thread, Daphne put the gown aside. She arched her back and rolled her head as she stood. Her life since leaving London had been anything but sedentary and now she could not sit for long periods of time. She'd found forgetfulness and peace in hard labor. It was only in the quiet moments that the reality of what she'd become caught up with her.

The faint click of the kitchen door opening drew her attention. Olivia must have come back for something. The housekeeper was always leaving her supper or her mending before going back to the cottage by the gate to her property.

"Olivia?" she called. "What did you forget?"

When there was no answer, an uneasy shiver shot up her spine. "Olivia?" She snatched the scissors from her sewing box and whirled to the back hallway as soft footsteps approached. "I…I have a pistol," she warned.

"Si, an' you will use it, too." A tall Spanish beauty appeared in the doorway. Her long dark hair hung loose to the small of her back and she had the confident look of a woman who knew her own worth. She gave Daphne a saucy grin. "I think you will have to be more ferocious than that if you want to stop someone, *querida*. If I had been the thief, you would be much the poorer now, eh?"

Daphne exhaled and dropped her scissors. "Why did you not answer me?"

Olivia shrugged. "I wished to see what you would do. I worry about you when I am not here."

Daphne turned away from her to hide her annoyance. Olivia meant well, but she could often be trying. "I got on quite well before you came along," she snapped.

"Si?" Olivia laughed and shook her head. "And that is why you are here on St. Claire? Because you 'got on' well?"

Daphne had learned almost the same day she arrived on the island that Olivia was a conscienceless busybody. Thank heavens she was discreet. And thank heavens Daphne had been careful to bury her secrets deeply beneath the rain tree behind her house.

"I suspect I am here for the same reason you are, Olivia," she answered.

Olivia gave a weary shrug. "Men," she said. "They are the reason for everything, eh? But I came back tonight because I forgot to put the little William's letter where you could see it. It is in your desk."

William? She went to the escritoire in one corner of the room. Her spirits lifted and she smiled as she opened the thin little letter and saw the child's bold writing. "Do you mind if I read it now, Olivia?"

"I will go, *querida*. Tomorrow, eh?"

"Yes, tomorrow." Daphane sighed, settling into her chair again. She read the words quickly, then went back to savor them a second time.

Her son was doing well. His letter was filled with news about his friends and classes. He'd finished his exams and had been promoted a level. He had grown two inches since last Christmas. The headmaster and his wife had invited him to stay with them over the Christmas holiday again, but he begged to be allowed to come home. He was homesick for her and St. Claire, he wrote, and promised he would be no trouble.

Trouble? That he could even think such a thing cut like a dagger to her heart. Of course he was no trouble, and she would give anything to have him with her every single day. It tore at her very soul to spend so much time apart from him, but the danger of having him where he could be found if she was discovered was too great. Oh, but surely she could risk having him for the Christmas season? A month? Two?

She withdrew a sheet of paper from the escritoire drawer and scribbled a few lines. Words of encouragement and love, and the promise that she would send for him soon. She folded her letter, sealed it and placed it on the foyer table to take with her to town tomorrow. She would post it by packet to a neighboring island, where it would be routed to Charleston—the only way she could be certain her letters wouldn't be traced.

Music floated on the sultry island breeze. Chandeliers cast a gentle glow through the grand ballroom. Were it not for the smell of salt air stirring the draperies and the humidity, Hunt could well imagine himself at a state dinner at Whitehall. On his left, Governor Bascombe introduced him to yet another island notable while, on his right, the chargé d'affaires, Mr. Doyle, kept the line moving.

Hunt shook the newest arrival's hand. "Nice to meet you, Mr. Goode," he said. "I believe we are neighbors, are we not?"

"Aye, Lord Lockwood. Our lands adjoin to the east. Glad you've come. Now you can straighten out that factor of yours."

"Prichard?" Hunt asked in surprise. "Has he encroached on your land or business?"

"In a manner of speaking. I can't keep workers. Prichard pays yours too much, so mine keep wandering off to New Albion."

"Have you tried paying yours more, Mr. Goode?"

The man gave him an incredulous look. "Profits, Lord Lockwood. That would cut my profits."

"Ah, yes," Doyle interrupted smoothly. "A man must make a living, mustn't he? Have you tried the hors d'oeuvres, Mr. Goode? They're delicious. You'll find them in the drawing room."

"Nicely done, Doyle," Hunt said when Mr. Goode had shuffled off to the drawing room. The chargé was the type of man who had always been popular at school—charming, good-looking and the sort one wanted on one's cricket team.

The tall, fair, solidly built chargé grinned. "Mr. Goode has a tendency toward confrontation. Easy enough to manage when you see it coming."

Hunt was about to reply when he caught a flash of shimmering plum from the corner of his eye. He refocused on the captivating creature. Mrs. Hobbs. Bascombe had been wrong. She'd come. Dare he hope she'd come alone? He gave a polite half bow and excused himself.

She had her back to him and he took a moment to admire the curve of her swanlike neck and the set of her shoulders. Her sun-streaked hair, done in an interesting twist at her nape, glowed in the candlelight. He could smell her scent—not vanilla and sugar, as it had been in her shop, but something more tropical. Oleander? No, gardenia. He inhaled deeply before speaking.

"Mrs. Hobbs. I am delighted to find you here."

She spun and left him bemused. The cut of her gown was both innocent and bold, revealing the valley between her breasts and suggesting a hidden lushness. And was that a hint of black lace beneath the plum silk? Lord! Was she wearing a black chemise? His mind ran riot with the fantasy and his body responded shamelessly.

"Mr. Hunt," she said in a low, throaty voice, obviously unaware of what she was doing to his pulse. "I wondered if you might be here tonight." She offered her hand, as gracious as any duchess.

Mr. Hunt? Then she still didn't know who he was? He bowed over her hand and held it fast. "Have you come alone, Mrs. Hobbs? Might I importune you for a waltz?"

She glanced around and took note of Governor Bascombe, still in conversation with Mr. Goode near the punch bowl.

"You can pay your respects to our host afterward," he said. "In fact, I will be pleased to take you to him myself."

A shadow of indecision passed over her features and he thought she might refuse. Then she looked up at him and when her uncertain green eyes met his, he could see her surrender. Whatever internal battle she had been waging had just been lost. And he'd won. Still holding her hand in his, he led her to the dance floor.

She tilted her chin to look up at him and an enigmatic smile curved her full lips. She looked so exactly like a woman who'd just tempted fate that he grinned back.

"It's just a dance, Mrs. Hobbs. I'm not going to devour you," he said, not entirely certain that was the truth.

She laughed and moistened her lips as he led her into the dance. "It's just that…it has been a while, Mr. Hunt."

"Really? How long?"

She shook her head. "So long I cannot remember. Six, seven years?"

"Ah, since your husband died."

"Long before that. I…we did not mix in society much. My

husband did not like to dance, and he did not like me to dance with others."

And yet, as they danced, he'd have sworn dancing had been second nature to her. "Where was that? London?"

"Yes. It seems like another lifetime ago."

He found it hard to believe that he could have missed her, even in the height of the seasonal crush. He had no doubt she was a part of the ton, even if only on the periphery. Could she have come to town when he was away on business?

"You have not forgotten a single step," he said, and led her into a quick turn.

She tilted her head back and laughed. "I shall hope I keep my balance."

"Follow my lead, Mrs. Hobbs. *I* shall keep your balance." He should be doing his job—meeting and charming the locals, ferreting out information about the islanders, pirates and the leeward side of St. Claire—but he didn't care. He'd rather dance with Mrs. Hobbs than breathe at the moment.

"How long have you been on St. Claire?" he asked, still curious how he had ever missed meeting her in London.

She glanced away and sighed. "A little more than five years."

"Less than ten?"

He felt her resistance to his questions in the stiffening of her spine and her unwillingness to meet his gaze. Mrs. Hobbs was hiding something. He'd seen the signs too many times to be fooled by it now. He shouldn't be surprised. After all, most of the English occupants of the West Indies were hiding from something or looking for a fresh start. Had she just wanted to find a life away from painful memories after her husband died?

He glanced sideways at her hand on his shoulder. Her wedding ring was gone. That was interesting, as was her pretty blush when she noticed the direction of his gaze.

The music ended and he released her with a reluctant sigh,

remembering his promise to deliver her to the governor. He offered his arm and led her toward the reception line, which had halted in his absence.

"Ah, here you are," Bascombe said as they approached. "We've been waiting for you, Lockwood. But now that I see what has delayed you, I completely understand."

"Lockwood?" Mrs. Hobbs looked up at him in surprise.

"Oh? I thought you'd been introduced." Bascombe looked between them with a touch of reproach, as if to say that they shouldn't have danced without a proper introduction. "Lord Lockwood, may I present Mrs. Daphne Hobbs? Mrs. Hobbs, please meet Reginald Hunter, Lord Lockwood."

Unbelievably, Hunt saw a veil drop over her features, as if she had just shut herself off from him. She performed a graceful curtsy and bowed her head. "Lord Lockwood. So pleased to meet you."

If they had not been surrounded by people, he might have told her to call him Reginald, Hunt or Lockwood, but not Lord Lockwood, or my lord, or sir, or any of the other words that would put distance between them. He bowed, lifting her hand to his lips. She met his gaze over her hand and her expression was guarded. When he released her, she moved away, as if she'd been just another guest waiting in line to meet him.

Oh, no. There was nothing he could do about it at the moment, but he was not about to let her close him out so easily.

Daphne sipped a glass of wine as she stood in the shadows and watched the reception line dwindle. Whatever tryst or liaison she'd fantasized about with Mr. Hunt was now an impossibility. As Lord Lockwood, he would mix with the same society she had fled. He would have heard the scandal concerning her. She was not naive enough to think such a delicious bit of gossip would have been hushed up. She would wager everything she owned that Lord Lockwood would know the name Lady Barrett. It was not every day a peer's wife murdered him and escaped the country with his family's jewels and the heir to the title.

As soon as she could make her plea to Governor Bascombe, she would excuse herself and leave. Furthermore, she would ask Hannah to wait on Lockwood if he came to Pâtisserie again. She would immediately remove herself as far as she could from his notice. She'd only been successful in remaining undiscovered all these years by avoiding encounters such as this.

Finally, Governor Bascombe exchanged a few words with Lord Lockwood and moved away, leaving Lockwood with the chargé. She seized the opportunity and went forward to take the governor's arm.

"Thank you for inviting me," she said as she led him toward a balcony overlooking the bay.

"Not at all, m'dear. Thank you for coming. You've always refused, and that's what I told Lockwood."

"The invitation was his idea?"

"Imagine my astonishment to learn that you'd never been formally introduced. Ah, well, that's fixed now. A very clever way for him to arrange a proper introduction. I think it's plain that you can expect even more attention from Lockwood."

Daphne looked over her shoulder to see Lockwood deep in conversation with a local planter. How extraordinary that he would request an invitation for her.

But she could not think of that at the moment. A quick glance right and left assured her that they were quite alone on the balcony. "Actually, I wanted to speak with you, Governor Bascombe. I have a favor to ask."

"Well, now. I hope it is within my power to grant."

"The favor is for a friend of mine. Captain Gilbert. He makes the run from London to Washington and St. Claire, and then back to London. He is here at least three times a year."

"Yes. I've met the man. Quite competent."

"I'm glad you think so, sir. You see, I thought it might make good business sense to offer him a patent to carry official government documents."

The governor just stared at her, speechless. No doubt he was not accustomed to women meddling in state affairs. This was going to take a little finessing.

"I am concerned, sir, that Captain Gilbert may discontinue the run if it is not more profitable. As he is one of the most reliable shippers to make port in St. Claire, I think it would be expedient to make him the offer. I must say that I depend upon him for my supplies of untainted flour and a number of spices. He has even been known to take small orders for cloth and other items. I'm certain there are some items that you and Mrs. Bascombe have come to rely upon. Surely it would be a detriment if he should forego St. Claire in the future."

"Er, yes," he replied. "Hmm. I suppose there would be no harm in it."

She gave him an admiring smile. "The only one who could say nay is the king, and I do not think he would have much interest in such a matter."

The governor rubbed his chin. "I will take the matter under advisement, Mrs. Hobbs."

"That is all I ask, sir. I trust your judgment and know you will make the right decision."

Governor Bascombe preened as she led him back into the glittering ballroom. The interview had gone marginally better than she had anticipated. She'd summon her gig and be home within an hour.

* * *

Scarcely attending the conversation, Hunt watched the doors to the balcony until he saw the governor and Mrs. Hobbs reappear. He had a sudden twinge of jealousy that Mrs. Hobbs and the governor might be…no, impossible! The man was nearly twice her age, and his manner, when he introduced them, had been quite formal.

"I say, Lockwood, I cannot blame you! Mrs. Hobbs is rather tempting, is she not?" his companion asked.

Unaccountably annoyed by Doyle's comment, he shrugged. "I've scarcely seen lovelier. Does she have…is she involved with anyone?"

Doyle chuckled. "Not that anyone knows. She's quite reclusive. Believe me, if I'd found an opening, I'd have tried. She has a Spanish housekeeper, and the rumor is that they are—" He paused and gave an eloquent shrug.

"Impossible," Hunt said.

Doyle laughed again. "Ah, you've been struck by the thunderbolt. As delectable as she is, she really is not suitable, Lockwood. Well, for a discreet affair, perhaps, or to be your mistress. But how would you ever explain that Lady Lockwood had been a tradeswoman? She'd never fit in, you know."

Lockwood was well past worrying what was suitable and what was not. There was a world of difference between taking a mistress and getting married. He watched as she curtsied nicely to the governor and headed for the foyer. Ah, the innocent dove! Did she really think she'd escape unnoticed?

Chapter Four

Daphne stood on the bottom step as she waited for her gig to be brought around from the stables. She could still hear the strains of a waltz, and sighed. She'd enjoyed her dance with Lord Lockwood. Perhaps too much.

Back in London, the year she had been presented to society, she had loved to dance and had often waltzed until dawn. Barrett had dogged her every footstep and courted her relentlessly. At first she'd been flattered, but when he'd somehow bribed her brother, she ceased to be amused. In the days and years that followed, Lord Douglas Barrett proved to be as bullish and relentless a husband as he had been a suitor.

She shuddered at the memory and closed her eyes against the visions. She had lived the horror too often and dared not give it a foothold now. Her peace had been too hard-won.

A breeze tugged a few long strands of hair loose from their pins and caressed her cheeks. She brushed them back impatiently, thinking that she was coming undone in more ways than one.

"Do you have a chill, Mrs. Hobbs?"

Oh, that deep baritone! She did not need to open her eyes

to know who had joined her. A frisson of warning raced up her spine. She placed a smile on her face before she turned. "Lord Lockwood. Shouldn't you be at your party?"

He grinned and shook his head. "I've met everyone, Mrs. Hobbs, and as far as I'm concerned, the best part of the party is right here."

A scorching heat infused her cheeks. How could he unnerve her so? Could anyone so glib be trustworthy? "Then it is a pity that I am going home."

"Can I persuade you to honor me with one more dance?"

In the moment of her hesitation, a stable boy brought her gig around from the stables. She shrugged. "Sorry, Lord Lockwood, but here's my gig. Nellie doesn't like to be kept waiting."

"And who can blame her?" He went forward and stroked Nellie's forehead. The mare blew out softly and pushed her nose against Lockwood's shoulder. "A beautiful girl should never have to wait. Where's your driver?" he asked.

"Here," she admitted, tapping a finger against her chest.

He seemed at a loss for words for a moment, then regained his composure. He took the ribbons and flipped the boy a coin. "Bring my horse around, will you, lad?"

The boy was off at a run and Daphne realized what Lockwood intended. "Please do not inconvenience yourself, Lord Lockwood."

"You cannot expect me to stand by and allow you to hazard weather, brigands and a broken axle alone?"

"I am not your responsibility, sir. And I drive the road alone every day."

"In the daylight," he amended. "There are hidden dangers in the dark."

Not the least of which was him. "Really, my lord, there is no need—"

"I won't hear of it. If you will not permit it for your sake, permit it for mine. How would you expect me to live with myself if anything should happen to you on your way home tonight? What if you were attacked by brigands? How could I ever call myself a gentleman again?"

She paused. This was not like Barrett's heavy-handed manipulation. Lockwood was half cajoling and half serious. She almost believed he really *was* anxious for her safety. "There are no brigands on St. Claire," she said, only half convincing herself.

His forehead creased and doubt narrowed his eyes. "Are you certain?"

Was she? Crime was more prevalent on St. Claire than in London. The waterfront brought all types here, most of them trying to hide aboard a ship or lose themselves in a new land.

Her indecision made up his mind. The stable boy arrived and Lockwood looped the reins of his horse to the box behind the passenger compartment of the gig. He handed her up and waited for her to settle herself before climbing in and taking the ribbons. At the end of the drive, he asked, "East or west, Mrs. Hobbs?"

"West. Are you certain I am not taking you out of your way?"

"I am now." He turned west at the end of the drive onto the coastal road.

She looked sideways at him and realized that this was what she'd wanted. Despite her protests, she'd been secretly hopeful that he'd find a way to persuade her. Oh, but what was she thinking? She should be avoiding him, praying he wouldn't remember her face five minutes after he embarked for London!

Tomorrow. She'd avoid him tomorrow. And every day after that until he was gone.

"How long will you be on St. Claire, Lord Lockwood?"

"Longer than I'd originally planned." He gave her a crooked smile and her heart lurched. "And we need to come to an agreement about the way you address me. Reginald, Hunt or Lockwood would be my choices. I'd rather leave my title behind, if it's all the same to you."

"But why? A title is a great advantage in society."

"Not when it puts distance between me and what I want."

"What do you—" She cleared her throat and turned back to the road. "A fortnight, then? Or longer?"

He laughed and she knew he was amused by her embarrassment. "A fortnight at the least," he said. "A month at the most."

She gazed out at the passing landscape, eerie in the night shadows, and clasped her hands in her lap, wondering what she should do. Lord Lockwood was an outrageous flirt, yet she was captivated by his easy charm and intrigued by the hint of danger beneath it. And tempted—for the first time since…

"What brought you to St. Claire, Mrs. Hobbs?"

"A frigate, Lord Lockwood."

He grinned but did not press. Instead he reminded her of his wishes. "Lockwood. Reggie. Hunter. Hunt. Surely you can find one you like?"

She breathed deeply and exhaled her tension. It was only a ride home. He did not seem like a Reginald and Hunt seemed somehow too…intimate. "And what brought *you* here, Lockwood?"

His pause was fractionally longer than natural and she realized he was hiding secrets of his own. "I've been debating whether to sell my interests here or to keep them."

"Are they profitable?"

"Moderately so. Since I am a planter, my profits are tied to seasonal vagaries."

She nodded. "As are those of most islanders who are not engaged in shipping and trade. But since St. Claire is small, I doubt it will ever compete with other islands in goods or shipping."

"Is that your conclusion, or that of most islanders?"

"Mine, I suppose. When the St. Claire Planters' Society decided not to cultivate sugarcane, it limited growth. Most of our exports, with the exception of mahogany, are delicate or perishable, which makes transport difficult."

"Do you disapprove of that decision, Mrs. Hobbs?"

"I do not necessarily see growth as a desirable thing." More settlers from England would mean more likelihood of recognition.

He nodded and looped the ribbons through his left hand with the casual grace of one accustomed to taking the reins. With his right hand, he swept the moonlit vista ahead of them. "It would be a shame to lose all this. But I find myself wondering what the attraction might be for a woman like you. In London, you'd easily make a good marriage and have a life of ease. Instead, you've chosen to labor on a distant island with an uncertain future."

"Some things are preferable to marriage, Lockwood." As soon as the words were out, she realized what she'd given away. She cleared her throat and hastened to add, "And the…memories were too painful to remain in London."

"You could have removed to the country."

"I did not want my husband's family managing my life." She frowned at him, hoping that would be enough to discourage further questions.

Undaunted, Lord Lockwood seemed to consider her statement. "Hobbs. Hmm. I wonder if I knew him. I believe there are Hobbses in Devon, are there not? What was his given name?"

"I would not imagine you ever met him. We did not travel in such lofty circles as yours."

He glanced at her in surprise and she wondered if he had detected the lie in her voice. "I did not mean to offend you, Mrs. Hobbs. You think I'm prying, do you not?"

"Aren't you?"

He looked apologetic. "In a manner of speaking, I suppose I am. I tend to see the world as a Chinese puzzle. I want to know how all the pieces fit. The curse of an orderly mind, I fear."

Some of her tension eased and the edge of panic receded. "I dislike speaking about the past. The memories are painful."

"Then we shan't," he said. "What shall we discuss instead?"

"You, Lord Lockwood. Why is it that every time I ask you a question, you give me a short answer and turn the conversation around to me again?"

"I swear I'm not as meddling as you think. I'm new to St. Claire and want to know everything about it. But I promise to leave you alone. Shall we discuss the island?"

That should be safe enough. "Of course. Our main exports are—"

He guffawed. "I do not want the tour lecture, Mrs. Hobbs. Tell me what sights are worth seeing before I'm off again."

"The waterfall on Mount Colombo. That is my favorite, if your time is limited. Take a picnic lunch, since there are no stops between."

"Is there a walking path?"

"An easy one. I've walked it with my son."

There was silence for a moment, and then Lockwood turned to her with a puzzled expression. "Oddly enough, I hadn't suspected you had children. Perhaps because you look so young. How old is your son, or is that prying?"

She'd have to be more careful about volunteering information. She couldn't blame him for his curiosity. "He is eight years old, and away at school."

"Ah. And are there more?"

"No. Only William."

Another long pause, and then he said, "That must be very lonely for you, Mrs. Hobbs."

She blinked and cleared her throat. She was *not* going to cry in front of Lord Lockwood. She drew herself back to the subject at hand. "There is a coral reef beyond the settlements where the mountains begin on the northwest side of the island. They are beautiful, and the water is so clear that you can see the most amazing fish. Do you swim, sir?"

He nodded.

"Then I would definitely recommend the trip, although it is not a simple one. There are no boats for hire there, and no towns. The reefs are too treacherous for ships to anchor or even send a tender ashore."

He stared at her again before he spoke. "I shall put that on my list. Anything else?"

"Not that I can think of at the moment. If something should occur to me, I shall send you a note."

"No need. I'll be stopping by your shop. You can just tell me."

How could she be both anxious to see him and dismayed at the prospect? It wasn't logical in the least, and yet he seemed to create these paradoxes in her.

"What can you tell me about Blackpool, Mrs. Hobbs?"

"Not much, I'm afraid. We keep to our side of the island and they keep to theirs."

"I've been thinking that I'd like to see a town built on cliffs. If I can find a spare day or two, I believe I'll go."

"I hear large ships occasionally moor offshore, but the rip currents are treacherous for small boats and skiffs. I wouldn't recommend it, Lockwood."

"Thought I might walk overland. Have a peek at the waterfall and volcano on my way. I'm the consummate British traveler, you know."

She laughed. "Even overland, I wouldn't recommend it." The inhabitants of Blackpool were determinedly unfriendly. And there were darker, unsubstantiated rumors that some visitors never returned at all. She would hate to have Lockwood suffer a similar fate.

He was silent for a time, as if he were digesting the information. When he finally spoke, it was not what she expected. "I confess that I suspect a conspiracy here. Every time I mention Blackpool, I'm met with silence or abrupt warnings to stay away. What is over there? Cannibals?"

Heavens! She wished she could laugh at that, but no one really seemed to *know* what went on over there. "I assure you, I have no idea. The mystery existed before I arrived in San Marco and I've never gone there. I have known people who have been there, but they do not speak of it."

"By the saints! With a temptation like that, I'm amazed that half of San Marco has not gone to see for themselves."

The comment made her smile. She'd thought the same thing. "I do not know what to tell you, Lockwood. You now have the sum total of my knowledge of Blackpool. But it is your turn. Tell me what has passed in London the last five years."

"I fear only more of the same. Prinny overdrawing the royal coffers, riots over the price of corn, the Spa Field riots, general social unrest—but you do not want to hear this."

"Oh, but I do!"

She was so eager that he raised his eyebrows in surprise.

"Well, at least tell me the *on dit*. Men are no good at gossip, but I shall take what I can get."

What a clever little jibe to loosen his tongue. "Ah, the *on dit*. Well then, you knew, of course, that the Burlington Arcade opened in Piccadilly? Two floors of excellent shopping, or so I've been told by my sister. I have been shopping there, myself."

"No!" She feigned a delightful disbelief. "What did you purchase?"

"Wedding gifts."

"For whom?"

"Ah, a sad story, that. You knew that Princess Charlotte died after giving birth to a stillborn son?" He waited for her nod. "Yes? Well, it was truly scandalous what happened next."

"What?"

"Since Prinny has no other heirs, the royal dukes raced to the altar with suitable women in tow. Clarence wed Princess Adelaide, Kent wed Mary Victoria, Cambridge wed Princess Augusta. I vow, 'twas impoverishing me to buy wedding gifts that year. Kent has won the race for England's future by producing a daughter, Princess Victoria. The entire country is praying for her health. And for a son."

He had hoped to amuse her, but she turned thoughtful at this news. "Heirs," she said with a wistful sigh. "They are important, are they not? Do you have an heir, Lockwood?"

"Aye. Three of them. My brothers, Andrew, Charles and James."

The road veered into the deep canopy of overhanging trees and the night became somehow more intimate without the light of the moon.

"No heirs of your own?" she asked.

"Not yet, Mrs. Hobbs."

"Do you not want to marry?"

He winced at the surprise in her voice and fought the impulse to tell her the truth—that he couldn't live a lie. More to the point, that he couldn't subject an innocent woman to the life he'd led and was still living. That he'd never marry, never risk the revulsion of his wife when she found out who he really was. If he dared to share the truth, she would flee, appalled by his past and the things he'd done. No, he'd have to give her the expected response of half-truths, omissions and lighthearted lies.

"I haven't reached my ripe old age unattached by avoiding women, Mrs. Hobbs. On the contrary, I've been searching high and low for the right one. Ah, the rigors I've endured! The disappointments."

"The rejections?"

"Dozens."

Now she laughed outright. "I am loath to call you a liar, Lockwood, but that just does not seem possible."

He shrugged. "I suppose you'd be right. I've never actually had the opportunity to propose. I seem to always come up late. My friends snatch up the good ones."

"Have you ever thought of fighting for the one you love?"

"An interesting concept, that," he admitted. "Perhaps I have not loved deeply enough to do so. But my sister swears she will choose me a wife if I do not come up with one soon."

"I shall hope, for your sake, that she has excellent judgment."

"She does. She is the only one of us married and is the youngest of us all."

"That must aggravate the matchmaking mamas at Almack's. Four eligible men, none of them married? You must be the talk of the town."

Were they? He wouldn't be surprised. Ah, but he and his brothers had avoided Almack's for the past five years. The atmosphere was too cloying and the almost unseemly forwardness of mothers desperate to marry off their daughters was too unsettling.

"My dear Mrs. Hobbs, I am more like most men than you'd suspect. Society has become stale and I would like to believe I could find friendship and affection with a woman who would be willing to cast her lot in with mine and, if fortune favors us, have a gaggle of little Hunters. Failing that, my brothers will provide heirs aplenty."

"Yet I must maintain that the only obstacle to your goal is you. If you wanted a wife, Lockwood, you would have one."

She waved at a gate just off the road. "Here. This is Sea Whisper, my home."

Ah, this was convenient. Should he tell her that his plantation adjoined her property? He turned the gig down the drive and passed a small gatehouse cottage with a light in one window. Mrs. Hobbs, noting his interest, said, "My housekeeper lives there. This is far enough, my lord. No harm could possibly come to me on my own land."

He drew up and paused with the reins in his hands. He did not want their ride to end. "Thank you for your company, Mrs. Hobbs."

She tilted her face up to his and smiled. "Thank you for your escort home, Lord Lockwood."

In the moonlight filtering through the oaks and cypress, she took his breath away. It had been months—nay, years—since he'd kissed a woman as enticing as this one.

Slowly, allowing her to escape if that were her wish, he bent to her lips. To his profound relief, she did not demur. On some level, she must have been expecting it. The dark fan of her lashes lowered as he hovered, barely touching, unwilling to deepen the contact until he had a response. When her lips parted ever so slightly, he was quick to take the gift she offered. Her mouth tasted of a subtle honey blended with flowers and heat, as delicious as any of her confections.

He met her tongue, shared his fire and hunger with her. A shivering sigh was her only response, as if she were struggling to regain her senses. Dear Lord, he knew *he* was lost. A single kiss, and he wanted Mrs. Hobbs with an intensity that nearly doubled him over. Wanted to lose himself between her heated thighs, to bury himself inside her and hear her sighs of passion.

Instead, she placed one trembling palm against his chest and pushed him away with a little gasp. "Please, I…that was a mistake, Lockwood. It must never happen again."

What a sweet little fool she was if she thought they could recork that bottle. Once opened, that particular brew was too intoxicating to leave untasted. But he'd grant her the illusion of control, and he'd wait for the inevitable outcome. Because he had no doubt they would become lovers.

He smoothed a wayward strand of hair back from her cheek and passed her the ribbons. If she was expecting an apology, she was not going to get it, nor would she get a promise it would never happen again. He grinned at her bemusement and stepped down from the gig. Unfastening the reins of his horse, he mounted as she pulled away down the drive.

"Sweet dreams, Mrs. Hobbs," he called after her.

Gasping, Daphne woke in the middle of the night, sitting up, sweat soaking her thin nightgown and tears dampening her cheeks. She threw her covers back and staggered to her feet, wishing she could cast off the haunting memories as easily.

What had brought them on—the memories of terror and pain she had so carefully buried, suppressed with hard work and denial? Just surviving—keeping William safe from his greedy uncle, preparing him to claim his rightful inheritance and escaping the hangman's noose—had consumed her days and nights. That had become all she knew of life these last five years.

Then, Lockwood's kiss! That one small intimacy had awakened the dormant part of her—the woman she had been before Barrett. Before the nightmare marriage and that final bloody night. That she could even think of the sweetness of a kiss again, or the aching of her heart for something she'd never thought to have, was completely unacceptable. She had denied herself for five years. Surely she could deny Lockwood for a few weeks?

Chapter Five

"You're awfully quiet this morning," Hannah said. "Did you enjoy the governor's reception?"

Daphne sighed and continued to roll the pastry dough out until it was paper thin. "It was not as tedious as I feared it would be."

"About time you got out, I'd say," Hannah commented as she added wood to the fire beneath the oven. "I wondered how long it would take you to come out of mourning."

"Oh, that happened long ago. And last night does not mark a change—it was simply the exception to a very strong rule."

"I wouldn't dismiss the notion, Daphne. There may yet be someone who can turn your head and carry you away."

Reginald Hunter's face flashed before her, and she blinked. No. Never. Not on a cold day in hell. If he remembered her, and if he should see her portrait somewhere, she'd be arrested and taken back to England—and she'd do no more than step off the ship before she'd be hanged. What would become of William then? Barrett's brother would take custody. She doubted William would survive his Uncle Alfred's care. He was every bit as brutish as Barrett had been. But once William achieved his majority, Alfred would hold no power over him. Only then would William dare return to England.

The shop bell rang and Hannah hurried to see who it was. A moment later, Captain Gilbert peeked around the kitchen door and grinned at Daphne. "I stopped by to thank you, Mrs. Hobbs. I just left Governor Bascombe. He summoned me this morning and we've had a most interesting interview. It seems I'm to have the patent to carry government documents between here and London."

She wiped her hands on her apron. "I hope that will make your circuits more profitable."

"By a far sight, Mrs. Hobbs. And I understand I have you to thank for it."

She was slightly abashed to have been caught in her machinations. "Oh, no, I wouldn't say that, sir. I simply mentioned your name."

"Not the way the governor retells the story." He grinned. "He told me that you have shunned island society since your arrival, and that you suddenly showed up when least expected. He said you were a woman with a purpose, however, and that you left once you'd accomplished that purpose."

She grimaced that she'd been so transparent. "I made a suggestion. That is all. Please do not make more of it than it warrants."

The shop bell interrupted them. Even with Hannah in front, Daphne seized the opportunity to halt the conversation. She left her rolling pin on the worktable and hurried into the shop.

Lord Lockwood stood at the counter, bending over the pastry tray, his hands clasped behind his back. When he saw her, his lips curved in a smile.

"Good morning, Mrs. Hobbs," he said, his voice soft and warm.

"Good morning, Lord Lockwood," she murmured. She felt Captain Gilbert come up behind her.

"'Lo, Lord Lockwood," he said.

The warm smile changed subtly to one of polite formality. "Captain." He nodded. "How's the provisioning going?"

"Slowly, I fear. Looks like it will take a fortnight to have the cargo aboard and make ready to sail. Mrs. Hobbs, however, has just seen to it that I keep making the run from London."

A flicker of something feral passed through Lockwood's eyes. "Did she? Well, I'd guess she could be persuasive."

Heavens! Did he think she'd persuaded the captain with favors? She started to deny it and then decided it would be better for Lockwood to believe anything that would make him keep his distance.

Captain Gilbert, however, was quick to sort out the misunderstanding. "Mrs. Hobbs was kind enough to speak to Governor Bascombe on my behalf. I've been given a patent on carrying official documents and correspondence between St. Claire and London."

"I see," Lockwood said.

But he didn't. The hardness that settled around his features told her that.

The uncomfortable silence drew out until she remembered herself. "Oh, sorry. Can I get something for you?" She moved behind the counter and fussed with a rack of cooling bread.

"Something smells good, Mrs. Hobbs. What do you have cooking?"

"Cobblers, but they won't be ready for hours."

"Ah, well, I won't have time to wait."

Impulsively, she tore off a length of paper and placed a cherry tart in the center. "A poor substitute, Lord Lockwood. I regret the cherries were not fresh, but preserves suit quite well." She folded the paper over it and tied it with the blue ribbon. "Careful, or the crust will split and the filling will make you sticky."

He accepted the package with a slight bow. "I am in your debt, Mrs. Hobbs."

"Not in the least, Lord Lockwood. I regret it is all I have to offer at the moment."

"I will be pleased to take whatever you offer, Mrs. Hobbs." He gave her an appraising glance. "Whenever you offer it."

Her mind went blank and she could only nod and hurry back to the kitchen, mumbling an excuse about the dough rising. The low voices of the two men carried to her, but she could not make out their words. She did not like the idea of Lockwood questioning Captain Gilbert.

The shop bell rang again and a moment later Captain Gilbert appeared in the kitchen doorway. He leaned one shoulder against the jamb. "Once again, I thank you for your efforts on my behalf, Mrs. Hobbs. If ever there is anything I can do for you, I stand ready and willing."

"Just keep bringing me newspapers, Captain."

At quarter past eleven that night, Lockwood found the abandoned hut without trouble. Layton's directions had been quite precise. He waited in darkness, melding with the shadows of a massive oak. When Oliver Layton arrived and dismounted, he watched while the agent checked the brick over the lintel for messages.

He came up behind Layton and tapped him on the shoulder. Layton jumped and spun around, his pistol drawn and cocked. "Sweet Jesus," he cursed in a whisper when he saw who it was. "I could have killed you, Lockwood!"

"Not with your throat slit," he mocked. "Island life is making you sloppy."

The man shrugged good-naturedly. "Lesson learned. But what are you doing here? Have you found something out?"

"I'm just getting started," Hunt admitted. "I did a little quiet questioning at the reception and discovered a few interesting tidbits. Nothing concrete at the moment, but I will let you know should anything come of it."

"Is that all?" Layton frowned.

"Guard your tongue with the harbormaster."

Layton raised his eyebrows and gave a succinct nod.

"I heard a piece of gossip that the American president has authorized the formation of an antipiracy squadron. If it's true, we might find some help there."

Layton laughed. "They've got their hands full trying to protect their own ships. Aside from that, it will be another year before such a squadron is outfitted and ready to sail. Heaven knows it will take a year before our own government decides what to do with the information *we* gather. And yet I had the impression that events here were critical and urgent."

Hunt thought of the dwindling fortunes in London and of the unknown man who had secretly betrayed them all. And what Layton didn't know was that their government had sent *him* to deal with the situation. "I've given up trying to second-guess the government," he told the agent. "Have you heard any rumors of corruption or collusion on the part of local officials?"

Layton raised an eyebrow. "If you mean the harbormaster, nary a whisper. Is that something I should pursue?"

"Not at the moment," he answered, unwilling to expose the Foreign Office's suspicion.

When Layton turned to go, Hunt ventured another question. "Ever patronize Pâtisserie?"

A roll of the eyes gave him the answer.

"Which little delicacy do you favor?"

"Mrs. Breton. Hannah. Those curves haunt my dreams."

"Have you wooed her?"

"Good God, no! A longshoreman wouldn't have a ghost of a chance with someone like her."

"You're not a longshoreman."

"Aye, but she doesn't know that. Yet."

"I've been curious about the proprietress—Mrs. Hobbs. Have you heard anything about her?"

Layton shook his head. "No. Shall I—"

"No. Just idle curiosity." He'd investigate that little mystery on his own. All the same, there was something not quite right about that whole arrangement. "Keep a weather eye on the shop, Layton. I'd hate to see them become embroiled in this. It promises to get ugly."

An hour later, close to midnight by the position of the full moon, Hunt found he was unable to sleep. He slipped naked from bed and pulled on his trousers, poured himself a glass of brandy and went to stand on the verandah overlooking the ocean. The full moon above the bay was reflected in the placid water.

Leaning one shoulder against the brace of the overhang, he let the rich warmth of the brandy seep through him. His mind wouldn't let go of the various tactics for his mission. Tomorrow he would study his map of St. Claire and get his bearings. Then he'd begin his search for the notorious pirates, Captains Sieyes and Rodrigo, and his investigation into St. Claire's complicity, or lack of it, in the pirate conspiracy.

Once he had formed a strategy and committed to a course of action, he wouldn't feel so on edge. He mentally ticked off a number of ploys and their advantages. He'd taken the first step by entering San Marco society. Even a colonial outpost observed protocol and decorum. And there was nothing like a drawing room for cultivating confidences and gossip. He'd found that people often did not realize the small gems of information they possessed. Until they knew the puzzle and how to put it together, they didn't even recognize they held the pieces.

The cry of a night bird broke the stillness and alerted him that something was amiss. He walked, silent and barefoot, down the steps onto the path leading to the beach, every sense attuned to danger. He caught his breath and stilled when he saw what had disturbed the peace.

Daphne riffled the surface of the water with her bare toe. Still water made her nervous. She had learned that it was an omen of storms to come. An errant breeze lifted her hair in a little swirl and carried the scent of rain with it as she walked along the edge of the ocean.

She loved the freedom on St. Claire—or, perhaps, simply the freedom of not being Lady Elise. No appearances to keep up, no social obligations. No hiding of bumps or covering of bruises. She could stroll the edge of the ocean at midnight in nothing but her knee-length chemise with complete freedom. No one to see her. No one to care. No one to gossip.

Though she usually slept well, tonight a persistent restlessness troubled her. Every time she relaxed, her thoughts wandered back to that unexpected kiss with Lord Lockwood. How could she have known the unsettling emotions that would evoke? All day, her head had been filled with visions of a dark curl falling over a forehead above deep blue eyes and a mouth curved in a smile. Oh, that smile! It did strange things to her insides. Things she'd never felt before. Things that had kept her awake tonight and longing for something she knew she could never have. Something that was a lie at its core.

She stooped and picked up a conch shell. Wading into the water to her calves, she let the waves dampen the bottom of her chemise to weight it from rising in the wind, then retreated to the sand before it became soaked. She hummed a new tune she'd heard in town—a seaman's chantey.

The lights of San Marco shimmered across the bay, reminding her how remote her home was, for all that it was barely five miles from town. When she'd come to St. Claire, she'd wanted to hide away, keep William safe from any chance of recognition. Then he'd grown and changed, turning from a sickly boy to a strong lad. When he'd been old enough, she'd sent him away to boarding school—away from her—to keep him safe. If Barrett's brother managed to trace her, he wouldn't find William.

She shivered at the thought. Or was it the rising wind? A cloud passed over the moon and she looked up to find the stars replaced by sudden dark clouds. A storm had whipped up out of nowhere. She glanced over her shoulder, dismayed to find that she had wandered beyond the boundaries of Sea Whisper and would be caught in the impending storm.

"Did you miss me, Mrs. Hobbs, or are you lost?"

She gasped and whirled toward the sound of the deep voice. There, before her, was the cause of her sleeplessness. Lord Lockwood. Her heart thumped at the sight of his bare chest. Strongly muscled, clearly defined, softly matted with dark hair and tapering into a narrow waist, it was the most stirring sight she'd ever seen. He was barefoot, dressed only in trousers, and those compelling eyes were watching her with a mixture of wariness and amusement as he twirled the stem of a white wild orchid between his index finger and thumb.

"Oh, I…what are you doing here, sir?"

"This is my land, Mrs. Hobbs. You are a trespasser, so a better question might be, 'What are *you* doing here?'"

"You…own New Albion?" She'd heard of the absentee owner of the neighboring plantation, but she'd never expected to meet him. Indeed, she scarcely talked to the overseer, Mr.

Prichard. How ironic that Fate had delivered Lockwood to her doorstep, or her to his. "Why did you not tell me last night when you brought me home?"

"I told you that you were not out of my way."

"Oh, well, I did not mean to intrude. I shall excuse myself."

"I thought for a moment that a naiad had surfaced."

She smiled at his attempt at humor. "Sorry to disappoint, Lord Lockwood."

"No disappointment at all, Mrs. Hobbs." He came closer and Daphne's heartbeat sped. "And I would be pleased if you would call me Hunt. Or Lockwood."

She started to curtsy and then realized how absurd the scene was. Heavens! She was in her chemise! She dropped the conch shell and crossed her arms over her chest. "Again, I apologize for my interruption."

He caught her shoulder as she turned to go. "A welcome interruption," he said. "I could not sleep, either. Are the nights on St. Claire always so sultry?"

"N-not always."

"I like what it does to your hair," he said, lifting a strand that had curled in the humid heat, then tucking the wild orchid behind her right ear.

She froze. Under any other circumstances, his familiarity would be insulting and presumptuous. But there was something otherworldly about this night, something almost destined, and he did not seem insulting. To the contrary, his expression held admiration and…desire? Her pulse quickened and she licked her lips, gone suddenly dry with anxiety.

He stepped closer still and she had to tilt her chin to look into his eyes. He slipped his hands around her waist and drew her against his chest with gentle pressure.

A reckless yearning seized her and she lifted on her toes to meet his descending mouth. The touch of his lips was gentle, tentative, neither beseeching nor demanding. He was teasing, heightening the sensation, making her want him. Waiting for her to ask for more.

A wave washed around their ankles, unbalancing her and making her cling to him for support. Lightning flashed across the sky and a warm tropical rain began to fall. The drops trickled over her face, down her neck, between her breasts. His hand, exquisitely gentle, lifted her chin and he kissed her deeply again, coaxing her, nibbling at the corners of her mouth until she opened to him. The other hand drew her closer until her breasts flattened against his chest and a hard swelling pressed against her lower belly. Then she ached for that, too. How odd that in all her years with Barrett, she had never once felt this need.

"Oh!" she breathed, aghast at her own thoughts. Where had this wantonness come from? "I…should go. The rain…"

"Let me shelter you," he said in a dark velvet voice.

She knew what would happen if she stayed. She'd sworn not to let any man possess her again. She'd clung to her independence. But independence did not banish her loneliness and longing. In the five years since…Barrett…she hadn't been more than mildly tempted, but this man was different. There was a promise of pleasure in his eyes and a deep magic in his touch.

He stroked her spine from the nape of her neck to the small of her back, pressing her closer. "It's a dream," he whispered, his breath tickling her ear. "Just a dream. When you wake, it will be your secret. No one else's. No words will ever be spoken. Can you let yourself dream, Daphne?"

Dream? It had been so long. Did she even remember how?

"A dream," he murmured again, his lips brushing hers. "In a dream, nothing is forbidden."

She slipped her arms around his neck to drag his mouth

down to hers. A moan started somewhere deep inside him and he tilted his head to nuzzle her neck as he lifted her off her feet. He carried her up the steps of a cottage and across the mahogany planks to what must be his bedroom.

He placed her on her feet, lifted the chemise over her head and dropped it on the floor in a sodden heap. Heedless of her damp skin and the sand clinging to them both, he lifted her again and laid her against the pillows. She held her breath as he unfastened his trousers and let them fall.

He was lean, well-sculpted and beautifully proportioned. And, heaven help her, he was twice the man her husband had been. In every way. Logic mingled with anxiety and she began to panic. What had she done? Three days ago she hadn't even met this man, and tonight she was naked in his bed. It was wrong. It was madness.

And she wanted it more than she'd wanted anything in a very long time.

Can you let yourself dream, Daphne?

He lay down on the mattress beside her. A kiss—a single kiss—and she was caught in a vortex dragging her deeper and deeper. He pulled her to him, pressed himself against the length of her. She trailed her fingers down his side, enthralled by the solid strength of the man in contrast to his exquisitely gentle touch.

Lowering his head, he paused to kiss a tender spot where her neck met her shoulder, and a deep shudder went through her. Then his tongue trailed to the hollow of her throat, and she could feel the heat of his lips against her flesh.

"Sweet Daphne, your sighs are an aphrodisiac."

She moaned at the deep warm rumble of his voice, and he moved lower still, capturing one tender nipple between his lips and drawing a tingle up from her belly. She felt herself dissolving, becoming fluid beneath his hands, and when those hands moved downward over her stomach to glide past her nether hair to find her entrance, she bit her lip to hold back an outcry.

Passion? Need? Possession? What were the feelings overwhelming her? She couldn't name them. She only knew she didn't want them to stop. And when he began stroking her, she gasped, wondering why she'd never felt such intimacy and surrender with Barrett.

And then, in the back of her mind, she heard a nagging voice—her conscience?—warning her. *If you surrender to this man, you'll never be whole again. If you let him make love to you, you are lost. He will learn your secrets and betray you, and when he does, you will truly die inside.*

"No," she sighed with the last of her will. "I cannot do this." She struggled to sit up, her limbs as heavy as if she'd been drugged.

Hunt looked confused and reached out to her. "Daphne, I will not hurt you. If you do not want this…"

Want it? Oh, yes, she wanted it with every tingling nerve, every throbbing pulse, but she could not. The memory of Barrett made it impossible. Would always make it impossible. Because his ghost always reminded her that she was a fraud. That she was a murderess and, given half a chance, that she'd do the same again. That she was hollow and had nothing inside to give.

She scooped her chemise off the floor and ran from the room.

Chapter Six

Chirping insects. The deep croak of frogs. The eternal sound of the waves. Yes, the storm had passed, leaving peace in its wake.

Hunt rolled over, the sheet twisting around him. His first thought was of the gift the storm had brought and then taken away. He sat up and stared at the pillow that still held the impression of her head. A wild white orchid was all that remained. If not for that, he could have dreamed her. Ah, but he could still smell her. Warm ambergris, orchid and sea spray. And woman. And, God, what a woman.

He stood and pulled his trousers on. Not bothering with shoes, he went down the verandah steps to the sand. An edge of watercolor blue stained the eastern horizon. Dawn was not far.

He found the place where they'd met, marked by the conch shell she had dropped, abandoned in the sea foam now. He picked it up and stroked the smooth pink inner curves. As smooth and delicate as Daphne had been.

He returned to the house and stood in the bedroom doorway, staring at the damp impression of her chemise on the floor, remembering her as she'd looked when he removed it. A flash of lightning had revealed her, flushed, trembling, her skin glistening from the rain, her sun-streaked hair curling down her back in a riotous wet windblown tangle and a wild orchid tucked behind her ear. She had looked like Venus rising from the sea.

There'd been something electric in the air. A tingling certainty. Something fated. They'd both felt it beneath their skin. They'd known from the moment they saw each other on the beach how it should end. It had been absurd to resist. Pray Daphne would realize that soon. Pray a fortnight would be sufficient to take his fill.

He placed the conch shell on his bureau and went to find the brandy bottle. Blast! Now he was drinking his breakfast!

Hunt pulled himself back into the moment and resettled in his chair on the governor's terrace overlooking the bay. Every time he let his guard down, his thoughts drifted back to orchids, soft flesh and hard passion. Damn! Was there no escape from the spell Daphne had woven around him? "I'm sorry," he apologized. "You were saying?"

Gavin Doyle cocked an eyebrow and gave him a slanted grin. "I was saying that there's nothing to see in Blackpool. The governor would prefer you stay on this side of Mount Colombo."

Would he? "Have you been there, Doyle?"

"Once," the chargé admitted. He poured another cup of dark, bitter coffee for Hunt. "Not worth the trouble. The people are unfriendly, the women are not attractive and the terrain is challenging. I'd rather climb an uncomplicated mountain than traverse those cliff paths. The houses literally hang off the rocks. One good shake, and the whole town would tumble into the sea. But it is the potential danger that is the governor's concern."

"Danger? Are the inhabitants *that* unfriendly?"

Doyle gave a short laugh. "That is the gossip. Every time someone disappears, it's said they've gone to Blackpool. Whether that is true remains to be seen. I'm of a mind to think the disappearances are due to common kidnapping or conscription. Ships have need of crew. When one sailor runs off—" He shrugged. "Replacements must be found, one way or another."

That was a logical explanation, but Hunt wondered if it was true. "What is Blackpool's raison d'être?"

"Fishing," Doyle said with a little snort of disdain. "And logging. Mahogany grows in the mountains and along the cliffs. I gather they fell them, strip the limbs and roll the logs into the inlet, where they lash them together until a shipper comes by for them. Cabinet makers in London and New York are crying out for mahogany, but there's sure as hell no sign of anyone getting rich in Blackpool. I believe they barely eke out a living."

"Why does everyone seem so indifferent to them? You'd think Blackpool was a different country."

Doyle raised an eyebrow. "It damn near is. The people there even contract their own supply ships. Believe me, they want nothing to do with us, nor do we wish to have dealings with them. It's not exactly a secret, just an unspoken understanding."

"Is it possible that the settlers are engaging in illegal activities?"

"Like wrecking?" He shook his head. "Not likely. There aren't enough ships coming by to make that lucrative."

Hunt narrowed his eyes and glanced out over the bay. Only three ships bobbed in the harbor. This was testament, he supposed, to the fact that St. Claire was a small, sleepy island. But that fact did not mean it had no secrets. On the contrary, he suspected that most of the islanders were escaping some unpleasantness in their past. Even Governor Bascombe's assignment to St. Claire was his atonement for a diplomatic blunder in a far eastern country. Where better than a distant and ignored island of exiles to find a fresh start? What better place for chicanery?

What better place for treachery?

He sipped the strong coffee and mulled over the governor's request. Only Oliver Layton knew his true purpose on St. Claire. If he continued to make an issue of Blackpool, the governor was sure to suspect an ulterior motive.

"Not Blackpool, then, but I'd still like to see more of the island before I leave," he told Doyle.

"How long do you plan to stay?"

Originally, he'd meant to stay two weeks, but he was four days into his investigation and had made no progress toward his two goals—to discover whether the pirates had a nest on the island and to find out who might be feeding them shipping information. And, as luck would have it, he'd found another strong inducement to stay longer. "Not sure," he admitted. "Perhaps a fortnight, perhaps two."

"I see," the chargé mused. He tented his fingers together and narrowed his eyes. "I believe that is longer than you planned, is it not?"

Hunt laughed. "Has the governor asked you to ferret out that information?" He did not like the idea of being pinned down, least of all by political officials.

Doyle gave him a self-deprecating smile and spread his hands wide in a gesture of surrender. "You've found me out. Alas, I was to be more subtle and not make you feel unwelcome. I am also to offer my services in any way to make your stay enjoyable. At least, until I leave."

Any way but a trip to Blackpool, Hunt thought. The man needed diverting. "Are you being reassigned?" he asked.

"I'm being called back to London. I was only assigned to St. Claire to cover Bascombe's frequent trips home when his mother was ailing. She's passed now, so I shan't be needed here anymore."

Frequent absences? Warning Hunt away from Blackpool? Was this more than simple coincidence? He'd have to proceed cautiously or he'd tip his hand. "Too bad. I shall have to remember to offer my condolences when next I see him. Meantime, tell me about Mrs. Hobbs."

"The little baker?"

"One and the same."

"As I told you at the reception, I really do not know much about her. She was established here before my assignment several years ago. She's quiet. Hasn't mixed in society until the reception night before last. I was astonished to see her there. She has been somewhat insignificant in society, and only her consequence as a merchant lifts her above the ordinary. Her manners are impeccable but I am told that she is painfully shy. On the rare occasions I have spoken to her, she has been quite standoffish. I must say, however, that she looked very different at the reception—a damn sight better than her common garb. I wonder if it could have been the candlelight."

Candlelight? Was Doyle blind? "Then you cannot tell me anything about her background?"

"Sorry. A small task to find out, if you'd like."

Suddenly, Hunt *didn't* like. In fact, he didn't want the polished chargé d'affaires anywhere near Daphne Hobbs. "Never mind. It was just a passing curiosity."

Doyle gave him a canny grin. "Passing? I think there's more to keep you on St. Claire than your plantation, eh, Lockwood?"

That was an impossible question to answer. Say *aye,* and Doyle would have a reason to give Daphne a closer look. Say *nay,* and he'd subject himself and his own activities to closer scrutiny. "Idle curiosity, Doyle. Don't give it another thought."

"How can I help it? I hear that she's been invited to the

Grahams' picnic this evening. I'll be attending, as the governor is under the weather. Perhaps I'll have occasion to talk to her. Or to sample her wares." Doyle tapped one finger against his cheek thoughtfully.

Hunt tightened his jaw to keep from making an imprudent reply. If Doyle sampled anything, he'd regret it. Hunt had decided to send his regrets to Mr. Graham, but if Daphne would be there, he'd reconsider.

He stood, and his chair scraped back along the terrace flagstones. "Thanks for the coffee, Doyle. Give my regards to the governor and tell him that I've made note of his warning."

"My, you are becoming quite the social butterfly," Hannah teased as she looked over Daphne's shoulder.

Daphne studied the handwritten invitation to an evening musicale and picnic hosted by the Grahams, a prominent family on St. Claire. Had Lockwood engineered this invitation, too? Of course, she would send her regrets.

"Oh, no," Hannah said, with a single look at her mulish expression. "You will accept that invitation, Daphne Hobbs, and you will have fun. You have a nice gown upstairs, and—"

"But I really do not want to—"

"So you say, but I think otherwise. Your step was lighter and your smile readier after the governor's reception, and I think you found something to interest you there. You're too young to give up on life."

"There is no future in—"

"Oh, bother! Who says you need a future? Just enjoy what you have at the moment."

Just a dream… Can you let yourself dream, Daphne? Lockwood's words kindled a languid heat in her center as the memory washed through her. Oh, how disconcerting the whole incident had been!

She *had* let herself dream. For the first time in her life, she'd followed her heart and dared to dream that there might be something more than self-loathing and pain in a man's arms. She'd have been better off not knowing what could have been.

Hannah took her hands and squeezed them. "Damn the future, Daphne. Whatever joy you've found, take it and do not ask for more. Tomorrows are for virgins and kings. You have a right to find some happiness, however brief."

Oh, how seductive Hannah's words were. Could she risk so much for a few brief nights in Lockwood's embrace? Could she live with the regret all the long empty nights ahead if she didn't?

Hannah hung her apron on a peg and headed for the door. "I'll be upstairs applying an iron to your dress, Daphne. Hurry up and close."

Damn the future…. Yes, she would find some way to forget Lord Lockwood later.

She put her broom outside the kitchen door and untied her apron. She'd have to clear the shelves and hurry upstairs and change before she could leave for the Grahams'. The shop bell rang with insistence and she frowned. This would have to be Pâtisserie's last customer of the day.

She was not surprised to see Mr. Lowe. He was her only customer from Blackpool and always arrived a few days after a supply ship put into port. He had told her once that Blackpool did not have a bakery, so her sweets were always a treat when he brought them back. He was a good customer and always paid in cash, but the way he watched her made her uneasy.

"Good afternoon, Mr. Lowe. What can I get for you?"

"That's dependin' on what you gots, Mrs. Hobbs." The man smiled. Daphne tried not to blink, as she often did when she noted his absent and broken teeth.

"Just what you see on the shelves, sir. You may have whatever you want for half price, as I am about to close for the day."

"Aye? Well, then, I'll take it all."

"All?" She looked at the row of crusty breads and the glass case still bearing tarts and biscuits. "Are you certain?"

"It'll keep a couple of days, will it not, Mrs. Hobbs?"

"The biscuits, yes. And the breads, so long as you do not dislike them a little dry. But you will have to cover the tarts if you hope to keep the insects out."

"Aye, Mrs. Hobbs, just likes I always does."

Daphne was not one to look a gift horse in the mouth. She turned away and ripped a length of brown paper from the roll to begin wrapping the purchases. "And who eats all this, Mr. Lowe? Surely not you?"

The man laughed. "Nay. Not I. I likes the biscuits and bread, but it's the charge man who likes the sweets. Well, and the biscuits, too."

The charge man? Ah, the man in charge. That was a rather quaint way to refer to an employer. But then everything about Mr. Lowe was quaint. Or sinister. Or perhaps she only thought that because he was from Blackpool.

"What is his favorite?"

"He likes the lemon and ginger best, Mrs. Hobbs. Says he cannot get enough of 'em."

"Ah, then I am pleased I have some left. Anything else?"

"Cap'n likes the meringues, but they don't last too good and I ain't leavin' until tomorrow night. Might come back for 'em tomorrow, though. That'd make 'im happy."

"And it is always nice to keep the charge men happy, is it not?"

He gave her an odd look and then laughed. "Aye. Nice."

Scarcely five minutes after his arrival at the Grahams' picnic musicale, Hunt watched the color rise in Daphne's cheeks as he bent over her right hand and drew it to his lips. Clearly, she was wondering if he would mention what had passed between them last night. He wouldn't, of course. He was still that much of a gentleman. But he hadn't promised it wouldn't happen again.

"I did not think I would see you again so soon, Lord Lockwood," she said, almost stumbling over her words. Her hands were trembling and he feared she'd spill the wine in the glass she held in her left hand.

"Then I shall count myself most fortunate, indeed, Mrs. Hobbs," he said, playing the game of polite formality to appease the island gossips. He released her hand and turned to his hostess, plump, graying Mrs. Graham. "Thank you for including me in such a lively event."

"Our pleasure, Lord Lockwood. After all, you are one of us now."

"One of you? Ah, an islander." He grinned. "Yes, I can see why so many people have made St. Claire their home. It has so much to recommend it."

Daphne met his gaze over the top of Mrs. Graham's head. She blinked and then covered her mouth with a fan. To hide a smile?

"Yes? Well, we think so, of course," Mrs. Graham said with a gracious nod. "I hope you will consider extending your stay with us. We rarely have such a charming visitor."

Oh, he was charming enough. Men like him learned to use charm and social skills to hide what lay beneath. "You flatter me, Mrs. Graham. I am not in the least charming. My sister reminds me of that fact often."

She and Daphne laughed and he found himself wondering about Daphne's background. Did she have brothers? Sisters? Were her parents still living? Would he and Daphne have anything in common at all? How odd that they'd spent such intimate time alone, and yet he knew so little about her. He must remedy that.

"Be that as it may, Lord Lockwood, we are delighted to have you here," Mrs. Graham insisted. "The musicians are setting up on the terrace, and you will find seating on the lawn. Hurry if you wish to claim a chair, otherwise you will find yourself sitting on a blanket. Oh, dear! That is Mr. Graham calling me." She turned to Daphne and said, "I am really loath to leave you when you have only just met and are so unfamiliar with our modest little house. And I fear dinner will not be served until after the musical presentation."

"Thank you, Mrs. Graham," Hunt said, trying to hide his satisfaction. "I am certain Mrs. Hobbs and I shall get along just fine. I shall look forward to conversing with you later." He waited until the hostess was out of earshot and then turned to Daphne. The awkward moment had come. They were alone.

He offered her his arm, and she took it with seeming reluctance before speaking in a rush. "Mrs. Graham has placed hors d'oeuvre tables beneath the striped awnings, and footmen are—"

"I see," he said, lifting a wineglass from a passing footman's tray. "This will do quite well for the time being. I find that food is the furthest thing from my desires at the moment."

She lowered her lashes as he led her toward the small hill overlooking the ocean. He regretted teasing her. Daphne Hobbs was too vulnerable, too sweet, to play these social games. Nothing in her common background had equipped her for the wordplay to which the haute ton was accustomed.

He relented with a little smile as they arrived at a small bench overlooking the ocean. "I meant to come by Pâtisserie today, but business kept me occupied. When I heard that you'd be here tonight, I hoped I would run into you."

She gazed out at the ocean and a bank of clouds forming

on the horizon. "Lord Lockwood, I…had a dream last night. It was a lovely dream, a moment of madness, but I would change it if I could. And now…"

Yes, he'd suspected she'd feel this way. All he could do was reassure her, since he had no intention of promising it would not happen again. "If you fear that I will tell, or that I will demand more of you than you are prepared to offer willingly, then set your mind at ease. I will never betray your trust, Daphne."

She released his arm and turned to face him. "I would expect no less of you, Lockwood, but that was not my meaning."

"Pray enlighten me."

She sat on one edge of the carved stone bench and patted the space beside her in invitation. "I cannot explain my behavior, least of all to myself. Last night was…undeniable. I've never done anything remotely like it before—it was out of character for me. What I meant to say is, well, we are virtual strangers."

"Not after last night."

"Nevertheless, whatever madness possessed us then has passed now. You must know that there can be nothing more between us, do you not?" No games, no demurring, just a straightforward, candid assessment.

"Nothing more," he acknowledged, "but, I pray, nothing less."

She did not answer immediately. He watched as she smoothed her skirts and considered the veiled question. "You have the manner of a man accustomed to getting what he wants. Is that due to your title, Lockwood, or self-confidence?"

Now he, too, gazed out over the ocean. "I became the sixth earl of Lockwood four years ago. My father married late in life and was quite elderly by the time I was grown. Before he passed, I was sent to tour our family holdings. The trip took me, literally, around the world. In short, Daphne, I am difficult to surprise or shock. I think I have experienced as much as any man, and that my understanding of the world and its workings is as good. I know that few things are as simple as black and white or right and wrong. And I know what is possible and what is not."

"You mean to reassure me, do you not? That I cannot shock or surprise you?"

"I do," he admitted, taking a drink of his wine.

"Thank you."

Her soft reply evoked a surprisingly visceral response in him. He realized that he wanted to protect her from further pain, stand between her and whatever had hurt her. Ah, but that was going farther than either of them wanted. In two weeks, perhaps less, they'd be strangers again. But first— "Tell me about Daphne Hobbs."

Her pause was so long that Hunt wondered if she'd heard him. "I have one brother," she said at length. "He is older, and my mother died giving birth to me. I think my father did not care for me, because he seemed to forget that I existed. When he died, he bequeathed me my mother's sewing basket and a quilt she made for me whilst she was carrying me."

Hunt tried to hide his outrage. "No trinket? Nothing of value?"

"Mother's jewelry went to my brother as a part of his inheritance, and for his bride to wear." She shrugged and lifted the wineglass to her lips. "But I am well-pleased. To have something she made for me, and to have the selfsame tools she used, was a gift more precious than gold."

"But nothing from him? What memento do you have of his?"

She turned to look at him, her eyes wide with wonder. "Heavens. I had not thought of it, but he left me nothing of his. Though I was not married yet, he had already done his duty by me in providing my dowry."

"And now your father and your husband are both dead. I

am sorry for your loss, Daphne. That is much to bear. At least you have your brother and your son."

She took another drink and did not volunteer more. "I believe you told me you had three brothers and a sister. I could feel sorry for her if your brothers are as waggish as you."

He laughed. "Sarah has set us all back on our heels more than once. She holds her own."

She gave him her first completely unguarded grin. "And you adore her. I can hear it in your voice. And you said she is married?"

"Quite happily. She has three children now. Two boys and an infant girl. And your brother? Does he have children? Is he helping you raise your son?"

"I have lost touch with him. We were never close. He and Papa were ever together—hunting, gambling, riding and drinking. I think they were the best of friends. No room for a frail girl in their world."

"Alone? You were raised alone?"

She closed her eyes as if looking back to some distant day. "I was allowed to share my brother's tutor but, when I was not romping through the Devon countryside, I recall sitting on a stool in the kitchen most of my childhood. I loved the chatter, the smells, the warmth. Cook fed me sweets and mussed my hair. 'Twas she who taught me to make bread and pastries. I loved her dearly. My brother discharged her when he married. I wasn't allowed to see her again."

Hunt clenched his jaw in anger. He had seen other families like this—where the sons were valued and the daughters a nuisance.

Oddly, it did not surprise him that Daphne had been raised in a family prosperous enough to hire servants. Her manners and speech were impeccable. And no wonder she had learned to cook.

"Why did your brother not take you and your son in when your husband died?"

There was a long pause before she answered, as if she were deciding how much to tell him. "Do not criticize him, Lockwood. That was my choice, and I chose not to throw myself on his mercy. I have not regretted my decision."

What brother worthy of the name would turn his back on his widowed sister and his nephew? Hunt set his glass on the bench beside him and took her hand. A delicate shiver shot through her, and it occurred to him that Daphne was unused to sympathy or support.

"If you ever need help, Daphne, please know that there is nothing I wouldn't do, no resource I wouldn't tap for you."

She looked up at him, those green eyes glistening in the dying light. "Your generosity astounds me in view of the fact that we have known one another so short a time. You are an uncommon man, Lockwood."

God, if she knew the kind of man he really was, she'd run as fast as she could. "I think I know the sort of woman you are."

She emitted a sardonic laugh. "I wish *I* knew the sort of woman I am. I am astonished by my own actions of late."

He cursed inwardly when Mr. Graham called him to come settle a dispute over a game of tennis. He released her hand and stood with an apology. "Daphne, please do not leave until we talk again. And that woman? I like her, no matter who she is."

Chapter Seven

*A*nd she *likes* you. *Far too much.*

Daphne stood to watch the cloud bank turn from gray to deep violet in the fading light. How, she wondered, did she keep getting herself deeper in trouble?

In all her years of running and hiding, watching over her shoulder, she'd never once doubted herself. Never once regretted all she'd left behind. But now, because of Lord Lockwood, she felt so…adrift. She had, quite literally, nothing to offer him. How appropriate, then, that they'd agreed there could be nothing more between them. *But, I pray, nothing less.*

A frisson of pleasure raced up her spine at the thought and she gave herself a mental shake. The strains of a violin reached her and she turned back toward the house.

Guests has taken the available seats facing the terrace, where a quartet was tuning their instruments. Late arrivals settled themselves on the blankets scattered on the grass. Little girls held hands and skipped in circles while little boys played Wild Indians, whooping and chasing one another with makeshift slings and bows and arrows. Darkness was closing in rapidly and gaily colored lanterns strung from the trees lit the fairy-tale scene.

Daphne strolled toward the group, still holding her wine-glass. She knew so many of these people, and yet she had never mingled in their society. All she knew was that this one liked soda bread, that one favored tarts, yet another had a penchant for meringues. They smiled and nodded at her politely, and she nodded back.

Alone, she found shelter in the shadows beneath a massive oak. She would stay for only a few pieces and then take her leave. If she remained for the picnic supper, she would have to make polite conversation. Heaven knew, she was sorely out of practice in that regard.

She became aware of a movement to her right and turned. The chargé d'affaires was approaching. She had always avoided anyone connected with government and law with great diligence, so she and Mr. Doyle had never exchanged more than a few words, and those at her shop in town.

She gave him a faint smile and turned back to the music, hoping he would pass her. That was not to be.

"Ah, Mrs. Hobbs," he greeted her in a theatrical whisper. "How diverting to find you at yet another island function. I thought they held no attraction for you."

"Never think it, sir," she said in a like tone. "But I live far from town and coming in again for a social event is really too time-consuming."

"Yet you attended the governor's reception, and here you are tonight. Dare I hope this signals a change in your previous policy of avoidance?"

She glanced down at the toes of her slippers. "The invitation reached me at an opportune moment, Mr. Doyle. Even so, I am afraid I must leave early."

He sighed. "And just when I was about to invite you to sit at my table."

She was not naive enough to miss the suggestion in his voice. She looked toward the terrace, praying to find Lockwood and failing. "I fear I must decline, sir. But thank you for the invitation."

"Not at all, Mrs. Hobbs. There will be more opportunities, to be sure. Especially since you have decided to seek political favors."

That brought her around with a start. Had there been something sharp-edged in his voice? "Political favors? I do not take your meaning, sir."

"I hear you have acquired a patent for your friend, Captain Gilbert, to carry government communications."

"Oh, yes. But that was not political, Mr. Doyle. It was personal."

"Personal? I see."

She groaned. "I have given you a wrong impression, sir. I merely meant that I, as a tradeswoman, depend upon Captain Gilbert to deliver the items I need to run my business. If he should quit the St. Claire run, well, my business could suffer, and that of a number of other tradespeople."

Mr. Doyle nodded and hesitated before he spoke again, a hint of condescension in his manner. "I understand, Mrs. Hobbs, but perhaps *you* did not understand the correct protocol."

Ah! He was offended because she had not gone to him first. There must be little for him to do when the governor was in residence, and she had deprived him of an opportunity to be useful. "I apologize for overreaching you, Mr. Doyle. Forgive my lapse of etiquette?"

"I've been too harsh, have I not? You have *my* apologies. I merely meant to keep you company, as you appear to have come alone."

"Please do not concern yourself, sir. As a widow, I am quite used to being alone."

"Ah, yes. And how long have you been in that lamentable state?"

Daphne hesitated. She did not want to answer, but neither did she want to give him any reason to look deeper into her past. "Five years, Mr. Doyle."

"Was it sudden?"

She blinked. What an odd question. "No. He…it had been coming on for quite some time."

"And where did you say you were from?"

And here it was, come home to roost—the very reason she had not mixed in society and yet further proof that she shouldn't have come tonight. She took a deep breath, forced a smile and launched forth with a lie and a diversion. "I am from Ashford in Kent. And you, sir? Where are you from?"

He chortled softly. "I apologize yet again. I did not mean to pry, but I did not want to waste this occasion to get to know you, since such opportunities are so rare."

She spied Lockwood not ten paces away. Relief mingled with anxiety. What a choice! The frying pan or the fire? She barely hesitated. "Oh! There you are, Lockwood." She ignored Mr. Doyle's sigh of disappointment and prayed Lockwood would go along with her subterfuge. She turned back to the chargé. "Thank you, sir, for the…diverting conversation." She went forward and took Lockwood's arm. She could feel the tension in his muscles through his sleeve.

"Is anything amiss, Mrs. Hobbs?" he asked, glancing between her and Mr. Doyle.

Yes! Her life was unraveling and the last thing she wanted was for either of these men to discuss her or her past. "Mr. Doyle has been keeping me company until you could return. Shall we go?"

With a short glance at Mr. Doyle, he nodded.

* * *

The little vignette he'd overheard confirmed Hunt's suspicion that Daphne Hobbs was hiding on St. Claire. She'd told him she was from Devon, yet he'd just heard her tell Doyle she was from Kent. Which, if either, was the truth?

Her hand, resting on his arm, trembled. He glanced back at Doyle again. "Daphne, did Doyle—"

"No! No, of course not. Mr. Doyle has come to Pâtisserie many times, and we have exchanged pleasantries, but I found myself at a loss in conversation. I am certain that is my fault. I am not adept at social intercourse."

He placed his other hand over hers in a gesture of comfort. "I have never found that to be so."

"Nevertheless, I do not like to talk about myself," she confided in a whisper. "I have always been a wallflower."

He studied her as they strolled the perimeter of the gathering. Even in the darkness, her smooth hair gleamed with glints of gold in the lantern light. Her peach-colored gown, modest for the gathering, was nonetheless elegant in its simplicity and her figure was sweet perfection. How could anyone as stunning as Daphne ever be a wallflower?

"I think I'd like to go home now," she said in a quiet voice. "I shouldn't have come. I really am not comfortable here."

He wasn't surprised at her decision. She'd appeared ill at ease except when they'd been alone. "I shall escort you, Mrs. Hobbs. Shall we find our hostess and make our apologies?"

"After the drive from the governor's reception, you know an escort isn't necessary. And I think it would be slightly scandalous for us to leave together again. Wagging tongues, you know. Gossip is St. Claire's favorite pastime."

He breathed a sigh of relief. As much as he'd like to be with Daphne, he'd rather not leave the Grahams' picnic. There were men here he needed to cultivate—exporters, importers and merchants. Men who would be privy to the shipping news, who might provide a sudden insight or a piece of the puzzle.

Daphne must have sensed his relief, because she released his arm and made a small curtsy. "Thank you for helping me disengage myself from Mr. Doyle. I shall find Mrs. Graham and say my farewells." She turned and hurried along the pebble path to the house.

He watched, fighting the urge to call her back. A faint hissing passed by his right ear and then, without sound or warning, Daphne crumpled to the ground. For a moment, he thought she had tripped, or caught the toe of her slipper on a fallen branch, but there was something unnaturally still in her form. He had no conscious memory of moving, only of kneeling beside her and turning her to look into her face.

A trickle of blood oozed down her cheek from an ugly splotch near her temple. The skin had broken in an erratic pattern, as if it had burst from impact. He dragged her into his arms and bent over her, trying to shield her from whatever had done this to her. He glanced around in a slow circle, narrowing his eyes to peer through the gloom. Blast the darkness! The only indication of anything wrong was a small round stone, gleaming with a wet patch, that looked out of place on the path.

The guests broke into a spate of applause and the quartet began another set. He was about to call for a doctor when Daphne moaned and struggled to sit up.

"Wh-what…"

"Sh-h," he whispered, then immediately wondered whether his instinctive reaction to keep this event secret was the right one. His instincts won out. They'd saved his life too many times to second-guess them now.

He stood, lifting her with him. "Lie back," he instructed. "I will deal with Mrs. Graham."

"I do not want—"

"I will tell her it was an accident."

"W-wasn't it?"

He suspected there had been something quite deliberate about it. He could still hear the hissing sound. If one of the lads playing with a sling had misfired, surely he'd have come forward by now. But this was not the time to quiz Daphne about her enemies. "We'll talk about it later."

Before she could make much sense of what had happened, Lockwood had her in the gig and they were headed for Sea Whisper at a brisk pace, trailing Lockwood's mount behind. She had a vague memory of him reassuring Mrs. Graham that all was well. That one of the boys playing in the woods that bordered the lawns had mistakenly released his sling in Mrs. Hobbs's direction. No, no fuss, please, he'd instructed. He'd just see that Mrs. Hobbs got home safely. And, after he'd had Mrs. Graham wet his handkerchief to clean the blood from Daphne's face, they'd departed.

She was mildly nauseated and her head ached. A hard knot was rising where she'd been struck—so close to the temple that a half inch lower would have killed her. And again, she was in his lordship's debt. She'd wanted to protest that she could see herself home, but when he'd put her on her feet for a moment, she'd swayed and nearly fallen.

She knew he'd wanted to stay tonight, and that compounded her guilt. He'd rebuffed her feeble attempts at conversation and was concentrating on the road. He kept glancing over his shoulder and watching the mangroves on either side of them, almost as if he expected to encounter wild beasts.

"Are you unwell?" he asked. "Nauseated? I think you have a concussion."

Entirely possible. "I am sorry to inconvenience you, Lockwood." The gates of Sea Whisper loomed ahead. "Truly.

This is far enough. I can make it the rest of the way. Please, I have importuned you long enough." In truth, she did not like being in any man's debt, and she'd never invited a man into her house before. She was not certain she wanted to do so now. She tried to think if there were things in her house that could betray her. Things that would tell him who she really was. But her head ached and she couldn't concentrate.

A grim smile curved the corners of his mouth. "Not a chance I'll leave you looking so unwell, Mrs. Hobbs. You haven't importuned me at all."

A polite lie? She held her tongue while he drove through the gates and she noted the light in Olivia's cottage. This time he took her all the way to the house. Surely once she was inside and settled, he would leave. She attempted to stand and fell back into her seat, her head swimming.

Without a word, Lockwood hopped down and came to her side of the gig. He lifted her out, carried her to the door and kicked the lower panel by way of knocking.

She winced. "I do not have a butler, Lockwood. Or any servant living in. Just put me down and I'll be fine."

He juggled her weight to free his left hand, and opened the door. Olivia had left a lantern lit in the front hall and Lockwood passed through into the parlor. "Where is your—"

"To your right," she said, beginning to feel nauseated again. If she could just lie down and be still—

He was remarkably surefooted and had keen eyesight in the dark. He found her room without further directions and placed her gently on the bed.

"I shall keep my back turned while you change," he said, lighting the candle on her nightstand.

She nearly choked. "No! I…am too tired. If…if you would just help me with my slippers, I will be fine."

He sat beside her, and lifted first one leg and then the other to remove her light leather slippers. His hands felt warm and seductive as he smoothed her skirts down again. That charming smile that was not a part of him was back. "You are quite safe, Daphne. I would not use this situation to take advantage of you. Let go," he added. She couldn't make sense of the request until he tugged his handkerchief from her hand. He went to the pitcher and bowl on her washstand, wet the cloth again and returned to her.

"Lockwood, really, I am fine. You can go now."

"Sorry, m'dear, but no. I will be waking you throughout the night. In injuries such as yours, the patient can lapse into a coma from which they do not awaken."

That was a sobering thought. She lay still and tried not to wince as he dabbed at her wound.

"I see you're accustomed to this."

"Accustomed?"

"This is not your first such injury," he explained. "You have a scar just inside the hairline above this one."

Her heartbeat lurched. That horrible night came back to her in a rush—Barrett tackling her, her head cracking on the marble hearth, seizing the poker... Bile rose in her throat and she gagged.

"Breathe," he soothed as he braced her. "Breathe and it will pass."

After a moment the nausea receded and Lockwood eased her back to her pillows. She closed her eyes, exhausted and wanting to stop his questions.

His shoulder propped against the doorjamb, Hunt watched Daphne sleep until he was certain she was resting comfortably, then returned to her parlor and poured himself a glass of sherry from the decanter on a small sideboard. He sat on the sofa, the only piece of furniture that looked sturdy enough to hold him. In a moment he'd unhitch Daphne's gig and stable the horses.

He closed his eyes and rubbed the bridge of his nose. Her injury puzzled him. It was an impact injury, delivered by a blow with something not sharp enough to cut the skin, but with enough force to shatter and even kill. His original impression of a rock and a sling was likely correct. But delivered by a careless boy playing at Indians? *Not* likely.

What was far more likely was that she had, by her association with him, found herself the victim of an attack meant for him. Someone must know—or at least suspect—what he was doing on St. Claire and either meant to stop him or give him a warning to cease.

Damn. That would mean he'd been found out. But who knew of his errand on St. Claire? He and Layton. Eastman surely wouldn't have told Bascombe—unless he'd hoped to draw the man out at Hunt's expense.

"Son of a bitch," he murmured to himself. Eastman had used him as bait. At best, Hunt would discover the leak and plug it. At worst, he'd be dead and Eastman would know the information came from their agent, Layton, or Bascombe.

So which one was it?

"Perdition!"

Hunt leapt to his feet and turned to face the intruder. A woman, her arms and legs akimbo, faced him. Her olive skin was flushed and her dark eyes narrowed in suspicion.

"Where is Mrs. Hobbs?" she asked.

"Who the blazes are you?" he returned.

The woman did not answer and hurried down the hall to Daphne's room. A moment later she returned, looking even fiercer and carrying a poker. "What have you done to her?"

"Nothing," he said, keeping his voice calm and in

command. "She was at the Grahams' picnic and was accidentally hit with a rock from a boy's sling."

"You lie. Mrs. Hobbs does not go to picnics."

He shrugged. "Nevertheless. I drove her home but I did not think it wise to leave her alone."

"I am here," she challenged.

"Who are you?"

"I am Olivia Herrera, the housekeeper." Poker still at the ready, she advanced another two steps. "And who are you?"

Ah, this would be the woman who lived in the gate cottage. "I am Reginald Hunter, Lord Lockwood. I own the neighboring estate. New Albion?"

Some of the tension drained from her arms. She lowered the poker to her side and eyed him warily. "Si? New Albion?"

He nodded. "I am going to unhitch the gig and stable the horses. Then I am spending the night on the sofa. I suggest you go back to your cottage and get some sleep. Mrs. Hobbs will need your assistance in the morning."

"You should go, eh? I will spend the night."

Hunt grinned. "I am staying, Mrs. Herrera. You may stay or go, as you please."

And she did stay. He found a strong pot of coffee waiting on the sideboard when he returned from the stables. Later, as he sat on the edge of Daphne's bed to shake her awake, Mrs. Herrera watched him from the door of the small bedroom adjoining Daphne's. She gave him a wary nod and closed her door, as if to say she had decided to trust him.

She shouldn't. After the things he'd done—the trusts he'd broken and the men he'd killed in the name of God and Country—trusting him was like trusting a wolf to guard a lamb. He'd debauch Daphne in a trice if she were better. In fact, he planned on it.

Chapter Eight

"I do not think I like this new man of yours, *querida*."

Daphne winced with the dull headache and tried to push herself up against the pillows. "What new man, Olivia? I do not..." She stopped. Lord Lockwood, of course. She had a vague memory of him waking her through the night and making her tell him her name and his. He wanted to make certain she was lucid, no doubt, but the questions had annoyed her at the time.

"Perhaps *you* do not have him, but *he* has other ideas," Olivia informed her. "You know, *querida,* he has an interesting way about him. I do not know which surprises me more— that I followed his orders, or that you did."

Good heavens! She had. The thought disturbed her. She had fought too long and too hard to win her independence to forfeit it now.

Olivia gave a deep chortle. "Ah, *querida,* you wear your heart on your sleeve, eh? I wondered...*si,* I wondered. But be careful. He is a dangerous man." She put the lunch tray down on Daphne's bedside table and helped her to sit up. "This Lord Lockwood of yours left orders that you are to have only liquids today, until the nausea passes. If you have dizziness, you must stay abed. I would do it, too, *querida*. Something tells me this man will be back to see that we have followed his instructions."

"P-Pâtisserie. Hannah will be wondering what's become of me."

"I sent the stable boy to town to inform Mrs. Breton that you will not be in today, and perhaps not tomorrow. You need to rest, *querida*. I want you to have a nap after you eat."

Olivia placed the tray over her lap. Tea and broth. Lockwood must have inspired fear in Olivia if she'd followed his directions so assiduously. Daphne wondered what he had said. She had yet to find anything that intimidated the housekeeper for long.

"Please bring me my mirror." Gingerly, she pushed her hair back from her forehead to assess the damage. A huge knot of vivid dark blue pooled around the broken skin. She knew from experience that she would be able to hide the worst of it by parting her hair to that side, then shuddered, dimly recalling that Lockwood had asked her about that other scar.

"Do you wish to lie down again, *querida?* Here, let me help you."

"No. No, I want to finish my lunch." She steadied the tray and sipped her tea, sweetened with lemon and sugar. The broth was a little harder to stomach. Perhaps it was the salt. She tried again, determined to conquer her nausea. If Lockwood were coming back, she wanted to be presentable. And to give him no reason to spend another night.

Hunt stared at his desk. The maps, notes and pens were precisely as he'd left them, yet somehow not as he'd left them. There was a subtle change that was oddly *too* exact. Almost as if they'd been moved and then replaced in a memorized order.

He went to his bureau and opened the drawers one by one. There, too, he sensed that someone had gone through them. The care with which items had been replaced indicated the intruder knew he had ample time. Hunt had been gone all day, and then with Daphne all night. Prichard? One of the servants? An outsider?

He returned to his desk and sat. One by one, he studied the maps and notes to determine if there was anything to indicate his purpose on St. Claire. He'd been very careful to keep any trace of his mission hidden. Naturally, he would have maps of his land and of the entire island. There were no notations of areas of interest to him—coves where pirates might lay in, places where rendezvous might be held, trails over the mountains to Blackpool. Nothing to betray him. Likewise, the papers were innocuous. He'd learned long ago to phrase everything in code.

Questioning Prichard would do him little good. If the man were the guilty party, he would be prepared with pat answers. Yes, it would be wiser to lay a subtle trap to determine whether Prichard was responsible.

On the other hand, if it wasn't Prichard… He closed his eyes and made a mental list of anyone who could remotely be responsible. Layton, of course, because he knew why Hunt was on St. Claire. Governor Bascombe, because he appeared to have an interest in keeping Hunt from going to Blackpool and had suspicious, frequent absences. Captain Gilbert, because, as a seafaring man, he was bound to know more about the other side of the island than he was telling. Doyle, because…just because.

And because Hunt had stayed alive by being a cautious man, he added Daphne Hobbs to the list. She couldn't be personally responsible for the search of his things, but there was always her wary servant, Olivia Herrera. Daphne had secrets and a mysterious past. She could have reasons for her presence on the island, and other reasons for her sudden entry into society. Could she have made an enemy evil enough to injure her, as she'd been injured last night? Absurd! And yet he couldn't dismiss the idea. The only thing he knew for certain was that he couldn't afford to trust anyone and that Daphne had been someone's target.

He folded the maps, closed his journal and slipped them back into the drawer. The time had come to take action. The questions he'd asked had gained him only vague evasions. He had to turn this mockery of an investigation into something workable. His primary expertise was in managing a situation, not investigating it.

He stood, pulled a strand of hair from his head, wet it with his saliva and placed it across the narrow gap between the desk and the drawer. If anyone opened the drawer again, he'd know it.

Now, to bait the trap.

After spending the afternoon touring the remainder of the plantation—beside Jack Prichard, to give his story credence—Hunt dangled the bait. "Prichard, could you have Cook pack two or three days' supplies for me and also have a bedroll and oilskin ready by day after tomorrow?"

"Aye, my lord. Are you leaving?"

He smiled. Was that wishful thinking? "Just doing a little exploration. I've heard there's a cove protected by a coral reef where the fish are extraordinary, and I'd like to see the waterfall on Mount Colombo."

"Oh." The factor's face brightened. "You will be amazed by the beauty. Yes, I will see to it that you have everything you need."

"Good. I finished my records and accounts this morning, so when we're done here, I'll clean up and go visit a friend. I shall likely stay in town tonight."

"Then you'll be leaving St. Claire soon?"

"Another week, perhaps. I'm close to making a decision regarding New Albion and may sell it."

"Do you have a buyer, sir?"

"Not at the moment. Interested?"

"If the price is right."

"Hmm. We'll talk later, Prichard. For the moment, can you show me where the fruit is stored before it is shipped?"

"Ah, yes. We do not keep it too long. We prefer it to rot on the docks at the shipper's expense rather than at ours." He laughed and shook his head. "It's all in the timing, my lord. It's all in the timing."

When he returned to his cottage to clean up, Hunt sent a note to Governor Bascombe by messenger, telling of his planned trip to Mount Colombo and the reef coast. Then he left his own message for Layton behind the brick over the lintel of the gutted hut. Finally, he'd tell Daphne Hobbs of his plans, and then he'd wait. One of them was bound to take the bait. He prayed it would not be Daphne.

Daphne reclined on a woven rattan chaise beneath the rain tree, her eyes closed and her face turned to the setting sun peeking through shifting leaves. Her muslin dress afforded her only the lightest of layers between her skin and the warm breeze.

She heard footsteps, long and measured, and knew Hunt had returned. The edge of the chaise gave as he sat beside her. She kept her eyes closed, wondering if he would speak. Instead, he smoothed her hair back from her forehead and traced the edge of her wound.

A languid sigh escaped her lips. How odd that he should have such an effect on her. A heat having nothing to do with the sun seeped through her.

"Does the sun hurt your eyes?"

"A little," she admitted, and smiled in spite of herself.

"What do you find amusing?"

"That I should know you by your touch." She covered his hand with hers. "I fear that is not a good thing."

"Then we must disagree," he mumbled, "because I think it is a very good thing." He cleared his throat and trailed his fingers down the side of her cheek. "The skin is already mending and the bruise is fading to yellowish around the edges. With a little care, this injury will not leave a ragged scar as the last one did."

The reminder of her scar broke her lethargy. The setting sun ducked behind a cloud bank and she blinked to focus her eyes. "Thank you for seeing me home last night, Lockwood. I don't know how I would have managed alone. But you really did not have to stay. Olivia has been hovering all day. I have told her the headache is gone, but she will not listen."

He grinned. "I should stay again tonight, just to give Mrs. Herrera something to think about," he said.

"Entirely unnecessary."

"I would not be so sure. I want you to be very careful and keep watch." He paused and took her hand between his. "I've been thinking, Daphne. Is there a chance that you were a target of that rock? Do you know of any reason why someone might want to hurt you?"

She shook her head even as she thought of William's uncle. But no, he would simply have her brought up on charges of murder. No need to sling rocks. She was far more vulnerable than that.

He accepted her denial and dismissed the subject. "I won't stay, but I will be checking on you to reassure myself of your well-being before I leave for a day or two."

Leave? A sharp pain pierced her middle. "Where are you going?"

"Just to see a bit of the island before I return to England."

She breathed a little easier. "Will you be gone long?"

"A day or two. I've decided to see the coral reefs and the waterfall since they come highly recommended."

"Are you taking a guide?" She resettled against the chaise cushions.

"I doubt I'll have need of one."

"Then…you will be returning to England soon?"

He hesitated before he answered and she prayed he was changing his mind. "I have duties. Obligations…"

She nodded. "Of course you do. I just…it seems like such a long way to travel for so short a time. I wonder that you bothered at all."

"I was at liberty for the moment, and I had to make some decisions about New Albion." He breathed in as if he were bracing himself. "If I sell, I shan't be returning."

She gazed through the trees toward the ocean, thinking of the miles that would separate them soon. A hollowness swept through her, and a sense of loss. They'd never been intimate, hadn't engaged in courtship rituals or declared affection for one another, but her life would be somehow diminished when he was gone. Ah, but he would be better without her.

She stroked the side of his cheek, savoring the masculine hint of dark stubble. "So pensive, Lockwood?"

He caught her hand and held it. "Do you ever visit London, Daphne? Have you thought of coming back? If circumstances presented an opportunity, would you—"

"No," she gasped, sitting upright. She coughed to hide her astonishment. "That is, I have too many unhappy memories there. I do not think I could ever be at peace in England."

"Peace? Is that what you want?" He leaned closer, brushing his lips across her forehead. "Or do you want rapture? There's no peace in loving, I think. Only a constant hunger." And then he dipped to speak against her lips. "A burning need," he said, his breath hot and sweet.

Oh, he was right. She didn't want peace. She wanted *him.* She had always wanted the things she couldn't have—a large and loving family, a man who loved her above all else, a home that was a refuge from the world instead of a prison.

Reckless and dizzy, she parted her lips and he accepted her invitation—softly, at first, and then with deepening hunger.

"You should come inside, *querida,* before you become overheated."

Lockwood broke the kiss and scowled at Olivia. The housekeeper's double meaning did not escape them. Daphne's cheeks grew warm and Lockwood stood. He gave her a slight bow and whispered, "I will see you later, *querida,*" in a tone Olivia could not mistake for anything but sarcasm.

From his vantage point in the shadows, Hunt kept watch. The waning moon cast eerie shadows through the palm fronds and undergrowth. He'd left his horse far down the beach, in a hidden clearing near Sea Whisper. No soft whickering or shifting hooves would give him away. He waited through the tedium, through the stealthy movements of nocturnal creatures and the call of night birds.

But nothing revealed itself.

Two hours before dawn, a soft sound, almost a shifting of the breeze, alerted him that something had changed. The hairs on the back of his neck rose. This was not an innocent sound, but the hint of something furtive.

From the shifting shadows along the path from the road, Oliver Layton appeared. A sharp stab of disappointment burned in Hunt's breast. One expected betrayal from the enemy, but it was bitter as gall coming from a comrade. He scarcely breathed as he watched to see what Layton would do.

Soundlessly, the man climbed the steps and made a soft hissing sound. *"Lockwood..."*

Hunt held his breath. Was the call a greeting or a test of how deeply he slept? Layton thumped his door with one knuckle. *"Psst..."* When there was no answer, Layton went down the steps and passed Hunt's hiding place on his way to the beach.

Hunt had a gift for stillness and knew how to control his breathing so that it became a slow, soundless rhythm. And he knew how to wait. These things were just a small part of what made him an adept assassin—and unfit for anything else. There was more, but Hunt did not like to think of those things.

If Layton had not forced entry and was looking for Hunt on the beach, it was unlikely he meant harm. Nevertheless, he waited while Layton glanced up and down the beach and then returned to the wide verandah and sat down on the steps.

Torn between waiting and making himself known, Hunt chose to wait. If Layton was cunning, he could be trying to draw him out or see if he'd laid a trap. Well, Hunt was a very patient man. Half an hour passed, then an hour. Finally Layton took a scrap of paper and a small piece of lead from the pocket of his work shirt and scratched a few words. He slipped the paper under Hunt's door and disappeared the same way he'd come.

And still Hunt waited until he was finally convinced that no one else would be coming, when dawn was less than an hour away. He took the steps two at a time, pushed his door open and retrieved the note. He glanced at his desk drawer and noted the hair he had placed there was still there. No one had come while he'd been with Daphne.

He unfolded the note and read. *Lockwood, I must talk to you at once. Tomorrow night at the hut. Layton*

Tomorrow night. But, for the moment, he had to keep his promise to Daphne—that he'd come back to check on her.

* * *

Her room was dark and only the barest hint of growing light through her bedroom window signaled the coming dawn. Daphne breathed deeply of the cool predawn air, and a tingle made her shiver. There was something foreign in the air.

The house was silent, but she had the sense of another presence somewhere near. Not Olivia. She'd sent the housekeeper home well before midnight. She lay motionless, straining to hear a footfall, a sigh, a stirring of the still air.

Nothing.

Daphne…

Had her name been spoken? Or had she dreamed it? She blinked, trying to see into the darkened corners of her room.

As if a ghost were materializing, Lockwood stepped out of the shadows of the doorway. "Daphne? I thought you were sleeping. Did I wake you?"

She pushed herself up against her pillows. "Not you." She sighed. "Your scent."

He came closer. "Horse and leather?"

She shook her head. "Heat and…" *Sex! A heady blend of man and desire.* She couldn't say that, but it was not necessary. He knew what she was thinking.

He moved closer. "I would have knocked, but I didn't want to wake you."

And she knew that nothing as inconsequential as a door would have kept him out anyway. "I thought you had forgotten."

"God, no," he breathed, arriving at her beside. "I will never forget you, Daphne."

His words seared her conscience. She would never forget him, either, but her past committed them to a life apart. He had obligations, responsibilities and a bright future. She had no future at all.

And soon he would be gone. Could she let him go

without…without knowing what might have been? Without feeling his flesh against hers? Without discovering what lay beyond the seductive kisses and skillful hands? Without knowing if she could be a woman in full, or if Barrett's taunts were true? Was she hollow? Cold? Incapable?

She took his hand to place it over her heart. "Do you feel my heartbeat, Lockwood?" she asked.

He nodded, looking strained and tense.

"Remember it. And know that as long as it beats, I will remember you."

His eyes widened and he pulled his hand back as if he'd been stung. "Daphne, do not say goodbye yet. I am not gone."

She nodded, knowing he would be soon. She did not demur when he leaned closer and traced her lips with his finger. She sighed and lifted her chin. He recognized her wordless plea and met it with a kiss. She knew he wanted to finish what they'd begun this afternoon before Olivia's interruption.

He cupped her breast, moving his thumb in little circles around the aureole. Her nipple firmed and he groaned. "I want you, Daphne," he whispered. "Not this endless teasing. I want you fully, with nothing held back. No reservations. Without qualification. Yielding to me. I don't want a part of you—I want all of you. If you cannot give me that…"

She could never be wholly any man's. As long as she kept her secret, she would be holding back. And if she told the truth, he would turn away from her. What choice was that?

She offered her lips again and welcomed the smooth heat of his tongue and answered with her own hunger. She was unaware that she was crying until the salted taste of her tears came between them.

"The sweetest refusal I've ever had," he murmured.

She could have called him back when he stood and moved to her door. She could have lied and betrayed them both. But she let him go, and she knew she would regret that for the rest of her life.

Chapter Nine

Hunt sat across from Governor Bascombe and watched the man's eyes. The eyes always gave a liar away—a quick blink, a shift in direction, the inability to meet a direct look. Unless the person was a pathological liar, there was some indication of untruthfulness.

Bascombe twitched in his chair. He kept looking toward the door as if he expected someone. Unfortunately for him, Hunt planned to stay rooted until he had some answers.

"What was that?" Bascombe asked. "Doyle?"

Hunt nodded.

"Good man. Very conscientious."

"I gathered."

"Is that it? Is that why you've come? To ask after Doyle?"

Actually, he'd come to assess the governor. As a peer, Hunt was not used to being relegated to underlings. There had to be a reason Bascombe was always sending Doyle to deal with him. "I spoke with Doyle just the other day, Governor."

"Did he tell you he is being reassigned?"

The lie came easily. "No, he did not mention that. Where is he going?"

"Undecided yet. Back to London to begin with. Then… could be anywhere."

"Your request, sir? Or his?"

Bascombe shifted in his chair but met Hunt's eyes. "Mine, but he does not know that."

"Is his service unsatisfactory?"

"He is quite proficient. But…I have no need of a chargé. My family problems have resolved themselves. I plan on being on St. Claire for a good long while."

Most men would not relish exile on a tiny island. Most men would, in fact, be only too glad to leave a chargé in place and hie back to London. Why was Bascombe guarding his position so jealously? Because it would be easier to conduct his clandestine business without an observer? Because he was trafficking with the pirates?

"Glad to hear it, Governor," Hunt said. Then he couldn't resist a little probe. "Is Blackpool a part of St. Claire, or has it declared its independence?"

Bascombe's gaze snapped up from his glass of port and a deep flush invaded his cheeks. "Might as well have," he growled. "I cannot even find the name of a mayor or any official. Can't correspond without a name, damn it all. Who the deuce do I make my demands to?"

"Have you thought of requesting military assistance?"

Bascombe looked down into his port again. "By and large, St. Claire is a peaceful island. We have managed to avoid military oversight so far. Wouldn't want to change that."

"Why?"

"Once you've got them here, you cannot get rid of them. And God knows they bring as many problems with them as they solve. Changes the whole atmosphere of the place."

Hunt smiled. There was truth in his assessment. Unfortunately, Bascombe's motives were questionable. He could as easily be covering up a crime as maintaining the provincial way of life on St. Claire. Still, Hunt found it odd that Bascombe did not visit Blackpool or make any attempt to incorporate its people into island life or government.

He gave the governor a bored sigh and sipped his own port. "I must thank you for warning me about not venturing over the mountains."

"I did? Yes, well. Good advice, that."

"Do you really think it could be dangerous?"

"Reports…indicate that is the case, Lockwood."

Well, that was good enough for him. He'd leave tomorrow.

The night air hung heavy over the entire island. He could have cut it with the knife he kept in his boot, or captured it in a jar. It was oppressive, weighing down on him and making his light cambric shirt stick to his chest and arms. He hadn't needed a jacket or a waistcoat for his short jaunt to meet Oliver Layton.

Hunt stood in the shadows of the ruined hut. Layton would be along soon and he wondered if the man would be prepared for Hunt's plan. Dangerous? Perhaps. Necessary? Absolutely.

His horse whickered and tossed his mane. Within a minute, Hunt heard the soft plod of hooves as a horse approached. He stepped out of the shadows as Layton dismounted.

"I wondered if you'd be here," he said.

"You sounded urgent."

"Aye. It's the first piece of useful information I've been able to gather. These islanders are a closemouthed lot." He looped his reins over a low-hanging branch of a sheltering oak. "Where were you last night?"

Hunt ignored the question. He waited for Layton to approach. The edge of his sheathed knife pressed against his ankle as a reminder that Layton could be a traitor. A sudden weariness came over him. He was sick of suspecting everyone and trusting no one, and of his life depending upon that.

"Well? What is it?"

Layton ran his fingers through his hair. "The dock foreman asked if I needed some 'extra' work. I told him I wouldn't be averse to making a little extra money. He told me to come to the Blue Fin at half past nine last night."

Hunt rubbed the stubble along his jaw. "Did you go?"

"Aye. Along with four other men. We were taken to a schooner docked at the end of the wharf. She must have docked after dark, because she wasn't there before."

"Markings?"

"None. No flags, no name. Black sails."

Black? Hunt's interest was piqued. "And?"

"There were boxes and crates waiting on board. We unloaded and stowed them in the harbormaster's shed."

"Are they still there?"

He shrugged. "I doubt they would keep evidence around where it could be found. But that is not the interesting part."

If that was not interesting, Hunt didn't know what was. He nodded for Layton to continue.

"When we were done stowing the crates, we were led to a warehouse filled with fresh goods and some unmarked barrels. I know the smell of gunpowder, Lockwood, and those barrels reeked of it."

That *was* interesting. "Let me guess. You loaded them onto the schooner."

Layton nodded.

"Did you see any documents change hands?"

"It was dark, Lockwood. The captain and our foreman huddled together for a few minutes. He could have passed off some documents, but I didn't see any."

"Did you find out where the schooner was bound?"

"No one said, but I'd lay odds she was bound for Blackpool. She didn't look like she'd been rigged for a longer voyage."

"Then?"

"The foreman paid us each four pounds and told us we had been drinking in the Blue Fin all night."

Hunt paced while he put the pieces together. He was not surprised that Blackpool was acquiring provisions from San Marco, but gunpowder? Why would a small village on the far side of the island need gunpowder? Unless it was for pirate cannons. "How many barrels of gunpowder, Layton?"

"I could not count them all, but I estimate close to sixty or seventy."

"Perhaps we should pay a little visit to the harbormaster."

Layton backed up a step. "There's more. I bought a pint for one of the mates. Asked him who the schooner belonged to."

"I am willing to wager you didn't get an answer."

"I was warned off. I was told some high muckworm was behind this and not to think I could get more than I'd already been paid."

Cold invaded Hunt's stomach. Questions like that could get a man killed. Layton knew that. Why had he risked being hit over the head and dumped in the bay? "Good God, Layton. What were you thinking?"

"I was thinking it could be my last chance to find out what is going on. But you have the right of it. The man picked up his pint and went to another table. Today my mates have been giving me a wide berth. I gather I am a marked man."

"Collect your things and meet me at the gate of New Albion tomorrow at midnight. I do not want anyone knowing the direction we are taking. We're going to Blackpool on reconnaissance."

"D'you think we'll find pirates?"

"I think we could. If some 'high muckworm' is involved,

then it's someone in San Marco, and he's got to be channeling information to Sieyes or Rodrigo some way. I'm betting it is through Blackpool."

Layton digested this news and then asked, "What will you tell Prichard and Bascombe?"

"I've already told them I am going to see the coral reefs. They will not miss me for a few days. We should be back before they become suspicious. Layton, you are going home afterward. St. Claire is not safe for you now."

Layton rolled his eyes but did not protest. "And you?"

Hunt sighed as he gathered the reins of his horse and tried not to think of his other unfinished business here. "I'll be going back, too. It's become increasingly clear to me that St. Claire is only half the puzzle. There appears to be a chain of contacts. Our muckworm is not likely to be the source of information regarding fleet movements. That would come out of Greenwich, pass to our muckworm, then to Sieyes and Rodrigo through Blackpool." Yes. From the navy to Bascombe, Bascombe to Blackpool and Blackpool to the pirate fleet.

"If you suspect all that, why are we going to Blackpool?"

"To confirm it. And to sever the chain."

Daphne could not sleep. Her sheets were twisted and damp from her restlessness. A glass of wine did not help. Nor did three. It was the weather, she told herself. Oppressive. How could anyone sleep when a storm was moving in? She recognized the signs. She could feel it in the still, heavy air. Feel it all the way to her bones.

She paced barefoot until she loathed the sight of the four walls surrounding her. Before she was conscious of making the decision, she was on the beach and up to her knees in the welcoming sea. Her chemise swirled in the water, then clung to her legs when it receded.

A little of the tension drained from her shoulders but the odd restlessness had a stranglehold on her chest. What was wrong? What did she want?

The memory of that night of near insanity rose to her mind. How seductive Lockwood had been, how persuasive. How she'd wanted to surrender with every fiber of her being. The fear that she'd never be whole again—that he would betray her and leave her—had overwhelmed her. But the memory of it clung to her and haunted her nights.

She glanced west, toward New Albion. Yes. That was what she wanted. *Needed.* And not just Lockwood's company. She wanted his arms, his mouth, his hands. She needed him next to her, above her, inside her. Tears filled her eyes. Oh, poor Daphne! Pitiful weak creature that she was, could she trade one night of passion for a lifetime of regret?

To her shame, she could. She knew that now. He would be gone soon, and she would remain. But she would keep the memory of him. She would not live with what might have been, cursing herself for her cowardice and always feeling empty. She'd have the memory, if not the man.

And then she was running, her hair whipped back by the wind. She had to hurry, before it was too late. Before she changed her mind.

"Lockwood!" she called, and the sound of her voice was lost in the wind and the roar of the waves.

From the sand she could see the dim flicker of a candle from within his cottage. Whether he had heard her call his name aloud or merely sensed it, something summoned him from the darkness. He stepped out to the wide verandah and saw her.

She took one tentative step forward, then froze. Did he still want her?

The black sky flashed with a streak of lightning and Lockwood came down the steps toward her. What would she say? How could she tell him why she'd come and what she wanted?

She needn't have worried. He cupped her cheek, meeting her gaze and acknowledging her wordless plea with a nod before he pulled her into his arms. His kiss sped her heartbeat. She would not change her mind this time. She would not let her own cowardice cheat her of this.

Lockwood slipped his hands down her back, over the curve of her buttocks and along the back of her thighs, lifting her to fit against his groin. She wrapped her arms and legs around him as he carried her thus to the house.

When he placed her on her feet beside the bed, he stepped back, waiting for a sign from her. She was unpracticed in seduction, but she knew what she wanted.

She reached out and fumbled with the fasteners of his breeches. He seemed amused by her awkwardness and steadied her with his hands on her shoulders. Finally she accomplished her task, and she pushed the cloth down until he was exposed to her. She swallowed hard and gathered her courage at the sight of his erection.

He waited until she lifted her gaze to his. A smile curved his lips. He was so sure of himself, so comfortable in this strange seduction, that she blushed. Her cheeks burned with it and a shiver went through her.

He lifted her shift over her head and threw it atop his breeches, but he did not embrace her. He stepped back, his lips parted as he examined her. She wanted to yield to modesty and cover herself, yet she knew he deserved this moment for all she had put him through. There'd be no turning back tonight, and she would be somehow changed by morning.

She prayed that she could live without him.

Later. She would think about that later.

Lightning illuminated the room and thunder rattled the

windowpanes. There had been a storm the last time she'd been here, and it seemed as if it had waited for them.

He lifted her and laid her upon the cool sheets before settling beside her. She wasn't certain what to do. Barrett had never required anything of her. Just that she lay still and receive him. On the rare occasions when she had tried to move, or ease his weight from her chest, he had cursed her and warned her to be still until he was finished. But this man—she could not bear it if he thought her gauche or clumsy.

When he lifted her leg to ride his hip, a shocking hunger sped through her. She felt open to him, vulnerable yet aroused. She gasped, dizzy with longing.

Another roll of thunder nearly drowned her words as she whispered, "Will you hurt me?" Oh, Lord! Had that faint quavering voice been hers? How could she have revealed her deepest fears? Thank God he could not have heard it over the thunder.

His voice was half moan as he whispered, "Easy, Daphne. Breathe. How long since—"

"Shh," she said. Questions would only make her think. For once, she wanted just to feel and not think of the consequences. Just once, to follow her instincts and not worry about planning her every step and hiding her real self.

He nuzzled her ear, nibbling the lobe and running the tip of his tongue along the rim. She shivered with the strange deliciousness of it, and the wonder that such things could bring her pleasure.

He inched lower, resting his mouth against the hollow of her throat, against her wildly beating pulse, and she tangled her fingers through his hair to hold him close. Unsure of herself, she followed his lead. He groaned when she nipped at his earlobe. Then he lowered his head and suddenly she was on fire. He nibbled at her breasts, drawing forth an instant and overwhelming need. She was molten at her core and she strained against him.

He rolled with her until he was above her, braced on his forearms. Even through the darkness, she could see the exact shade of his eyes, the sheen of perspiration on his forehead, the faint smile lifting the corners of his mouth. And she could feel the hard length of his erection between them.

"Easy," he urged. "Slowly."

The crisp hair of his chest abraded her breasts and made them all the more sensitive as he started moving downward again. Desire and fear, conscience and passion, all whirled in confusing opposition, and she truly didn't know what would happen next. Barrett had never done any of this.

She hadn't thought she could want a man in this way, but she ached for this one, caught in a need so intense that she couldn't name it, couldn't even make sense of it or of the urgency that gripped her. "Now," she demanded as hard pellets of rain began to pound against the windowpanes.

He stroked her side and bent his head to tease her breasts, bringing them to responsive peaks.

"Quickly," she gasped. "Before I change my mind."

His voice came as a low growl. "There is more, Daphne."

"*Now.*" She caught her breath on a sigh as a crack of thunder overhead shook the rafters. "Please…"

He laced his fingers through hers and pressed them against the pillow. Holding her gaze, he lowered his hips the remaining inches between her thighs, easing his shaft downward. She bit her lip as he prodded at her entrance, expecting the old pain. Anxious to have it over with, she tilted her hips up to him and he gained a shallow entry. She closed her eyes, preparing herself for the inevitable intrusion, but yearning for it anyway. He prodded again and then again, each time deepening his penetration. Where was the hard push forward? The mindless assault on her body?

She burned inside, wanting him there, *needing* him there, and moaned at the almost magical moment he glided deep inside. Tears trickled down her cheeks into her hair. How odd, that at this exact moment, she felt whole for the first time.

"Stay with me, Daphne," he whispered.

She opened her eyes again and held his gaze as he moved within her, creating a rhythm that compelled her to match him. Joined with him, her passion rising, she was attuned to his needs, bound by his gaze and commanded by his rhythm. She arched toward him, taking him into her, greedy for him. Harder, faster, deeper. And when little frissons of pleasure built into wild rapture, he shuddered with his climax. And, just as suddenly, her world spiraled inward to the point where they were joined, then erupted in a dark brilliance.

She was panting, gasping, trembling, and long waves of pleasure were washing over her as Lockwood, still deeply rooted within her, smoothed her hair back from her face and whispered soothing phrases in her ear. He called her beautiful. Told her she was Aphrodite and that he'd never known such ecstasy and that he couldn't get enough of her.

Sometime later—hours or days, she did not know—he sighed against her temple. *Sleep,* he urged as he eased from her for the third—or was it the fourth?—time. *Rest, sweet Daphne.*

Ah, but how could she rest? She'd just done the most irrational thing of her life. She'd just bared her deepest passions to a man who could ferret out her secrets, who was a member of the ton—a man who, by careless boasting or idle curiosity, could cause her ruin or even death.

Oh, Daphne, you little fool. Was it worth it? she asked herself. And answered, *Yes. A thousand times yes.*

Chapter Ten

Hunt sat on the steps of the verandah watching the sun rise. He hadn't been surprised to wake and find Daphne gone, though she could only have been gone for a matter of minutes. She was the sort of woman he'd have to marry if he wanted to wake with her. And that idea was becoming more appealing by the hour.

When he'd seen her standing on the beach last night, he'd feared he was dreaming. Daphne had been frozen, almost as if she could not move unless he urged her. He'd gone to her, half afraid she'd bolt if he spoke and broke the spell.

He stood and plucked several stems of wild orchid near his door, then stretched, savoring the aches of arduous lovemaking. He'd gone slowly with her, fearing she'd bolt again if he gave her the slightest reason. Her question—would he hurt her—had been spoken so softly that he'd barely heard her, and it warned him she had not been treated as she deserved. Was this the key to her past?

But then, by the shy and almost desperate way she responded, he knew everything he needed to know about her. He'd stake his life that she had never done anything like that before. If she had taken lovers, she had done so only after long and patient wooing. And they'd been clumsy idiots. He recognized the first taste of rapture when he saw it.

Amazingly, he'd meant every honeyed word he'd murmured in the midst of the storm. Daphne had become everything to him. He was not a green youth, caught up in the throes of his first love affair. He was experienced enough to know the difference between infatuation and love, and worldly enough to know that he'd begun to love Daphne long before she'd come to him in the storm. Her quiet courage, her strength and determination, were the foundation. Her throaty laugh, the expression on her face when she looked into his eyes, the way she arched her neck and moaned when she reached her climax—those were the added advantages.

He wanted to take care of her, ease her way, lie down and get up with her and, if she were willing, get his sons and daughters on her. To hell with his friends and family if they could not accept Daphne as Lady Lockwood. He would make her his, and no one would stand in his way.

He tickled his nose with one of the wild orchids. The scent, uniquely Daphne's now, seduced him utterly. He would give her time to rest, and then he would go to her tonight before he left for Blackpool.

She should be exhausted, Daphne realized. She should be barely able to move. But logic had no place in her current condition. She smiled and pulled the chain that tipped the bucket over her head. The fresh cold water rinsed away the salt and the sand, reviving her as effectively as a sound sleep.

She wrapped her dressing robe around her and went into the cottage. The smell of eggs and ham reminded her that she hadn't eaten since yesterday afternoon. In the kitchen, Olivia turned to her, a hard expression on her face.

"I was…up early." That much was true.

"Do not lie to me, *querida*. I have been here for hours. I know where you were."

Daphne considered an evasion and then discarded the idea. She was an adult, after all, and a widow. She could do as she pleased. She went to the worktable and poured herself a cup of tea from the chipped china pot.

"Well?" Olivia insisted.

"I will not excuse myself, Olivia. And I have no need to apologize to you."

Olivia raised her eyebrows. She was not accustomed to such frankness from Daphne.

"Oh, what does it matter?" Daphne asked, half to herself. "He will be gone within a week. I just…" She shrugged.

"He is handsome," Olivia allowed. "And he has the look of a man who could bring your blood to a boil. But, *querida*, he is not a man to trifle with."

"There is nothing trifling about what we are doing."

Olivia shrugged and turned back to her cooking. "He will leave you with his seed in your belly. Then what, *querida?* Will you ask me for the name of the old Gullah woman in Blackpool who takes care of such matters?"

Daphne looked down at her flat stomach and placed her hand over it in a protective gesture. The thought of bearing Lockwood's baby bloomed in her, filling her with wonder. Could such a thing be? "I hadn't thought of that, Olivia. But no. I would not get rid of it."

"*Querida,* I have always known you are cut from fine cloth. I do not know what has brought you to St. Claire, but I know you are not the sort to give birth to a bastard. And what would you tell little William?" Olivia clucked her tongue and shook her head. "Sometimes you are so innocent. *Think, querida.* How would such a thing change your life? Your position on St. Claire? The good citizens would soon put the pieces together and know who had fathered your baby."

Her hand trembled and she splashed her tea into the saucer. She would have to move to a new island. Perhaps take refuge on San Juan or a Dutch holding. Olivia was right. She could not have a child. Such a thing could be disastrous, especially if Lockwood found out and decided to claim it.

"I was not thinking," she admitted.

Olivia nodded. "The madness will pass, *querida.* You will only miss him for a little while, and then you will forget him. Send for William to come for the holiday. He will cheer you. He misses you so."

She sat at the table and looked up at her friend. "Yes. He does, does he not?"

"So many letters lately, eh? A certain sign he wants to come home. There is another so soon."

"Another?" she repeated. "Letter?"

"Si. I have put it on your desk."

Daphne rushed into the parlor. There, on the polished surface of the escritoire, was a letter stained from travel and passage from hand to hand. Its origin was Charleston, but the envelope did not bear William's childish handwriting. She broke the seal and unfolded the page.

My dear Mrs. Hobbs,
It is with mixed emotions that I take pen in hand to inform you of a rather startling event.
Several months ago our modest school became the focus of flattering attention from abroad. We received visitors who, under the guise of evaluators, were engaged in interviewing our staff and students. They were,

they said, gathering data for a British catalogue of foreign schools of merit to assist wealthy families in finding suitable education for their sons. They were granted
access to all facets of Bridgerton Academy.

Their questions seemed logical. They asked the age
and nationality of each student, the number of years they
had been in attendance at Bridgerton, their curriculum
and the current location of the student's family.

An icy cold settled in the pit of Daphne's stomach and her
hand began to shake.

Remembering your instructions at enrollment of
young William, I thought I had successfully evaded the
pertinent questions. William, however, must have given
other answers during his interview.

Two days ago, our visitors were back, bringing with
them a man claiming to be Lord Barrett, who swore that
Master William is his son.

Daphne covered her mouth to muffle her outcry. Barrett?
But he was dead! She closed her eyes and could still see him,
lifeless and bleeding, on the floor of her bedchamber. It
couldn't be! There had to be some mistake. Alfred! Could it
be Barrett's brother?

Lord Barrett presented papers signed by the British
Consul authorizing him to remove Master William to
England forthwith. I denied that the child was any but
William Hobbs. However, William had given answers
in the previous interviews that identified him as the Bar-
rett heir.

You will understand that I had no choice but to com-

ply with their demands. I regret, Mrs. Hobbs, that you
did not fully inform me of the facts pertinent to Master
William's birth. Had I been warned, perhaps I…

She crumpled the letter in her fist, fighting tears and en-
croaching panic. William! He must be terrified! And if Alfred
had him, he was in danger of his life. Alfred would like
nothing better than to present William dead, and then claim
the title for himself and his sons.

"Perdition! What has you in such a state? Is little William ill?"

Daphne looked up to find Olivia in the doorway. "He…he
is gone. Taken back to England."

Olivia's eyes narrowed. "No. It is not possible. Who would
do such a thing?"

"I think it was his uncle."

"The wicked uncle, eh?" Her housekeeper sighed and
shook her head. "Do not look surprised, *querida.* I have
known for years. How could I clean your house, cook and
care for little William before he was sent to school, and not
know these things? I am sorry for you, but it was bound to
happen. Yes?"

Daphne shook her head. "No! I planned so carefully. I
guarded against…"

"But you had five years, eh? Long enough for William to
grow stronger. You must have known you would have to stop
running someday."

"I thought William would be safer away from me. I never
thought they'd find him. I feared they would find *me.* I cannot
think how—" The necklace! The one she'd sold in Boston for
the money to take them even farther away, and to fund their
new life. Once Alfred found that, he must have spent the last
years looking for her in America before he finally thought to
look for William instead. Oh, she should have kept him with

her! Stupid! She had been so stupid! She pounded the little desk with her fists and wept with rage.

"*Querida*," Olivia soothed, "collect yourself. You must trust now that William will be well. That your fears have been for naught. Eh? You cannot help him now."

She could. She would. With her last breath, she would find William and keep him safe. She stood and straightened her dressing gown, collecting her thoughts and beginning to make plans.

First, she would send a message to Captain Gilbert.

Daphne wrote notes to Olivia, giving her Sea Whisper, and to Hannah, signing over the deed to Pâtisserie. She'd sent a letter to the headmaster of William's school, then cleaned the house and finished the wash. And she'd taken her valise—the same one she'd used to flee England so long ago—down from the attic. She would pack her things in the morning, just before she left for San Marco. Once there, she would prevail upon Governor Bascombe one last time.

And the last chore, the one that would end her idyllic life at Sea Whisper, lay ahead. She walked out the kitchen door and took long strides toward the stable. Oh, she must remember to send a note to Timmy and ask him to pick up her horse and gig at the docks. She had a sinking feeling she was forgetting at least a dozen things, but her thoughts had been so scattered since reading the headmaster's note that she couldn't concentrate on anything for long.

She'd had a burn in her stomach all day. All her years on St. Claire, she had feared that someone would recognize her or that she'd be traced. But they'd found William, and that was worse. She took a deep breath and calmed her jangling nerves. She mustn't panic. Now, more than ever, she needed to keep her wits about her.

She took the shovel from the empty stall and went back to her garden. The sky had grown dark, and she hurried back into the house to fetch a lantern.

Exactly five paces from the trunk of the rain tree, she plunged the scoop into the ground. Although the earth was damp from the rain last night, she had to slice through grass and hard-packed sand. The task was not as easy as it should have been, and an hour later, the hem of her gown heavy with mud, she wiped her forehead on her sleeve. *How deep had she buried it?*

Another shovelful, and another. And, at last, a hollow sound and a solid *thunk*. She dug around the edges and then used the shovel to wedge the small chest away from the roots entwining it. She dropped the shovel and scooped the chest out of the ground.

For five years this proof of her crime had lain inert beneath the rain tree. Five years in which she'd learned to be strong and independent, learned to take care of herself and her son. Learned to trust no one but herself. And now it was over. She was back where she'd begun.

Tears blurred her vision as she carried the chest to the house and placed it on the worktable in the kitchen. The latch was rusted and the tiny key she'd kept in a stocking did not work. A knife from a drawer did.

Mud and rain had seeped through the cracks and warped wood, leaving the oilskin pouch in a bed of muck. She took the pouch to a pan and pumped water over it until she could untie the leather thong that held it closed. And there, on the dough board, she emptied the pouch.

The only jewelry she'd worn since that long-ago night was her wedding band, as an odd sort of penance. Now diamonds, pearls, sapphires and rubies flashed at her, dazzling in their brilliance. Necklaces, rings, bracelets, earrings and hairpins scattered across the table. The Barrett jewels. William's inheritance.

A sharp intake of breath spun her around. Lockwood stood there, his attention riveted on the small scattering of gems. She'd been so intent on her task that she hadn't heard him come in. Dear Lord! How could she ever explain this?

"Daphne," he murmured. "Where…how did you come by this?"

Tears sprang to her eyes. She could not bear to see his anger and disappointment when he learned of her perfidy. Oh, but did he have to know her whole sordid past now? She was almost certainly going to her disgrace and death. She couldn't take Lockwood's scorn with her. He would know soon enough but, please, God, not tonight.

He blinked and turned his attention to her, then closed the distance between them and gathered her into his arms. "Daphne, is this your secret?"

She managed a nod.

"Did you steal them?"

She nodded, then shook her head. Perhaps it was stealing, but she was holding them for her son's future. He was, after all, the rightful owner of the Barrett jewels. Or would be, if his uncle let him live that long.

"You are overwrought. Come." He led her to the pump and held her hands under a stream of water.

She felt the heat of his chest against her back, the strength of his arms around her and the tickle of his breath in her ear as he whispered, "Easy, Daphne. I will make it right. We will get through this. Just trust me. Tell me what's wrong. What has upset you."

She turned in his arms and looked into his eyes. But she couldn't trust him. She couldn't trust anyone. William's life was hanging in the balance. "I…cannot."

She thought he would curse her or demand to know, but he merely smiled as if he understood her fears.

He brushed the hair back from her forehead and ran his finger along her old scar. "What happened here, Daphne? Who did this to you?"

"No one. I...fell."

"You are a poor liar. Do you think there is anything I cannot keep you safe from? Anything I would not do for you?"

Her heart twisted. "You barely know me, Lockwood. Perhaps you do not know me at all."

"I know enough. Trust me. Tell me why you are hiding on St. Claire. It has something to do with this scar, does it not, and the jewels?"

Everything to do with them. "I...I need time to think." She sighed. "This is all so confusing. Happening so fast."

"Time? I can give you that, my dear. I will be gone tomorrow, and perhaps the next day, but when I return, we will talk. There are things we need to settle."

Ah, he, like she, would be gone in the morning. By the time he came back, there would be nothing left to settle. She laid her cheek against his chest and nodded.

"I love you, Daphne."

Her heart stopped beating. He loved her? How cruel! How utterly absurd! And how bittersweet to realize that she loved him, had for days now, but had never expected that love to be returned. And now she wished it wasn't. Everything would be so much easier if only she could make a clean break.

"Did you hear me, Daphne? Do you understand what I'm telling you? I want you to marry me."

"I love you, Lockwood, and I will give you all I *have* to give. All that is in my power." *Tonight. And pray it would be enough to last a lifetime.*

His eyes softened. He kissed her cheek and the scar on her forehead. She knew he was telling her that he'd take care of her. But it was too late for that.

She slipped her arms around his neck and came up on her toes to reach his lips. He was exquisitely gentle, but she did not want his gentleness. She wanted his passion, fierce and hot, as it had been last night. She moaned and trembled with the memory of what he could do to her.

When he felt her hunger, he lifted her and carried her to her bedroom. Tonight there was no room for hesitance or uncertainty. Tonight they tore at each other's clothing until they were at last flesh to flesh with nothing to separate them. When he nipped at her breasts, she grew damp with longing. She pulled him to her and wrapped her legs around him, wanton and greedy.

He met her urgency with an almost violent passion, driving into her in one long thrust, filling her with himself. He was claiming her, making her unfit for any other.

She arched and moaned. "Yes, Lockwood…please. Again."

And he did. Again. And again.

Chapter Eleven

The trek over the mountains had taken longer than Hunt had anticipated, and their arrival in the small town had been delayed until late afternoon. They had left their horses in a clearing off the track a mile or two down the mountain. The dark suspicious faces of the villagers gave no opening for conversation or questions, and narrowed eyes followed them as they wove down the steep narrow lanes in search of a tavern or inn. Everything about Blackpool was unwelcoming.

A cluster of small stone huts perched precariously over the deep cove, at least one hundred feet below. The only way up the sheer cliffs was a square platform operated by a windlass. One small schooner, dark sails lashed to the masts, was anchored in the cove and tossed like a cork on the rough currents. No wonder ships did not routinely anchor here—they'd be dashed against the sheer rock walls and sink.

"That's her," Layton whispered. "That's the schooner we loaded three nights ago."

Hunt committed the schooner to memory. If he saw her again, he'd remember her. She was sleek, low and dark—more of a smuggler's vessel than a pirate ship.

"Jaysus," Layton whispered. "You'd think we were lepers."

Hunt gave him a grim smile. "Not far from the truth when you consider why we've come."

"Let's have done with it, then, and not linger. I've no wish to have my throat slit in my sleep."

"I am as anxious as you to be back in San Marco, but we cannot rush this, Layton. Subtlety is what we need at the moment, and a touch of patience. It should not take too long to get what we want."

They found a small tavern and sat at a table in one corner. Again, Hunt kept his back to the wall.

A short, stout man came toward them, wiping his hands on a dirty apron. "Whadya want?"

"Chowder?" Hunt ventured. "And ale?"

Layton nodded his agreement.

The man did not move. Did not even blink. "You stupid?" he asked. "Strangers don' come 'ere for the chowder. Whadya want?"

Layton half rose from his chair with an angry expression and Hunt waved him back. "Food. And the answer to a question."

"What that be, stranger?"

"Food first."

The proprietor looked at him with grudging respect before he shuffled back to the bar.

The distant clang of a ship's bell carried from outside. Was there a new ship in the cove announcing her presence?

The proprietor yanked a chain hanging from a beam and, somewhere outside, an answering bell sounded. Damn clever. Now everyone in Blackpool and the cove below had been warned that there were strangers in the village.

"That was a challenge, Lockwood. Was it to warn the villagers or the ship?"

"Shh. Challenge or not, we do not rise to it."

"I've barely seen a dozen people. They likely chop strangers up and put them in the chowder."

Hunt gave Layton a quelling glance. He inclined his head to the back door. "Do you have to visit the privy?"

Layton grinned. He stood, ambled out the door and returned a few moments later. He sat back in his chair, crossed his arms over his chest, donned an expression every bit as sullen as any they'd seen and gave Hunt a faint nod.

So he'd been right. There was a new ship in the cove.

A man dressed in work garb with a red kerchief around his neck opened the door and peered into the gloom. He studied them for a long moment, then shut the door.

"Taking a report to his friends, no doubt."

Hunt agreed with a nod. "It shouldn't be long, now."

"I was more at ease at that French tavern in Marseille near the middle of the campaign," Layton admitted. "That, at least, was war and we all knew the rules. This is…different."

Hunt sensed it, too. The danger was nearly a physical presence. He gave the tavern keeper a hard look. The man pulled a tap and poured two tankards of ale. He brought them to the table and slammed them down, sloshing foam on the sticky surface.

Layton spun a coin on the tabletop and grinned when the man snatched it up.

What was wrong with Layton? It was almost as if he were trying to start a fight. "Contain your antagonism, Layton, or wait outside."

Layton gave a long-suffering sigh and then took a drink from the tankard. He made a face and an obvious effort to keep from spraying the ale onto the table.

"Come, can it be that bad?"

He nodded and Hunt took a cautious sip from his own tankard, expecting the ale to be watered down or stale. But it was bitter with an odd bite. Gunpowder? Was the contamination deliberate, or a faint reminder of the original use of the cask? He met the tavern keeper's gaze.

Deliberate. And, if Hunt was any judge of character, a warning. It was becoming increasingly clear why the civilized side of the island never ventured here. These people gave new meaning to the word *inhospitable*.

Daphne stood in front of Governor Bascombe's desk, feeling rather like a naughty child called to account for her behavior. "A family emergency," she explained. "Completely unexpected. The point, sir, is that it changes my circumstances and I am not likely to return to St. Claire. I have deeded my estate to Mrs. Herrera, and my business to Mrs. Breton. I believe all my accounts are paid and I should have no outstanding debts."

The governor nodded and tented his fingers as he studied her. "Then why have you come?"

"I wanted to ask you, sir, for a personal favor."

"Have another friend who needs a patent, madam?"

The slight edge to his voice made Daphne uncomfortable. She wondered if he regretted having granted Captain Gilbert the patent. But she had no time for hesitation now. "No, sir. I simply wanted to ensure the smooth transfer of my property. Mrs. Herrera and Mrs. Breton are unaccustomed to the intricacies of title transfers, taxes and such."

She removed a list from her reticule and slid it across the desk to the governor. He opened it and scanned the lines. "As you can see, it is a list of property and how I have disposed of it. There will, of course, be sufficient funds in my accounts to cover the costs of transfer. I do not know anyone else I trust who can oversee this task."

He looked up at her and nodded. "I shall oversee the transfers, if that is what you are asking, Mrs. Hobbs. Most generous of you. I see here that you are giving your horse and gig to Timmy Adams. Very compassionate. The lad has a mother and brother to support. With his own horse, he can hire out."

She closed her reticule, relieved that he had consented.

"But would you not rather sell your property? Surely you will need money upon your return to England? I am bound to say that this looks almost like a last will and testament."

That was closer to the truth than he could possibly know. She forced a smile and said, "I suppose it is a sort of ending to my life here on St. Claire. But is it not said that all good things must end sometime?"

In the harbor, the *Gulf Stream*'s bell rang the call for passengers to board. The governor nodded again and she stepped back from his desk. "Thank you, Governor Bascombe. I knew I could count on you."

Her hand was on the knob of his door when the governor called her back. "Mrs. Hobbs, I wonder if you might do *me* a favor."

She was hardly in a position to refuse. She returned to his desk and inclined her head. "My pleasure, sir. Name it."

After an aggravating pause, he opened his middle desk drawer and removed a small oilskin packet sealed with string and wax. "When you arrive in London, would you see that Lord Eastman gets this?"

She took the packet from him and glanced down at it. "Are you certain you do not wish to include it in the courier's packet? I could give it to Captain Gilbert."

"No!" Governor Bascombe stopped and cleared his throat. "That is, I'd rather this remain a private matter. Never do to mix personal and official business, would it?"

"N-no," she agreed uncertainly. "But I have not met Lord Eastman. Where would I find him?"

"At the Foreign Office, m'dear. And one last favor?"

"Of course."

The governor sighed and shrugged, his manner belying any particular importance. "Give it into his hands only, eh? Don't want it languishing on some clerk's desk for weeks before it gets to Eastman."

She nodded, relieved to know this was not an important document. She would put it in her writing box to keep it safe. "Of course not, sir. I shall deliver it upon my arrival."

The gloom outside thickened and the tavern keeper lit the hanging lanterns with a piece of kindling he drew from the fire heating the chowder pot. Muted conversation carried to them from outside. Hunt couldn't make out the words, but they stopped abruptly when the door opened.

A huge man with black hair and a florid complexion crossed the threshold and halted to stare at them. The man hitched his ragged trousers up, glanced at the proprietor, then at their tankards and then back at the tavern keeper. Clearly, he was not pleased that the man had served them. He and his companions went to the counter, followed by the man with the red kerchief, and spoke in low tones with the proprietor. He wondered if these were new arrivals from one of the ships in the cove.

"Pirates?" Layton muttered.

"Don't know, but I'd wager my title and fortune that they know where to find them. Too quiet to be a pirate town, but there's something illegal going on here. Smuggling?"

"What the hell is wrong with these people?"

Hunt smiled in spite of himself. "Not so complicated, Layton. They do not want to hang. For all they know, we could be government men."

Layton gave a short laugh and looked away from the

group at the tap. "If something does not happen soon, we'd better leave."

Hunt was inclined to agree. He'd never been in an odder situation. He held the tankard to his lips, then put it down again, suddenly wondering if the gunpowder had been added to mask a drug.

The giant in tattered trousers advanced until he stood over their table. "Name?"

Hunt pushed his tankard away and stood. He was nearly as tall as the man and wanted him to know he wouldn't be intimidated by size. "Lock," he said, using one of his aliases. "Yours?"

"Saldon. What you want?"

"Chowder."

Layton snorted in amusement and Saldon gave him a look that could have curdled milk.

"We don't hold with jokers in Blackpool."

Hunt shrugged and drew Saldon's attention away from Layton. "Not joking, Saldon. Can a man get a bowl of chowder in Blackpool?"

"Y'didn't come all the way from San Marco for chowder, Lock."

"I want some now. I do not like to do business on an empty stomach."

"Mathers, get 'em chowder!" Saldon called to the proprietor, then turned back to Hunt. "What you want?" he asked again.

Hunt sat and gestured to an empty chair between him and Layton. "I am looking to do some business."

"That so? What kind of business?"

The silence stretched out as Hunt deliberately kept Saldon on edge. "The kind I wouldn't want to do in San Marco," he said at last. "A mutual friend sent me. Said we might strike a bargain."

"We don' 'ave mutual friends, Lock."

He nodded. "Well, then. You're not the man I was sent to see."

The proprietor brought two bowls of steaming chowder with spoons. Hunt and Layton applied themselves to the meal and ignored Saldon. To Hunt's relief, the chowder was remarkably good and he did not have to pretend to have an appetite.

A grin spread over Saldon's florid face. He lifted Hunt's tankard and sniffed. "Ol' Mathers up to his tricks?"

Hunt pushed the bowl away and did not answer. With a glance, Layton followed suit.

"The man you come to see got a name?" Saldon asked.

"I was told he'd find me."

"Name Rigo mean anything to you?"

Rigo? Rodrigo the pirate? The bloodthirsty villain who, along with the French pirate, Sieyes, had half the Caribbean quivering in their boots? He shot Layton a warning glance. "Maybe. He around?"

"Might be, dependin' on why you want 'im."

"I told you. Business."

Saldon glanced over his shoulder at the tavern keeper. "You got a room, Mathers? Lock an' his friend, here, might be too late to go down the mountain tonight."

The proprietor grunted and headed off to a darkened back stairwell. A moment later he was back and growled something about the room at the head of the stairs. Hunt wondered how much the man would fleece him for chowder and a room.

His initial objective had been to evaluate the town and to see if there was any indication of a pirate base. But now he had an opportunity to learn much more. If he could verify that either of the ships in the cove belonged to a pirate, he could safely conclude that there was some complicity from San Marco. And that would mean that someone in San Marco was passing information to the pirates through Blackpool. According to Layton, the schooner he recognized had been loaded with supplies. If they were being transferred to another vessel, then the connection was made.

Saldon went back to the bar. A moment later, one of his companions hurried out the tavern door.

Layton leaned across the table to whisper, "What the hell are you going to do if Rodrigo actually comes?"

"Fabricate a story," he admitted. "Keep it suitably vague and allude to my superior. If I can lead him into mentioning a name, we'll have all we need."

"And how the hell do we get out of here?"

Hunt grinned. "We'll have to make something up." He'd been in worse spots and might have relished the challenge a week ago, but he had Daphne to think about now.

He remembered her as she'd been last night—demanding instead of pliant, aggressive instead of passive, desperate, as if…as if it were the last time?

Suddenly, he was impatient to finish here. He needed to get back to San Marco. No, to Sea Whisper.

The tavern door opened and Hunt noted it was full dark out now. Two men entered—one a wiry individual with stringy brown hair, the other a dark man dressed in a lace-trimmed shirt with a gold loop through his left ear. They glanced toward Hunt's table, then went to the bar. The first man looked over his shoulder and narrowed his eyes before turning his attention to his companion's conversation.

A moment later, the dark man crossed the room and sat in the chair Saldon had recently vacated. He looked between the two of them and raised one thick dark eyebrow. "Lock?"

Hunt acknowledged the question with a nod.

"You desire to do the business?"

The accent was heavily Spanish and Hunt shot Layton a warning glance. "Depends," he said. "Who are you?"

The man's lips split in a wide grin. "I am the man who does business in Blackpool."

Rodrigo. It had to be. Hunt had better come up with a suitable story quickly. He stalled by taking a drink of the noxious ale. "A mutual friend recommended you. He said you could handle anything. Is that true?"

Rodrigo grinned. "His name, this friend yours?"

Hunt donned a wary expression. "You first."

"I have many friends, Britisher. But not to do the quibble, eh? I talk only private. Better that way, eh? No witnesses." He laughed and gave a meaningful glance at Layton.

With a jerk of his head, Hunt sent Layton to the bar.

"Private!" Rodrigo shouted.

One of his men grabbed Layton by the sleeve and dragged him out the back door, followed by the proprietor. Rodrigo turned back to Hunt. "Now we are alone. Speak."

"Our…mutual friend told me you might be willing to handle a small matter for me."

"Small?" Rodrigo laughed. "No one comes to Rigo for small matters. An' who is our mutual friend, eh? Your king?"

A chill went down Hunt's back. Did this man suspect who they were? There was nothing for it but to bluff. "What makes you think I'm here on the king's business?"

Rigo tilted his head toward the door. "Your friend. One of my men has recognized him from the other side. He has been asking around, eh? Prying. If he is the mutual friend who told you I could help, he was lying."

There was a muffled cry from the back.

"If you listen carefully, Lock, you will hear the splash, eh? This is how we deal with meddlers and liars. Your friend is no more."

Hunt controlled his breathing as rage gurgled upward. He did not even blink as he summoned the dead calm that had gotten him through such situations in the past. Only a cool head would serve him now. The knife in his boot would serve him later.

"You do not care?" Rigo grinned. "Good. Then you will not miss him. Now what is this business of yours?"

"I want someone kidnapped," he said. "If I give you the sailing schedule and name of a ship, can you capture it and remove this person?"

"You want the ransom?"

"I want him dead."

"And the rest of the ship?"

He shrugged to indicate his indifference.

"Ah. Good. More for me. Now, this person's name?"

The first name that came to his mind was one of the few men he knew to be as deadly as he. And a man who would relish the chance to kill a man like Rodrigo. "Lord Auberville."

"The terms?"

"No terms. You get the schedule and the ship. I get Auberville."

Rigo sat back and crossed his arms over his chest. "And how will I know this is not a trap to draw me out?"

Hunt gave him a cold smile. "I'd say that is your problem. Goes with the territory, does it not? Verify my information with your own source."

"You do not lie to me, Lock, and give me false promises or silly plans. I like this. I will think on it, eh?"

"When will you give me an answer?"

"In the morning."

In the morning, Hunt would be gone. And so would Rigo. He stood. He had an even chance of making the pirate believe his next ploy. "I'm going to bed. I'll expect your answer in the morning."

"What? No camaraderie? No friendly attempts to make me trust you?"

"I've no interest in being your friend. Business is another matter. Mind you have an answer for me in the morn." He turned his back on the pirate and walked toward the stairs, the hairs on the back of his neck prickling.

He heard the pirate's chair scrape back on the wooden floor and a muffled snort of laughter. But he reached the stairs without hearing the telltale slide of steel against leather. And he reached the room at the head of the stairs without another sound.

Inside, he slid the bolt into the lock, leaned back against the door and closed his eyes. Layton. My God, Layton. They'd both known the risks, had been warned countless times about coming to Blackpool, but Hunt still knew this was his fault. His nod had sent Layton out the back door and to his death. How would he live with that now? Atone for it? But perhaps he *wouldn't* have to live with it. Odds favored him joining Layton before the night was done.

His room was on the second level in a back corner of the tavern. One window overlooked the cove, while the other looked out over the back courtyard and privy. As he suspected, a man stood guard outside. Someone would also be posted at the foot of the stairs until they decided what to do with him. This room was a prison and as effective as any cell in any dungeon.

He took a quick survey. The window over the courtyard had been nailed shut but the one over the cove swung open silently. They hadn't bothered securing this one, since the sheer drop into the cove would prevent escape. He pulled the sheet off the bed and tore it in lengthwise strips, twisted and knotted them and then tied the improvised rope to the foot of the iron bed. He pushed the bed as close to the window as he could without making noise, then slipped his knife from his boot and clenched it between his teeth.

Before he could think twice about the consequences of a failed knot or a weak weave, Hunt was dangling over the cove, swinging in a sideways arc from the makeshift rope. On the third swing, he came close enough to the side of the tavern to leap for the edge of the cliff.

For one breathless moment, he thought he'd misjudged the distance in the dark. Then he landed against the cliff edge, dug his fingers into the ledge and forced the toe of his boot into a crack in the rocks. A shower of pebbles loosened and tumbled into the water below. If anyone heard, they did not come to investigate.

He pulled himself up and rested for a moment, staring down into the inky darkness. The crash of waves as they broke against the cliffs, gave him chills. Somewhere down there, Layton…

But he couldn't think of that yet. He stumbled to his feet and kept in the shadow of the tavern. His knife in his hand now, he debated the wisdom of killing the guard. If he could do so silently, if he could be sure it would be a clean kill… But Hunt's objective was not to escape. He glanced again at the cove before he edged around the side of the tavern and into the darkness, taking the path that led toward the platform lift Rodrigo would use to return to his ship.

He melded into the darkness, knowing how to use it to his advantage. In the end, he did not have long to wait. Rigo soon arrived, speaking to his companion, one of the men from the tavern. The Spaniard was issuing instructions.

"Throw him over the edge like his friend, eh? We shall collect their bodies in the morning, if the fishes do not dine on them. Too bad we must kill him, eh? I liked this man, Lockwood. My friend would never use my name. He sends only you, eh, Lowe?"

Rigo came within inches and was only a foot past Hunt when Hunt reached out, seized him around the shoulders and drew his blade across Rigo's neck. Rigo never had a chance to defend himself. Just like Layton.

Lowe stood frozen and the moment drew out, though it could not have taken more than mere seconds. Let Lowe live and give him the chance to send up an alarm? Kill him and forfeit any chance to find out the traitor's name?

Lowe made the decision. He opened his mouth to shout a warning to his comrades and Hunt did the only thing he could. He heaved Rigo's body at him, sending them both spiraling off the cliff. Lowe's scream echoed into the night, then was swallowed by the endless hiss of waves.

Hunt was halfway back to San Marco before he realized that Rigo had known his name.

Chapter Twelve

~~~~~~~~~~~~~~~~~

London
December 11, 1820

Odd how she had forgotten the gaiety, both forced and natural, of London gatherings, Elise thought as she stood in the ballroom of Lord Bainbrook's town house. Not that everything was superficial—absolutely not. For instance, the way society was cutting her was quite sincere. In the two weeks since her arrival in London, she'd encountered countless cold shoulders, a few direct cuts and one or two hostile glares. Even her brother had not responded to her letter informing him that she had returned to England.

She had expected no better. A woman who abandoned her husband was bad enough, but a woman who kidnapped the heir and stole the family jewels was quite beyond the pale. She wondered if the men feared she might be contagious to their wives.

This was to be her punishment. And a quite effective one, too—sentenced to stand at Barrett's side and act the part of a repentant wife while he took various opportunities to demean and embarrass her. And, of course, to wear the jewels she'd stolen—even the necklace she'd sold in Boston. She touched the cold stones around her throat, as effective as any noose. Diamonds. Would she ever like them again? Their glitter? Their fire?

"I knew you'd enjoy the irony, my dear," Barrett whispered as he tightened his grip on her arm. "It cost me a fortune to buy that back, but it was the first step in tracing you. I like showing them off to the ton now—you and the jewels."

She shrugged. "We needed food and shelter. It was a calculated risk."

He pinched the back of her arm. "One you regret now, eh, m'dear?"

"The only thing I regret is sending William to school in Charleston. You wouldn't have found us if I'd sent him to San Juan."

"The *only* thing you regret?" he asked, his voice dripping venom.

"That, and not staying long enough after I hit you over the head to finish what I'd started."

He laughed. "Thank you for not disappointing me, Elise. It makes my victory so much sweeter. I shall always remember the look on your face when you came running to William's rescue and found me waiting instead."

"*That* makes your victory sweeter? I'd think it would make it more difficult for you to get a good night's sleep."

He gave her a cold smile. "I am not worried in the least. You will not attack me again. Not as long as I have William. My brother knows where he is, and he knows what to do if anything happens to me. No, Elise, it is in your best interests to keep me alive and happy. You'll keep our bargain, because you really have no other choice. And do not think to tell anyone, or ask for help. That would end our little game, and William would have to pay the price."

Their bargain. Was there ever a more desperate attempt at survival than the iniquitous bargain she'd struck with her husband? If there was, she didn't know of it. Yes, she'd stand at his side, and she'd play the part of a repentant, dutiful wife. But he wouldn't use her. He wouldn't visit her room at night. He wouldn't avail himself of her person. Somehow, she couldn't even bear the thought of that after...

After Hunt. After lying beneath him, knowing his touch, his reverence for her body and his attention to her pleasure. To lie with Barrett now would be profane. She shivered just thinking of it.

"You promised I could see William next week," she reminded him. "If you do not produce him happy and well, our bargain is void."

"And then what?" Barrett sneered. "What can you do? I'm within my rights to discipline my wife and my son in any way I see fit. Why, I can even have you brought up on charges of attempted murder, and I will, Elise, if you attempt to leave me. How often do you think you'd see the brat if you were in gaol?"

"What?" she scoffed. "And have all of society know the details of our marriage? You may be within your rights to beat your wife and children, Barrett, but it is considered déclassé. Are you willing to face the polite censure I am enduring?"

"After what you've done, no one would blame me. In fact, I think it is expected. Anyone would do the same. Half the ton believes I am a saint for taking you back."

"The other half thinks I am a fool for coming back," she muttered under her breath.

"You were more biddable before you had your little taste of freedom, m'dear. You didn't talk back so much then."

"I am not the same woman you tried to kill that night,

Barrett. I am stronger and I have learned to fight for myself. You will not like the woman I have become."

His expression turned ugly. "I did not like the woman you were. And what else did you have a little taste of, Elise? Did you spread your legs for another man? Did you give him what you refused me?"

"Afraid you'd come up wanting in comparison, Barrett?" His grip on her arm constricted to the point of sharp pain. She would have bruises tomorrow.

"Don't bait me, wife, or you'll be sorry."

She was already sorry. Sorry that she'd ever married Barrett, sorry that he hadn't died when she'd hit him over the head, sorry that he'd found William. And—*God forgive her*—if she could, she'd do it all again, but this time she'd finish it.

She could not even imagine the form Barrett's vengeance would take if he knew about Hunt. Or if he knew that the moment he stopped watching her so carefully, she'd search for William, and when she found him, she'd do whatever she must to keep him safe this time, even if it meant killing Barrett.

"Smile," he warned. "Here come our host and hostess."

Hunt sipped his whiskey and listened to the faint strains of the orchestra as he watched Lord Eastman scribble the last of his notes behind the desk in Lord Bainbrook's library. Looking up for verification, Eastman asked, "So you killed Rodrigo?"

Hunt nodded.

"One less parasite in the world, if you ask me," Eastman muttered as he added another line to the report. "Thanks for managing that situation."

"It wasn't an assassination," Hunt told him, unable to summon any real regret. "It was personal."

A shrug was Eastman's only reply. "And Blackpool?"

"Not a pirate enclave." He stood and went to the sideboard

to pour himself another glass of whiskey. "More of a pirate sanctuary."

"What the hell does that mean?"

"There was no government that I could determine. No pirate lairs or hideaways. There's an uneasy peace, often violated, and a brooding atmosphere. The only law is the law of lucre. Visitors are discouraged. No one appears to have a past or a future. In fact, the only conversations I heard were in hushed tones, and the violence was quick, and then covered over as if it had never been. Inhospitable."

"Would you recommend a bombardment of Blackpool?"

Hunt fought back his raw anger at Layton's death. There was no room for a personal agenda in such decisions. "I wouldn't think so. The population is too small to make it worthwhile. Send a ship of the line to San Marco every month and word will filter to Blackpool. Eventually they will find the proximity to be bothersome and they'll find another hole."

"Yes…" Eastman tapped his finger on the polished surface of the desk. "About that, Lockwood. Why do they allow it to exist? Isn't Bascombe doing his job?"

"I suspect Bascombe is deep in his cups half the day. Many of the duties fall to Mr. Doyle, the chargé there, though I gather he is hamstrung much of the time. According to Layton and a few of the natives, Blackpool is simply ignored as if it doesn't exist. Easier, I suppose, than trying to enforce law there."

"Or could it be that Bascombe is in league with Blackpool or the pirates?"

"I did my damnedest to make that connection, but I couldn't find a tangible link. The only thing I can say for certain is that Rodrigo knew my name. That would indicate some form of communication between the two towns, would it not?"

"That would be logical. But who is that person?"

Hunt drew the moment out by taking a long drink of

whiskey. When he'd taken this assignment, he'd have been willing to tell Eastman anything. Today, he didn't trust anyone. There were several possibilities—Eastman among them. He had no doubt the information regarding ship movements was sent to Blackpool by someone in San Marco, and therefore the spy was either present or had contacts on the island. Expediency warned him to keep the information to himself. "Too soon to tell. I am exploring a few leads. Meantime, I'd appreciate it if you didn't tell anyone about our conversation."

"Never think it, Lockwood. That's why we called you in on this. Your discretion, you see. No one knows you are on assignment for us."

He laughed. "It is that *we* I am worried about, Eastman. Who are *we?*"

"Auberville, and the secretary."

Lord Auberville? Hunt trusted him implicitly, and he trusted the foreign secretary, but anyone—*every*one—else was open to scrutiny. "Is that why you asked me to meet you here? Still keeping me out of the Foreign Office?"

Eastman stood and tucked his notes into his jacket. "Precisely. Now go enjoy yourself."

"I'm going home. I've barely been there long enough to change clothes. I imagine there's a stack of correspondence waiting for me."

"Half your cronies are here tonight, Lockwood. Take a few minutes to say hello. Oh, and catch up on the scandals." He laughed and shook his head. "Truth is stranger than fiction, it seems. Would you believe Barrett's wayward wife has come back?"

Hunt tried to remember the scandal. Something about the wife running away in the middle of the night, taking the only child with her. He hadn't paid much attention at the time, since he'd never met the wife and despised Barrett and his ilk—brutish men who bullied their way through life.

"She's back, eh? Well, I might have to see this oddity." In fact, he'd had just enough whiskey to be curious about what sort of woman would willingly return to Barrett. She must have been terribly down on her luck. Or dreadfully ill-favored.

Eastman left the library first. Hunt waited a full five minutes before venturing out. He nodded to a few friends, had a short conversation with his brother, Charlie, promising to meet him at home later and then claimed a glass of wine from a footman's tray. Time to go in search of the wayward lady.

As he entered the ballroom, he noted a cluster of women whispering behind their fans. Ah, scandal was brewing already. He gathered Lady Barrett would be hard-pressed to find friends if she did not already have one or two in the aristocracy. He followed the line of their gazes to a couple standing with their backs to him, seemingly in conversation with Lord and Lady Bainbrook. Barrett was pinching the back of his wife's arm, out of sight of his host.

His gut twisted. The color of her hair? The slender line of her back? No, he was imagining things.

"…this evening. Thank you for inviting us, Lady Bainbrook."

The voice. A chill of anger and betrayal swept through him. He could never mistake that voice. Questions, logical and otherwise, raced through his consciousness. *Later. He would deal with his questions later.*

He stood behind the couple, nodding at Lord Bainbrook. Noting Bainbrook's distraction, the couple turned, as he knew they would. Daphne's eyes widened and a flash of terror passed over her face, so quickly gone that he realized he was the only one who'd seen it. That look, brief as it was, gave him great satisfaction—small payment for the pain she'd caused him.

Barrett gave him a cautious nod. "'Lo, Lockwood. Haven't seen you around for a while."

"Haven't *been* around for a while," he replied. He met Daphne's widened eyes. Was that a plea he saw? Too bad. "I don't believe I have met your…wife?"

If Barrett was discomfited by Hunt's lack of a formal greeting, he recovered quickly. "Oh, of course." He turned to Daphne and said, "Madam, may I present Reginald Hunter, the Earl of Lockwood." He turned back to Hunt and continued the introduction. "Lord Lockwood, may I present my wife, Elise, Lady Barrett."

So that was Daphne's real name? Elise? She offered her hand, looking as if he might bite it. Ah, but he had much more interesting plans. He took that delicate hand, still roughened from hard work, bowed over it and lifted it to his lips. Her fingers trembled like a sparrow's heartbeat. Deliberately, insultingly, he lingered over the kiss, releasing her hand only after Barrett cleared his throat.

"Charming," he pronounced as he turned back to Barrett. The man looked angry, but no angrier than Hunt was. Barrett was a viscount and Hunt outranked him in the peerage. There was no question of Barrett issuing a challenge unless Hunt's attentions to the viscountess were far more blatant. That was coming. "Where have you been keeping yourself, Madam?"

Elise's lips parted in a gasp. Lord Bainbrook and his wife excused themselves quickly and turned away. He smiled with satisfaction.

"I…I—"

"She's been away, Lockwood." Barrett shot his wife a nasty look and Hunt was almost sorry for her. Almost.

"Ah, *away*," he repeated. "May I have the next dance, Madam?"

"I—"

"My wife does not dance, Lockwood. Never has."

Hunt gave the woman in question a smile. He and Elise knew that to be a lie. She had waltzed with him at the governor's mansion and had followed his every lead with grace. He watched her face for any sign of denial, but a mask had dropped and he might have been watching a statue.

"What a great pity," he said at last. "We shall have occasion to meet again, eh?"

His less-than-subtle suggestion had the desired effect. Barrett's brow lowered ominously and Elise's eyes widened. Oh yes, she'd come looking for him. If for no other reason than to beg him to stop his baiting.

He bowed sharply at the waist and walked away.

But she did not come to find him. Not her fault, he supposed, since Barrett didn't let go of her arm until they were ready to depart—almost as if the man were afraid she would bolt again. But he had seen no signs of mutiny in Elise. In fact, he'd seen no signs of life at all beyond her trembling hand. Clearly, she was afraid Hunt would betray her. As to that, he was still undecided.

Back in Bainbrook's library, Hunt helped himself to another glass of his host's excellent whiskey and sat in one of the leather chairs before the fire. He hated having the answers to his questions within reach and still denied. Why had Elise left St. Claire without a word? Why had she lied about who she was? Why had she given herself so sweetly to him when she could never be his? Had it all been a lark to her when it had meant the world to him? She'd made a colossal fool of him.

He'd done all manner of dark deeds in the name of God and Country—he had been conscienceless, killed, stolen and even kidnapped the enemy. He had done the dirty jobs no one else would take. Jobs that eroded one's soul despite their necessity for the safety and security of the nation. But he'd never added adultery to his list of sins. Until now. Until Elise.

God, there was nothing left in him now that was untainted. Nothing sacred. What few scruples his country had left him, Elise had stolen. He swallowed the whiskey and closed his eyes, relishing the burn as it traveled down his throat and heated his gut. Would that it could scald the anger and shame from him.

"You're looking grim, Lockwood."

He opened his eyes to find Tristan Sinclair, Lord Auberville, at the sideboard pouring himself a brandy. He groaned. "Go away, Sinclair."

"And let you wallow in whatever the problem is? What sort of friend would I be?"

"Better than you know. My thoughts aren't fit to speak aloud."

"Ah. A woman." Sinclair sat across from him. "I'd say you are in deep."

"Drowning," he admitted. "Tell me about Lady Barrett and do not ask me why."

Sinclair's right eyebrow shot up and a wry smile curved his lips. "Very well. Five or six years ago, just before you got back from the continent, Lord Barrett was hit over the head. His wife, his son and the Barrett jewels disappeared. Though Barrett never said, conjecture had it that his wife had had enough of his escapades and escaped his yoke. He tried to preserve his reputation, but it was never quite up to snuff anyway. Now that she's back—and the jewels with her, I might add—the gossip mill has it that she regretted her…ah, lapse of good manners, and has come to her senses. All very simple, and a tale told every day in some part of the world."

Come to her senses? She had preferred Barrett to him? Well, why not? His sins were doubtless darker, though less apparent. Yes, it all made sense now, down to the glittering diamonds circling her slender neck.

Sinclair cleared his throat. "So, Eastman says you have information regarding our little problem."

"Little problem? I could wish it were little. Did he tell you what scant progress I've made?"

"He said he was vastly encouraged by the way things are developing. No answers yet, but a narrowing of the possibilities."

Hunt glanced at the closed library door and lowered his voice. "I believe the problem has its source at very high levels and that the answers to our questions lie here, in London, and not the Caribbean." He paused as he remembered giving Auberville's name to Rodrigo. The pirate was gone now, but God only knew whom he might have told about Auberville. "By the way, stay out of the Caribbean until this is over."

Sinclair frowned but did not ask the obvious question. Instead, he asked, "You have not told Eastman your suspicions?"

Hunt shook his head, then smiled when Sinclair gave a soft whistle. "I am going to track the insurance records from Lloyd's, check bank accounts, perhaps engage in a little 'investing.'"

"Money. The root of all evil." Sinclair raised his glass to Hunt in a salute. "If you need anything, you know where to find me."

Chapter Thirteen

Late the following afternoon, Hunt turned the key in the lock of his office door on Bow Street. It gave and opened easily. Everything remained the same—his desk, his chairs, the one dingy window high in the wall that admitted light from the grate on the street above. He crossed to his desk and found a light layer of dust covering the blotter, stacks of papers and old reports. He had expected to find the office reassigned. After all, he'd turned in his resignation before taking the assignment with the Foreign Office. He sat behind the desk and uncapped the brass inkwell.

"Damn! Howe said he'd seen you come in, but I did not believe him. Are you not supposed to be in the West Indies?"

Hunt smiled at his brother-in-law. Ethan's office was just a few doors down the hallway. "Just got back yesterday. How are you, Ethan?"

"I am well, and so is Sarah. And you will not recognize the baby. Sarah will be hurt if you do not come to dinner tonight. She'll want to hear the stories of your travels."

"Not exactly fit for a little sister's ears," he confessed.

"How did that go?"

He shrugged. "As I expected. Not a complete waste of time, but not particularly productive. Say, hasn't anyone read my resignation? My office looks untouched."

Ethan Travis grinned and sat in the chair facing Hunt. "Look in your drawer."

And there was his unopened resignation with the secretary's name on it. "How did this happen?"

"He knew what it was and told me to put it away until your return. He thought you would change your mind. I tried to tell him that would not happen, but…"

"He was right, Ethan. I *have* changed my mind."

His brother-in-law cocked an eyebrow. "May I ask why?"

"It is possible that I might need to kill someone before this is over and, if so, I will need the connections."

Ethan was speechless. He stared at Hunt for a long moment before answering. "I can see you are not jesting. Is there anything I can do?"

He gave a short bark of laughter. "Aside from killing for me, you mean? Thank you, but no. I'd like to wrap this up as quickly as possible. When I am done here, I am done with everything."

"That will make Sarah happy. I should warn you that she has a list of eligible misses that she is plotting to put in your path. She thinks one of her brothers should be married, at least, and you are her first choice."

Hunt opened the bottom drawer on the right of the knee well. The bottle was still there. He withdrew the brandy, uncorked the bottle and found two reasonably clean glasses. He poured a healthy draught for them both and raised his glass. "To eligible misses, none of whom will meet me."

Ethan looked wary. "Hmm. Were I a betting man, I would wager on my wife. She has a will of iron, you know."

"Yes, I do. But she has met her match. I have decided I am

not marriage material. Andrew will have to provide the heir. Tell Sarah…no, I will tell her. What time is dinner?"

"Eight." Ethan regarded him with a speculative look. "Have you talked to Charlie since your return?"

"Briefly. I had business out last night and we were to meet at home later, but I was gone longer than I planned. Haven't run into him today."

"Did I hear my name?" His younger brother came around the corner into his office. He glanced at the glasses and gave Hunt a grin. "Any left for me?"

"What are you doing here?"

"Work here," he said.

"The hell you do!" A sick feeling descended into the pit of Hunt's stomach.

"Sorry. It is a fait accompli. Too late to save me from myself."

"But why?"

Charlie leaned against the doorjamb, crossed his arms and met Hunt's eyes straight on. "You did not really expect me to dash about the ton and idle my days away, did you?"

"Why not? It has worked to keep you alive thus far."

"That was not living. I felt like a damn parasite. You may not be happy to see me here, brother, but here I am."

Hunt studied his brother's face. He recognized mutiny when he saw it. There was flint in his blue eyes. Charlie, for all his jesting, had a more serious nature than anyone knew, a nature suited to covert work. No one would ever suspect him of ulterior motives. But… "We will talk about this later, Charles. I need to discuss the exact nature of your duties with the secretary."

"Too late," Charlie said, pushing away from the doorjamb and dropping his arms to his sides. "I have been assigned to you."

Damn! How could he do what he needed to do with his brother watching over his shoulder? He would have to think of some way to keep Charlie occupied until he could finish this assignment. Something safe.

"No," Charlie said, reading his expression. "Did you think I did not know, Hunt? Did you think I haven't heard the whispers about you, noticed the way some of your colleagues are uncomfortable when you join them? I have known for quite some time what you do, and why."

Hunt turned to Ethan. "Tell him…"

"Sorry. He knows. He's always known."

He had suspected as much. Hunt had intended Charlie for the diplomatic corps. Ah, too late for that now. He sighed and poured a brandy for his brother. "Sit down, Charlie, and I will bring you up to date."

Who is that woman?

Elise stared at the face in her dressing table mirror. She looked only vaguely familiar—her eyes, her mouth, her nose—but somehow not familiar at all. How ironic that the woman she had pretended to be should be more real to her than her own self.

The little clock on her writing desk struck seven as she picked up her brush to run it through her hair. Behind her in the mirror, the sight of a chair propped beneath her doorknob was a stark reminder of what her life had become. She could not even leave her door open for her maid. She was a self-imposed prisoner without bars, a hostage to her son's safety.

She threw the brush down and stood, wondering what to do next. She couldn't think, couldn't eat or sleep. After the tedious voyage, broken only by occasional games of whist with Mr. Doyle and other passengers, she had sped from the docks to the house in Mayfair, leaving her things aboard to fetch later. Alas, no sign of William. Only Barrett awaited her.

He'd known she'd come. He did not have to find her. All

he had to do was claim William and let the headmaster do the rest. And the irony was that Barrett did not want either of them. A man with a runaway wife was the object of many jokes. He only wanted to exert his power over them, enforce his "rights" and, perhaps, regain his standing in the ton and his family's jewelry. He hadn't bothered to retrieve her things from Captain Gilbert until she'd told him she'd brought the jewelry back.

She glanced again at the chair beneath the doorknob. That was one right, however, that he'd never reclaim. Even though he had agreed to her terms, he had come to her door every night. She'd heard his wheezing on the other side of the panel, had seen the knob twist with excruciating slowness, as if he were testing it. After a moment, he would go away, apparently unwilling to fuel the servants' gossip by forcing the issue. But that day was coming. Already he was testing her door at any time of the night or day. He would not suffer her rejection long.

The worst of her regrets was Lockwood. Had she not known his passion, she might have been able to bear her husband's touch. Tears burned her eyes and she wiped them away with the back of her hand. Last night, facing his anger, she'd wanted to die. What was the use of trying to explain? Nothing could change the fact that she was Lord Barrett's wife. Or that she would remain such for as long as William was a hostage.

And now Lockwood hated her. His scorn last night had cut deeply. The look in his eyes had told her that his love had turned to ashes. His pain had equaled hers. The difference was that she would always love him, and he had already stopped loving her.

Even Barrett had remarked upon it. *I cannot tell which of us he dislikes most, madam. And neither of us has done him an unkind turn. Or is there something you are not telling me, Elise? Some clandestine meeting with Lockwood?*

She'd been tempted to tell him that Lockwood held the same crime against her that he did—desertion. But she denied any knowledge of Lockwood's motive. What an accomplished little tart she was becoming. Adultery, lying, theft, attempted murder—was there anything she hadn't done in the name of motherhood or love? Was there anything she would *not* do?

She silenced her self-pity, lifted her plum velvet evening gown over her head and smoothed it over her hips. Barrett would make her wear the amethysts with the gown, as if to tell the ton that *all* his jewels were back. She smiled when she realized he would have to open the safe in the library. He no longer trusted her to keep the jewelry in her room. That, it would seem, was the only mistake Barrett had learned from.

A soft click drew her attention back to her door. The knob turned slowly, then turned in the opposite direction. Chills raced up her spine and her heart squeezed as she watched the door give slightly under quiet pressure. The chair held and the knob was released. Soft footsteps continued down the corridor.

She gasped for air, unaware that she'd been holding her breath.

Yes, it was just a matter of time.

Elise stood alone near the fireplace at one end of the ballroom. She could not accustom herself to the frigid winter temperatures after the balmy Caribbean weather. If it were not so cold, she would be tempted to take a walk out to the gardens. Lord Carlin's winter ice sculptures were touted as amusing and unique.

Barrett, however, demanded that she remain prominently displayed where he could see her. Standing in conversation with two of his friends, he turned toward Elise and laughed. His friends laughed with him and she felt the heat creep up her cheeks. She had no idea what sort of lies he might be telling, but she did not care as long as he was not by her side.

She scanned the room again, looking for any familiar face, any *friendly* face. Alas, there were none. Barrett had refused to introduce her to anyone but their host and, without an introduction, no one engaged her in conversation. He deliberately intended to isolate her. Where were her former friends? She'd had few, since Barrett had begun cutting her off from them after their marriage. Would they even speak to her now?

She gathered her embroidered black kerseymere shawl closer around her shoulders as the clock on the mantel struck the hour of eleven. The deep fringe tickled her arms and she shivered. How long would she have to stay? The orchestra began another set and she moved toward the hallway. Perhaps she could escape for a few minutes and sit in the ladies retiring room.

A burst of laughter greeted her as she turned down the corridor. A large group was coming her way, and Lockwood was in the midst of them. She spun around but it was already too late.

"Ho, there, Madam," he called to her.

She affected a look of surprise and turned back. Surely he wouldn't embarrass her? "Good evening, Lord Lockwood."

That smile, that mocking smile, curved his lips. He had her on edge, and he knew it. "Good evening, Lady Barrett."

His companions paused and glanced curiously between them. If he did not speak soon, the insult would be obvious in his absence of an introduction. Lockwood allowed the moment to draw out before he relented.

"Madam, may I present my brother, Mr. Charles Hunter, and my sister and her husband, Lord Ethan and Lady Sarah Travis?"

The men gave her a polite bow while Lady Sarah, a lovely, slender woman with violet eyes, came forward and took her hand. "How nice to make your acquaintance, madam."

That was the first truly sincere greeting Elise had heard since arriving back in London. It was likely because Lady Sarah had not heard the *on dit* regarding her. "And yours, Lady Sarah."

Lockwood looked as if he regretted the introductions. "Go on without me," he told his party. "I'll find you in a few minutes."

She and Lockwood stood in silence until the others had passed into the ballroom. Then he turned back to her and said, "Well, here we are, alone at last, *Daphne*."

He used the name like a weapon to wound her. She lifted her chin and stiffened her spine to take his scorn. "I suppose an apology would not be enough?"

"You suppose rightly." His voice dripped sarcasm but his face remained impassive. To any observer, they might appear to be discussing the weather.

"Then there is no possible way I can make amends, Lord Lockwood, since I have nothing else to offer."

He ran one strong finger down her arm. "I can think of dozens of things. A baker's dozen."

Her knees weakened at the low tone of his voice and the memory of his intimate touch. "You know I cannot."

"You had no such qualms before. Why come all missish now? Is adultery not the same in London as it is in St. Claire?"

"I…I did not know that Barrett…" Oh, how could the truth make any difference now except to cause them both pain? Perhaps it would be easier if he thought the worst of her. "That he would find me," she finished in a rush.

"You made me an adulterer, Elise. That was one of the few sins left that I had not committed. Were you laughing when I told you I loved you? Asked you to marry me?"

She looked down. She could not bear the rawness in his tone, the anger and revulsion in his eyes. "It would be best if we did not speak again."

"Not so fast, m'dear," he said, staying her with a hand on her arm. "I am entitled to recompense, am I not? I think I shall take it a little at a time. Savor it."

"Barrett—"

"Is a toad," he finished. "And will not stand in my way."

Little matter that Barrett would take his fury out on her. Doubtless that would not stand in Lockwood's way, either. An angry retort hovered on her tongue.

"Well, well! What is this? A St. Claire reunion?"

Relief mingled with fear as she turned toward the voice behind her. "Mr. Doyle, how nice to see you again."

Lockwood scowled. "Doyle. What are you doing here?"

"In England?" he asked, a jovial smile on his face. "Has our little baker not told you? We were shipmates on the voyage home. I've been reassigned. I'll be bound for India come spring."

"You were traveling together?" Lockwood looked at her and she could see the disgust in his face. He suspected her of sleeping with Mr. Doyle! She shook her head, hoping he would believe her.

"Yes," Doyle said, evidently missing the tension between them and the implication of Lockwood's question. "And it would have been deuced dull without her. She was the only one on board who could play a hand of whist with any finesse. And imagine my surprise when she confessed she was Lady Barrett."

"She told you?"

"There…seemed no point in keeping the secret any longer, since I was coming back." Elise nearly choked on the words. "Mr. Doyle was kind enough to keep me from spending all day in my cabin."

"Yes," Lockwood agreed. "How fortunate you had him to…relieve your tedium."

Mr. Doyle glanced between them and frowned. "I say, have I interrupted something?"

"I was just leaving."

"What the devil got into him?" Mr. Doyle asked as they watched Lockwood disappear into the ballroom. "Is he angry? What did I say?"

"Nothing, sir. It was not you at all. I am afraid I have offended Lord Lockwood."

"You? Impossible. But let's not speak of Lockwood. I'd rather hear how you are getting on. I know you thought your husband was dead. Were you surprised? How did he receive you?"

"He expected me, Mr. Doyle. After all, he had brought my son back to England. He knew I would not be far behind."

"Yes, and how is little William? I know you had some misgivings regarding his health."

"William is…is well. I am here now, and Barrett has accepted me back."

"Ah, all is forgiven, eh? Well, he'd be a fool to turn you away, madam. You are a rare prize. I am only surprised that you were amongst us on St. Claire so long and none of us guessed." He leaned closer and whispered dramatically, "I'd have kept your secret, madam. I never give a lady away."

She merely smiled.

"I was sorry I did not get a chance to say goodbye to you when we docked. I went looking for you, but Gilbert told me you'd dashed off the moment the gangway was down. Did you ever go back to collect your things?"

"Barrett sent for them," she said, having only a vague recollection of her valise arriving and being taken to the attic after Barrett removed the jewels. Those garments were far too light for a London winter. "But shall we talk about you, instead? India? How exciting."

"Yes, one of the northern regions. I am all enthusiasm. I've been taking lessons in Hindi, learning the history of the region and studying the political… But you are not interested in this. Shall we just say that I am embracing my new assignment and leave it at that?"

"If you wish," she allowed. In point of fact, she did not want to let him go. He was the one friend she had in London.

"Allow me to escort you into the ballroom. Will you dance?"

The thought of Barrett's scowl chilled her. "I fear my husband is a bit jealous. He does not like me dancing with anyone but him."

"Ah, well. I suppose I can understand his reluctance, since he has just got you back. I would likely feel the same."

"You are too kind, Mr. Doyle." *Much too kind.*

"Well, shall we go in? I'd like to meet this husband of yours."

"I am afraid he might not understand our friendship, sir. I shall be pleased to introduce you, but if you would refrain from mentioning that we were on shipboard together, I would appreciate it."

He gave her his first wary look, as if he'd just now realized that her relationship with her husband was not all it should be. "Of course, madam. As you wish."

Chapter Fourteen

Hunt stood next to the French doors in the ballroom, wishing he could get quietly drunk. He hadn't moved from his position in more than an hour, and each time a footman had passed him, he'd taken another glass of wine. Across the room, Daph—*Elise*—stood by the fireplace. After introducing Gavin Doyle to her husband, she'd been left alone.

The rich plum velvet of her gown was a perfect frame for her beauty, and reminiscent of the plum silk she'd worn in St. Claire. Her embroidered silk shawl glowed with rich colors that complemented her gown. She wore amethysts at her throat and in her hair, and she stood so still that she might have been posing for a portrait.

He sipped his wine and glanced around the ballroom. Barrett was circulating, greeting friends and enemies alike. Was he tpid to know the difference? Good God! Hunt it every time he thought of Elise in Barrett's orse by far than anything he'd imagined when one upon his return to San Marco.

had denied any knowledge of where she id, in fact, that her employer had been "different" since Hunt had arrived on the island. She accused him of driving Mrs. Hobbs away, of imposing himself on her and taking advantage of her vulnerability. She'd said much more, and by the time she was done, Hunt had come closer than he'd ever been to striking a woman.

Harder still had been facing Mrs. Breton. Hannah. She would never know, now, how Layton had felt about her. The impossible sadness of that brought a lump to his throat. And no, Mrs. Breton hadn't known where Daphne had gone or why, but she wished her well and hoped she would see her again one day.

When he'd found the *Gulf Stream* gone from the harbor, he had a sinking feeling in his gut. Not only was Daphne gone, but he'd have to wait for the next England-bound ship before he could get off the island. Had he planned to go after her? No. She'd made it clear that she did not want him.

What stung the worst was that she hadn't left word for him. Hadn't scratched a single line of explanation or apology. But she'd taken the time to deed her property to her housekeeper and her business to her friend. And she'd remembered to pack the pouch of jewels in the single valise Mrs. Herrera said was missing. She'd thought of everyone *but* him.

Or had *"Yes, Lockwood... Please. Again..."* been her way of saying goodbye? He still had the taste of her on his tongue, could smell the wild orchids in her hair and feel her heat as she took him deep inside. *Two months* had done nothing to dull that memory or quell the hunger. He finished his wine and looked around for a footman. Instead, he found Gavin Doyle.

"Admiring our mutual friend, Lockwood? She is quite a pretty picture, is she not?"

"Quite," he answered. He was not about to discuss the viscountess.

"I feel a little sorry for her. She looks a bit wistful—as if she belongs here, but is ill at ease."

Hunt shrugged. "She will adjust. How long ago did you arrive?"

Doyle frowned as if he were thinking. "Nearly a fortnight now. We had a speedy voyage. Captain Gilbert said the trade currents were assisting. No storms and just one rainfall."

Two weeks. Elise had been in Barrett's bed for two weeks. Hunt's stomach turned. He had better change the subject before he was tempted to put a fist through Barrett's face.

"I hear you've been reassigned."

"Yes. Delhi, India."

"When do you leave?"

Doyle gave him a curious look. "Trying to get rid of me?"

Hunt grinned. He hadn't been very subtle. But he had been curious about the reassignment ever since Governor Bascombe had told him about it. "Not at all. Just wondering. I hope they give you a chance to catch your breath before sending you off again."

Doyle relaxed and nodded. "I doubt I'll be leaving before February."

"Did you request India? Or were you content on St. Claire?"

"I was content, for the most part. But it never pays to get too comfortable. A man could wither and die in a place like St. Claire. Better, don't you think, to move on, if you want to advance and make a name for yourself?"

"So you requested a new assignment."

"Yes. There didn't seem to be much point in staying. Despite Bascombe's credentials, he was perfectly content to sit back and let me handle anything unpleasant or problemmatic."

This was interesting. According to Bascombe, *he'd* requested Doyle's reassignment. Another piece of the puzzle? "And you did not want to handle the problems?"

"More than willing," Doyle explained. "But with Bascombe always in the fore and taking credit for my efforts, it was time for me to move on. If I mean to build my fortune in the diplomatic corps—and I do—then I must be in a position to be noticed, eh?"

Two men, two different stories, two possibilities. One traitor. "Yes," he agreed after a moment. "I'd say you'd have to be noticed to advance."

"Besides," Doyle said as he tossed off the rest of his wine, "I always had the feeling that I was more in Bascombe's way than a help to him."

Still two possibilities. Either Bascombe needed Doyle out of the way so that he could conduct illicit business, or he wanted Doyle reassigned to keep him from trafficking with pirates.

Here was a job for Bow Street. Tomorrow he'd ask one of the runners to look into Gavin Doyle's background. And just for added interest, he'd ask Eastman what he thought. After all, he was the one who'd suggested that the leak was within the Foreign Office. Eastman would also be able to find out how Doyle's transfer came about—Bascombe's request, or Doyle's?

"Well, must keep moving," Doyle said with a touch of regret. "I have a host of people to greet here, and then I promised to meet a friend at Belmonde's later."

Hunt nodded, making a mental note of the notorious gambling hell. If Doyle had admittance to Belmonde's, he must pay his debts. But how much could he gamble on a minor government official's salary? Hunt and Charlie would have to drop in later for a hand or two. Meantime, Charlie could help him with another matter.

Elise held her breath as she watched Charles Hunter slap Barrett on the back and laugh. A moment later, they went toward Lord Carlin's billiard room. Oh, blessed respite. Perhaps now she could finally find the ladies retiring room.

"Looking for an escape, madam?"

Lockwood! She whirled to face him, took two subconscious steps backward and dropped a little curtsy. "Lord Lockwood," she acknowledged. She glanced toward the corridor where her husband had disappeared, hoping he had not seen Lockwood.

"You are safe for the moment," he said. "At least from your husband. My brother has challenged him to a game of billiards. I think we have a few minutes."

"For what?"

He grinned. "Have you seen Lord Carlin's portrait gallery?"

She shook her head. What game was this? Is this what he'd meant earlier about taking his revenge a little at a time?

He took her hand and led her up the stairs and down a hallway to a large gallery at the end. There were no chandeliers to light this room, not even a single candle. The only illumination came from moonlight filtering through a bank of tall windows along one side. The Carlin ancestors were silent witnesses on the other.

He spun her around to face him and then let go of her. "Why, Daphne? What game were you playing?"

"Elise," she corrected.

"Damn it! You know what I mean."

Yes. She knew. He wanted answers. And still she could not tell him the truth. But he deserved anything that would allow him to purge his anger.

"It wasn't a game, Lockwood."

"Lockwood? What happened to 'Hunt'?"

"I think it would be unwise of me to use that name. I do not want my husband upset."

"Ah, you haven't told him we met on St. Claire. Why, Elise? Would he want to know just how well we knew each other? What would he say if I told him we *knew* each other? In the biblical sense?"

"Please, leave me alone."

"It shouldn't matter to him. After all, you went from my bed to his. Was I so lacking in skill that I sent you running back to him?"

"Stop it! You have no right to question me."

"I will not stop until I know why. Why did you give yourself to me when you belonged to someone else? Why did you flee the first moment my back was turned?"

"Hunt, I…I had no choice." And she still had no choice. She had no doubt that Barrett would carry out his threat to harm William if she told anyone what he held over her head.

"No choice? The hell you didn't. You had *me*. I told you I'd help you. I swore that, whatever the problem, whatever you'd done, I'd make it right." He paced to a window and back again. The look on his face tore her heart in two.

He pushed his fingers through his dark hair. "And you could not give me the courtesy of a simple refusal. Instead, you lied. Even then, you lied."

"What lie did I tell?"

"That you loved me, too."

The tears she'd been fighting rolled down her cheeks. No, she hadn't lied. That, at least, had been the truth—was still the truth and would always be the truth. "I…I am sorry," she whispered. She wished he would strike her, or plunge a knife in her heart—anything that would ease his pain and anger.

"Sorry? You will excuse me if I cannot believe you, madam."

"What can I tell you? What will satisfy you? I had reasons why I could not tell you who I was."

"Theft? Kidnapping? Those are minor infractions for someone with your skills in duplicity, Elise. Have you done murder? Treason?"

"Would it matter?"

"Not to you, I gather. But then what matters to you more than yourself?"

You, she wanted to say. *And William*. There had been more truth and honesty in her years on St. Claire than there had ever been in London. She looked down, unable to meet his eyes—those heartbreaking eyes.

"Defend yourself, Elise." He grasped her shoulders and shook her. "Give me reasons, damn it."

"I am sorry." There was nothing else she could say.

"Sorry?" He tugged her into his arms and she landed with a soft thud against his chest as her shawl dropped to the floor. "How sorry, Elise? *This* sorry?"

His kiss was angry and demanding. It was undeniable. She yielded to it with her own hunger. The faint music from the ballroom faded and the laughter of guests below seemed as distant as a summer day. He backed her against the wall and slipped one leg between hers. She clung to him and drew him closer, accepting his tongue as well as the sharp bite of his fingers as they cupped her bottom and drew her against his groin.

"You are a fire in my blood, Elise. You burn away my memories of your lies and treachery until all I can think of is how you feel, how you smell and taste. Damn you for that, and damn you for your lies. Give me a single reason that I shouldn't tell Barrett about us."

"He would kill me." And William.

"Another of your exaggerations, Elise?" he asked, his breath hot in her ear. "He has taken you back, draped you in the very jewels you stole from him and presented you to society in a gesture of acceptance. His actions are that of a man smitten. And you'd have me believe he'd kill you?" He nibbled at her earlobe and she weakened. "Should I thank him for preventing me from making the biggest mistake of my life?"

She trembled with the effort to separate herself, but her will was not as strong as his. He held her against him and tilted her hips to cradle his erection through their clothes. Her heart pounded and she gasped with a surge of desire.

He reached down with one hand and swept her skirts up her leg. Before she knew what he intended, and long before she could find her voice to protest, he worked his hand past her garters and undergarments and found her center, damp with her longing. His finger slipped easily past the tender flesh and she trembled with the raw shock of the invasion.

"Ah, but *this* doesn't lie, madam," he said, slipping his finger deeper. "*This* much is true."

She moaned, whether with humiliation or the intensity of her need, she couldn't say. Both emotions mingled and she suddenly knew what it was to be shameless. He hated her and wanted to punish her, but she still wanted him, was ready to beg him to make love to her.

His voice dropped to a harsh rasp in her ear. "But it isn't enough, Daphne. God help me, it is not enough." He pulled his hand away and lowered her skirts.

She leaned against the wall, still trembling with unsated passion as he backed away from her. Cool, unruffled, he turned his back and went to stand by the windows. "Your husband will be looking for you soon, madam."

Elise arrived back in the ballroom before Barrett returned. He looked pleased until he saw her, and then came to her with a scowl.

"Where have you been, madam?"

She shook her head to deny that she'd gone anywhere. "Where have you been, Barrett?"

"Playing billiards with Charlie Hunter. I beat him soundly, by the way. Made ten pounds on him."

She had forgotten how her husband would wager on

anything from a spin of the *rouge et noir* wheel to how many leaves would fall from a particular tree in one day. And he'd always had the devil's own luck. He'd built his fortune on the misfortune of others, then used it to buy people, as he'd bought her brother, and thus her. She looked away, doing her best to ignore him.

"I know you've been gone, Elise. Where is your shawl?"

The portrait gallery! "I must have dropped it," she muttered. "Where?"

"I…" Telltale heat crept into her cheeks. "I shall go fetch it. I must occasionally…that is, the ladies retiring room provides certain services…"

Barrett chortled. "So modest, my little tart? Well, next time stay where I leave you. I was not gone long enough to cause you more than a little discomfort."

She gave him an angry glance but said nothing further.

"So you left your shawl in the retiring room? Come, I shall escort you there."

He gripped her elbow and began to pull her toward the corridor. She jerked her arm away and narrowed her eyes. "This ends now, Barrett. I have suffered your restrictions long enough. It is absurd that I cannot have even a few moments alone, greet acquaintances or attend to my personal needs. If you think this is making me look foolish, you are wrong. It is making you look absurd. Pitiful. So unsure of your own consequence that you must control your wife's behavior."

"You little—"

"You are making a laughingstock of us both. If you have meant to demonstrate to society that you do not trust me, you have done so. And now you'd do better to grant me ordinary freedoms before society begins to pity me and see you for what you truly are."

For one long moment, she thought he was going to slap her.

But it was worth the risk to gain the freedom she needed to find William. Though she'd kept her voice low, they had drawn the attention of couples close to them. Barrett managed to restrain his evil temper but his fingers bit into her arm. Gradually, he eased his grip and forced a smile to his lips for the sake of onlookers.

"Do not make me regret this, Elise," he said between gritted teeth. "You will pay for it if you do."

She nodded and breathed a tiny sigh of relief when she saw Gavin Doyle headed their way. The look on his face told her that he suspected conflict. Then his entire expression changed to one of open congeniality. This, she gathered, was what it meant to be a diplomat.

"I say, Barrett, was that not you I saw playing billiards with Charles Hunter? I was not aware you were a gamesman."

"I keep my hand in."

"Ah, I've never been much good at billiards, but I'm a fair hand at cards. Anything from whist to *vingt et un*. We shall have to have a game. I was just leaving to meet friends at Belmonde's. Would you like to come along?"

Barrett shot her a sideways glance. "Not tonight, Doyle."

"Any night, then. I am generally there after midnight." He bowed to Elise and gave her a wink, then inclined his head to her husband before he walked away.

The onlookers began to wander away, convinced that anything of interest was over. But they did not see Lord Lockwood heading their way carrying her shawl. Barrett followed her horrified stare and suffused with color.

"'Lo, Barrett. Madam. Did I not see you wearing this earlier?" There was something smug in his voice.

"It is mine," she confessed.

Barrett snatched it from Hunt's hand. "Where did you get it?" he growled. "Couldn't have been the ladies retiring room."

"No, actually, it was not." Hunt grinned, watching her reaction. The moment dragged out until Barrett realized Hunt wasn't going to volunteer the information.

"Well? Where was it?"

"On the floor."

"Where, damn it?"

Hunt frowned. "Contain yourself, man. It is not the crown jewels."

Elise closed her eyes. Could this night get any worse? "I want to go home, Barrett. Take me home."

Both men looked startled by her words. Absurdly, Barrett draped her shawl over her shoulders and guided her toward the foyer while Hunt looked thunderous.

Pray that would put an end to his taunting. She did not know how much more she could take without telling him the truth.

Chapter Fifteen

Gathering her heavy woolen cloak closer about her, Elise turned right on Great George Street to cut though Green Park. She'd been shopping longer than she planned and did not want to provoke Barrett's ire on her first outing alone. Well, alone but for her maid, who undoubtedly reported to Barrett.

"May we stop by the canal and watch the skating for a moment, ma'am?" Anne asked.

She nodded, tucking her fur-trimmed hood closer and pushing her hands into her muff. The poor maid was almost as bored as she. Perhaps if Anne were distracted, she would be more inclined to trust Elise, or at least not report her every move. Elise chose the path that led toward the south end of the canal and quickened her pace.

"Oh, ma'am," Anne panted, "please slow down. I cannot keep up with you."

Elise smiled and waited for the maid to catch up. She took the one small parcel from her and pushed it in her muff so Anne could warm her own hands. She'd purchased a pocket puzzle for William, praying that she would be able to give it to him soon.

Through the trees, she caught sight of crowds gathered along the canal. Vendors selling hot chestnuts and roasted potatoes called out their wares as they rolled their carts slowly along the path. Laughter and good-natured shouting lifted her spirits and she remembered why she had loved London so many years ago. Before Barrett.

She found a spot with a clear view of the canal and stopped to watch. Men and women glided effortlessly across the ice and a group of boys played a rousing game of curling with their brooms whisking every which way.

"Oh, ma'am, I wish I could skate!"

She turned to the maid and nodded. "You can. I shall hire you a pair of skates and you can twirl and turn to your heart's delight."

"I would be that happy if I could just stay upright, ma'am." She frowned and looked away. "But we should be gettin' on home soon."

"Perhaps tomorrow, then?" Elise wondered if she could ever win the girl's friendship.

"Well…"

She heard a loud roar of laughter and looked back out on the ice. She recognized the object of the teasing. Mr. Doyle had just taken a spill and was enduring the barbs of other skaters. How diverting to find him here.

"Mr. Doyle!" she called. He turned in her direction and she realized he wouldn't know her beneath her cloak and hood. She waved and called again, then turned to Anne. "Mr. Doyle is a friend of my husband's," she explained.

"My, what a handsome gent."

"Is he? I hadn't noticed," Elise teased.

They waited while Mr. Doyle got to his feet, brushed the snow and ice from his trousers and skated toward them. "Ho, there, Lady Barrett."

"Hello, Mr. Doyle. What are you doing here? I thought you'd be bent over a desk studying your history books or practicing your Hindi on some hapless scholar."

He laughed. "I was until my instructor urged me to take some fresh air. And you can see where that has got me."

"You looked as if you were having fun."

"Quite a lot of it, actually. Do you skate, madam?"

"I used to. Many years ago, now. I rather enjoyed it."

"Then meet me here tomorrow afternoon, and I shall take you for a turn around the ice."

She glanced sideways at Anne. "Thank you so much for the invitation, Mr. Doyle, but…"

"I shall ask your husband's permission tonight," he said, guessing at the reason for her hesitation.

"Tonight? Are you seeing Barrett tonight?"

"Why, yes. He sent an invitation 'round to my club to meet him at Belmonde's. I believe he intends to take me up on my challenge to a game of whist."

Elise frowned and lowered her voice so Anne wouldn't hear. "Be careful, Mr. Doyle. Barrett is uncommonly lucky. Many *former* friends will tell you so." He laughed, and she knew he thought that she was teasing. She was not. "He collects other men's fortunes like most men collect shillings. He buys people, sir. I pray you will not be one of them."

He looked uncertain as to how to respond. In the end, he decided to ignore her. "As the two of you seem to be inseparable, I shall look forward to seeing you this evening, madam." He bowed and turned back to the canal.

Belmonde's? Was that not a rather infamous gambling hell? She wondered if Barrett would actually take her to such a place. She turned to go, but Mr. Doyle's voice called her back.

"Oh, Lady Barrett, I assume you have heard the dreadful news?"

"Dreadful? No, I believe I have not." She could not imagine what dreadful news could be circulating now.

"Drat! What a deuced bad way to learn of it."

She walked back to him, fighting a sudden constriction of her heart. Surely Doyle wouldn't know anything about William? Or…or Hunt? "Tell me, Mr. Doyle. Please do not keep me on tenterhooks. It cannot be worse than my imagination."

"Why, it is Captain Gilbert. And I fear it is the worst possible news. He is dead."

"Dead?" She felt as if someone had knocked the wind out of her. He had been hale and hearty two weeks ago when they had docked. Perhaps a man of his age— "Was it his heart?"

Mr. Doyle's eyes dilated slightly and she realized he, like so many others, relished the telling of bad news. "Gads, no. It was murder."

She stared at him for a full minute before she could comprehend. "S-surely there is some mistake. He never spoke of enemies. Who would want to murder him?"

"They do not have any suspects," Mr. Doyle told her. "They believe the motive could have been robbery, since Gilbert's cabin was ransacked and he did not have any cash on him."

"They?"

"Bow Street, madam. The metropolitan police."

She pressed the sudden pain between her eyes and tried, unsuccessfully, to fight her tears. "I…I cannot believe this. He was such a good man. He always brought me papers and had a kind word. He was a good friend to me."

Mr. Doyle looked discomfited by her tears. He reached into his jacket, removed a handkerchief and pressed it into her hand. "Here, now, madam. I did not mean to make you cry. I just thought you should hear the news. Wouldn't do to have you read it in the papers, would it?"

"Th-thank you," she replied, thinking how absurd it was to thank a person for such a thing.

"I knew you were close friends by the way you used to visit. And he had you to his cabin for dinner several times, did he not? I do hope you have some gift from him, some memento, to comfort you."

"I…" She frowned. "I do not think so, sir. I cannot think of anything. He used to bring me newspapers…."

"Never mind, m'dear. 'Twas an idle thought. I am certain your memories alone will comfort you. Come now. Go along home, eh? Nice cup of tea should fix you right up."

Tea? Was he jesting? She looked at him again and saw a touch of anger in his expression. He, like Barrett, had no patience with women. She dabbed at her eyes and held his handkerchief out to him.

He shook his head and waved her hand away. "Quite all right, madam. You can return it another time."

She nodded and hurried toward Piccadilly Street, Anne behind her.

Hunt turned the wick higher on the lamp on his desk. He'd been poring over the ledger Charlie had brought him for over an hour. Remarkable. He had never suspected Charlie could be so bloody efficient.

He had the gist of it, but he wanted it in Charlie's words. "So what does this all mean, Charlie?"

His brother leaned back in his chair and propped his heels on the edge of Hunt's desk. "Well, when you compare—"

He waved his hand. "No. First tell me how you got this information."

"When Lloyd's heard that the Home Office was looking into the recent piracy, they were most cooperative. I vow, they'd have given me my own office if I had asked for it."

"And?"

"And they sat me down with their books. They are devilishly hard to decipher until one begins to see the pattern. You see, beyond the primary register, there are dozens of other records and cross-references. Lloyd's does not do the insuring. They have members—names, they call them—who do the actual underwriting. These are the companies and individuals who bear the risks. Each time an insured ship goes down, *they* stand the loss."

He remembered this much from Eastman's summary when he first urged Hunt to look into the situation on St. Claire.

"Take Auberville, for instance. He is one of the underwriters. When the *Empire* went down, he took a heavy loss, but when the *Natalie Jean* came in he made it up, and with a tidy profit. Not like—"

"Charlie, you are not using this assignment to look into our friends' finances, are you?"

"Of course," Charlie replied with a grin. "And our enemies', as well. If a name appears on the lists, I follow it to the final entry. I am looking into *all* the investors, Lord Lockwood."

Hunt snorted at this acknowledgement that he was Charlie's superior on the case. He looked down at the ledgers again—one for each investor in a pirated ship.

"The only way the underwriters profit is if the ships arrive safely in port. It's the ship's investors who stand to profit either way. If the insured ship arrives safely, the investor profits from the cargo proceeds. If the ship goes down, their investment is protected by the insurance."

"Then I was wrong about tracking our traitor this way?"

"No." Charlie looked excited now and removed his heels from the desk to sit forward in his enthusiasm. "Because there's another link to trace. Say, if you *only* invested in ships that were never attacked, or if you invested in a ship and insured it, too."

"Then you'd come out even?"

Charlie shook his head. "Not if you were the pirate. You'd have profit from selling the pirated goods *and* be paid back for your original investment by the insurers. Simple fraud. And, of course, piracy."

And murder, too, Hunt thought. "Diabolical."

"Wouldn't say that. He'd just be damn clever."

"I meant you, Charlie."

His brother grinned from ear to ear. "Wouldn't be the first time someone's thought so."

"How long will it take you to compare the lists?"

"A few more days. Then it will be up to you. I'm likely to come up with a dozen possibilities. You will have to determine which one is the traitor. I wouldn't know who'd be in a position to traffic with pirates."

"Get me the names, Charlie. I will do the rest. And tonight I shall reward your efforts with an excursion to the hells. How does Thackery's sound? And Belmonde's?" A knock on Hunt's office door interrupted them. "Come," he called.

His brother-in-law peeked in, donning his greatcoat. "Are you coming by for dinner? Sarah said your valet was still trying to make sense of your wardrobe and your cook hasn't fully restocked."

"She shouldn't be overseeing my house and yours," Hunt grumbled. "She has enough to do with the children."

Ethan shrugged. "She'll have it no other way. Says she is too used to looking after her brothers to stop now."

"Aye, that's why she's bride-hunting," Charlie said. "So she can hand us off to some other unwary female."

"Tell her I'll be there if she is not also having an unmarried female guest. Charlie, too."

Ethan nodded, then hesitated. "Hunt, did you know a Captain Gilbert?"

"I sailed with him on the outbound voyage to St. Claire. Why?"

"Dead. Murdered."

Gilbert? He frowned. "When? Who did it?"

"The same night he made berth. The killer is still unknown. Gilbert was found aboard his ship. The crew was on shore leave. His cabin had been searched and anything of value was gone. It looks like robbery."

"How?"

"Knife. His throat was cut. Odd for a robbery, wouldn't you say? If Gilbert resisted, he'd have been knifed from the front. A puncture wound is what we see in such cases. This looks more like someone surprised him from behind, then tried to make it look like a robbery."

"So you think it wasn't?"

"The circumstances are quite odd. Do you know of any reason anyone would want to kill Gilbert?"

Hunt shook his head, though instinct told him that this was far too coincidental to be a random event. The memory of killing Rigo and Lowe flashed through his mind. The pirates had known his name and his business on St. Claire. Surely it couldn't be retaliation? But he was not close to Gilbert. If they had wanted to hurt him, they'd have gone after Elise.

Elise. She would be devastated when she heard this news. He felt an unwelcome twinge of sympathy for her. It would seem he hadn't managed to hate her entirely.

Belmonde's was everything Elise imagined it would be— lush, opulent and decadent. The proprietors allowed no reason for a patron to leave the confines of their walls. Every need was catered to, every wish granted, from food and drink to private games in private rooms such as the one Barrett and Mr. Doyle had entered when they'd left her alone more than an hour ago.

Before he'd disappeared, Barrett had simply warned her to stay in the main salon and not to wander upstairs. She had not needed money, since there were wine fountains at each end of the dimly lit salon and she had no idea how to play the varied games in progress at the tables.

She recognized several men from various functions she'd attended since returning to London, but none of the women were familiar. When she'd seen a sporting young buck take one woman's hand and lead her up the stairs, she guessed at the purpose. Yes, Belmonde's knew how to keep their patrons happy.

She found a bench in a quiet curtained alcove and simply watched the people. Barrett's game of flaunting her everywhere he went was wearing on her nerves. The humiliation was her penance, but she would gladly face much worse to be with William again. The moment she found him, she'd find a way to leave Barrett.

When Mr. Doyle and her husband reappeared, they came toward her but entered an adjacent alcove and began whispering. She could not hear most of their conversation until Mr. Doyle raised his voice in an urgent whisper.

"By God, your wife was right. You have the devil's own luck! That was all I had, Barrett. You've cleaned me out."

"Stay away from my wife. I heard how you came when she called at the canal this morning, just like a whipped dog. But she's mine, Doyle, and I'll cut down anyone who interferes."

Elise found no pleasure in being right about Anne reporting to Barrett. And she was not in the least surprised at Barrett's possessiveness. Jealousy, not love, was his motive, along with a desire to punish and isolate her.

Mr. Doyle's answer was typically diplomatic. "I assure you, the lady has no interest in me, nor I in her. We are only connected by our voyage."

"Well, then, pay up what you owe, Doyle."

There was a short period of silence, and then Mr. Doyle's voice came again. "Give me a chance to win it back, Barrett. I swear I'm good for it."

She closed her eyes and said a little prayer for Mr. Doyle. He had the sound of a man obsessed, and if he'd fallen victim to Barrett, he was lost.

"I have some investments. I could give you a share."

"Why should I risk a share in your investments when I can have your cash?"

"No risk," Doyle assured him. "And I'll pay you half again what I owe."

Disgusted with her husband and embarrassed for Mr. Doyle, Elise could not listen to more. She stood and walked to the wine fountain at the far end of the room.

The sound of masculine laughter from the foyer drew her attention. Lockwood's brother-in-law entered the main salon, followed by two young men who looked remarkably familiar. A moment later, Lockwood and his brother, Charles, joined them. She smiled. No wonder the men looked familiar. These were the infamous Hunter brothers. The two she hadn't met, James and Andrew, if she recalled, had the same dark good looks as Hunt and Charles. She turned away when she realized that Ethan Travis had not brought his wife. No, this would not be the sort of place anyone would bring a wife. Anyone but Barrett.

Embarrassed to be found there, she filled her glass and skirted the edge of the salon to find another empty alcove. Alas, her plan went awry when Barrett spotted her and raised his voice.

"Where have you got to, woman?"

She changed direction and hurried to join him and Mr. Doyle. Perhaps she could steer them away from Lockwood's group.

Unfortunately, Lockwood was almost as determined to embarrass her as Barrett. He led his group in a path to intercept her and bowed. "Madam," he said with a sharp bow, his gaze snagging on her low décolletage.

She dropped a proper curtsy. "Lord Lockwood."

"I believe you've met Mr. Travis and Charlie? May I present my wayward siblings, James and Andrew? Lads, this is the legendary Lady Barrett."

James came forward first, lifted her hand to his lips and bowed. When he looked up at her over her hand, his eyes startled her. They were so exactly like Lockwood's that she nearly melted. He grinned and passed her hand to Andrew.

The family resemblance was not quite as strong in him and his eyes were a deep impenetrable brown. Andrew, she thought, would be a hard man to know.

As he released her hand and stepped back, he said, "Charmed to meet you, Lady Barrett. I must say that I am a bit surprised. I have heard of you—who has not?—but I never expected you to be so…"

"Charming?" Lockwood supplied with an edge to his voice.

"Beautiful," Andrew finished.

Elise was momentarily taken aback by his reference to her scandal, but there was something almost liberating about having it openly acknowledged rather than skirting the issue and making everyone uncomfortable.

"You must excuse Andrew, madam. His manners were neglected in our youth. Likely because he discovered a talent for avoiding our tutor."

She was about to reply when Barrett and Mr. Doyle joined them.

"Here you are, madam. Did I not tell you to stay put?"

"I went to fill my wineglass."

Her husband looked angry but could not express it in the face of so many witnesses. She supposed she would pay for her words on the coach ride home.

"A beautiful woman should not have to refill her own glass. I shall be pleased—"

"Do not make trouble, Andrew." Lockwood glanced at Barrett, clearly concerned that Barrett would issue a challenge.

Doyle stepped between the men and placed a hand on Barrett's shoulder. "We were just going to rejoin a game of *vingt et un*. Come, let's make a group, eh?"

Lord Ethan was quick to take up the invitation. "Lead the way, Doyle. But I warn you, we're a determined group."

They began to move away, but Hunt remained where he was.

"Coming, Lord Lockwood?" Doyle asked.

"Go on without me. I'll be along in a moment. I have some business to take care of."

Chapter Sixteen

Hunt's conscience tweaked him when Elise turned and hurried away. Aware that he was being watched, he went in search of rye whiskey. He needed something strong to kill the bitter taste of gall at seeing Barrett assert his ownership over his wife.

He turned around in time to watch the embroidered hem of her lilac gown disappear into an alcove. Good. They would be alone. He did not relish giving her the news of Captain Gilbert's death, and he certainly did not want to subject her grief to public scrutiny.

With a glance over his shoulder to be certain they would not be observed, he found her as she sat. She was startled to find him standing there and not altogether pleased, judging by the look on her face.

"I apologize for Andrew. He has not learned when baiting will not serve him."

"Baiting? I thought he was teasing Barrett."

Hunt laughed. "Not Andrew. He hasn't a frivolous bone in his body. He seems to have taken a dislike to your husband. He was trying to provoke him."

Elise's lips parted in surprise. "I misread him completely."

"Most people do."

"But I think I haven't misread you, Lockwood. You are here to cause trouble, are you not? If Barrett comes back—"

"Do you think I give a damn what your husband thinks?"

She winced. "No, I suppose not. In fact, if I had a pence, I'd wager you do not."

"You'd win."

"What do you want? Why did you follow me?"

"I thought you might want to know that your friend, Captain Gilbert, is dead."

Tears sprang to her eyes and spilled down her cheeks, and she dashed them away with the back of her hand. "I know. It is insane. Why would anyone kill him?"

He removed his handkerchief from his waistcoat pocket and lifted her chin on the edge of his hand. She did not resist when he dabbed at her eyes. "I am sorry for your loss, Elise. I know he was a good friend to you for many years. How did you hear? I gather it has been kept from the papers."

"Mr. Doyle informed me of it this morning."

"He called on you?"

"I met him skating on the canal when I was on my way back from shopping."

What bothered him more? That Doyle had known about Gilbert before he had, or that Doyle had been with Elise? Whichever, it put him on edge. "Does your husband know you were with Doyle? He does not seem as if he would tolerate your friendship with any man."

She looked a little bewildered by that, too. "He and Mr. Doyle have struck up their own friendship. It was Barrett who asked Mr. Doyle to meet him here tonight."

"And, of course, Doyle was only too glad to do it. How better to be close to you? And me, Elise? How shall I get close to you?"

"Please, Lockwood." She cast a panicked glance at the crowd in the salon. "Someone will see."

He closed the heavy velvet curtain over the alcove with a snap of his wrist. The space instantly became more intimate. "Now they will not."

"If only it could be that easy," she murmured. Her hands shook as she brought them up to press her temples. "What do you want from me, Lockwood? Answers I cannot give? Everyone wants something. An apology? An act of contrition? Do you want me to suffer? I think I can manage that, my lord."

"I do not want anything from you, Daphne." But that was a lie. He wanted the midnight back, and the storm. He wanted her writhing in his arms, calling his name, moaning as he filled her.

"Elise!" she cried. "Have you only come to taunt me?"

"Tell me why it cannot be. Why did you come back to Barrett, Elise? Why did you not tell me?"

"All those years, I believed I had killed him. Every time I closed my eyes, I saw him lying on my bedroom floor, his head gashed and blood everywhere. I was so certain…"

Some of the sting left him as he recognized the truth in her words. She had believed she was a widow. And her refusal to return to England made sense, too. If she thought Barrett was dead, she would believe herself to be a criminal. "But why did you come back, if you thought he was dead?"

"A letter…" she began, but then closed her mouth and shook her head.

"Were you *trying* to kill him, Elise? Or was it an accident?"

She groaned and he sat beside her. He didn't give a damn what was happening on the other side of the curtain, or that Barrett could return and find them there. He took her mouth and swallowed her gasp of surprise. She was sweet and warm, and her lips trembled when they opened to him.

"Please," she whispered, "*please* do not taunt me as you did in Carlin's portrait gallery. I cannot stop you, and you know it."

He was not ashamed of that incident. He'd wanted to shake her from her icy coldness, to remind her of what they had once been to one another. And to know if he had only dreamed her responsiveness. Furthermore, he could not promise not to do it again. "Elise…" he whispered against her lips. "Why did you not leave word for me?"

"I could not think what to say. I still cannot. *Tell* me what to say, Lockwood. What words will ease your mind? Give you peace and recompense?"

There were no words. There was nothing she could say that would make it right again—that could ever give them a future together. He reached out to her, then let his hand drop. He did not even have the right to touch her.

He stood and bowed before opening the curtain and leaving her there alone as he ran a gamut of curious stares.

Elise stared out the library window at the dirty slush melting in the morning sun and shuddered. She had forgotten that London was a very dangerous place until the news of Captain Gilbert's murder, and then their return home last night to find that the house had been broken into and searched. The servants had long since retired, but the thief had fled when Barrett's valet had heard a noise and gone to investigate.

She turned and faced the desk, where Barrett was poring over his records, comparing his inventory to the items in his wall safe. A careful examination of the rest of the house revealed that nothing of import was missing and that the thief had not been able to open the safe.

"Then what *is* missing?" she asked.

"My cash. Must've been fifty pounds in my desk drawer.

Looks like Smythe frightened him away before he could get to the rest."

The thought was not in the least comforting. What if they'd been home? Her stomach twisted with anxiety. "London is so bleak in the winter, Barrett. Can we not go home?"

He looked up from the ledger with a smug smile on his face. "I think I shall buy another estate, courtesy of Mr. Doyle's wagering. One in the north. When I'm tired of you, I can send you off to Northumberland." He laughed at the hope that must have shown on her face. "You are too transparent by half, Elise. Oh, you want to go away, but it isn't the robbery that has you troubled. You want to avoid society's curiosity, do you not? Their censure? Well, you've made your bed, dear wife, and you will have to lie in it."

He stood and laughed again at his suggestive metaphor and came to pinch her cheek with a cruel twist. She slapped his hand away, knowing there would be another bruise she would have to hide. But perhaps he was right, after all. Once they were back in the country, there would be nothing to prevent him from abusing her at will—no need for her to appear in public, no restraint on his evil temper. Surely that would be more dangerous than a mere thief.

She turned at a soft knock on the door. Smythe appeared, bearing a sealed note on a silver tray. "My lord," he said as he offered the note with a bow.

Barrett popped the seal and unfolded the page. As he read it, his eyes narrowed. "Why would Lady Sarah Travis ask *you* to tea this afternoon, madam?"

Lockwood's sister? She lifted her eyebrows. She knew Barrett had been opening her mail and burning anything he did not want her to see, but she had suspected those were notes from William. It had not occurred to her that she could be receiving invitations. "I really cannot say," she admitted. "I have met her, but we did not pass more than a few words."

"You may go," he pronounced.

"And if I do not wish to go?"

Barrett narrowed his eyes in a warning. "You will go, madam. And you will report back to me."

"What should I report?"

"Whatever they discuss. Whatever questions they ask. I find it far too coincidental that I keep running into Lockwood and his kin. They are up to something, and I want to know what it is. You, madam, will be my eyes and ears."

Was he jesting? But no, Barrett never jested. She held her quick refusal, knowing it would do no good. Later, when he demanded a report, she would simply tell him tea had been a purely social event.

"And do not lie to me," he added, apparently reading her expression. "Or your precious William will suffer for it."

She studied the ugly look on Barrett's face and asked the question that had troubled her since William's birth. "Why do you hate him so, Barrett? He is your son. Your flesh and blood."

"*Your* flesh and blood, madam. He looks like you and even sounds like you. There is nothing of me in him. He is a weak, puling little brat."

"Do you doubt he is your son?"

"I have wondered that from the day he came squalling into this world. I wouldn't put it past that ne'er-do-well sot of a brother of yours to pass off used goods. If the brat is mine, madam, I swear you drank a witch's potion to purge my influence from your womb."

Was he mad? "But…he is still your son."

"Only because I have no other at the moment. His real value to me is in bringing you to heel."

She tried a bluff. "No longer, Barrett. You have coerced me

from the day I arrived, all without giving me proof that you even have William, or that you have not already…already…" But she could not finish the thought, let alone the words. "After what you've just said, you cannot hold that over me without proof. Produce William if you think to use him against me, or I shall leave you immediately."

Barrett laughed. "So you have grown claws, little kitten. Very well, then. I shall have William here tomorrow afternoon. You will have precisely two minutes to assure yourself of his safety. That is all, madam, until I am certain I can trust you."

"What will that take, Barrett? How can I show you that you can trust me?"

"Do not betray the little trust I've given you so far. And open your bedroom door to me."

Dear Lord. She might have been able to justify spying on Lockwood's family, but how could she ever…no. Never. Not if hell froze over. Not if the sun fell from the sky. Not if…but she gave her husband a cool nod of acknowledgment.

A polite servant had taken Elise's bonnet and cloak and had escorted Anne to the kitchen. Elise stood uncertainly in the foyer, wondering if she was supposed to find the parlor or wait for another servant to appear.

Instead, Lady Sarah skipped down the wide staircase, smiling in welcome. "I heard the bell, but I had to put the baby back in her cradle. I hope I have not kept you waiting too long."

"Not at all, Lady Sarah. I—"

"Shall we dispense with formalities, madam? I would much prefer you to call me Sarah, and I would be grateful for the privilege if I could call you Elise."

Elise barely had time to nod before Sarah linked arms with her and led her toward a small sitting room behind the front parlor. "I hope you do not mind, Elise, that I have asked you to come earlier than the other ladies. I wanted a chance to talk to you alone."

"I do not mind at all," she said, a little breathless from Sarah's energy.

"You will learn that I am usually more subtle than I am about to be, but we haven't much time."

"I am not sure I know what you mean, La—Sarah."

"It is about my brother, you see." She sat on a small blue velvet sofa and pulled Elise down beside her. "To be frank, he came to me early this morning and told me that he thought you might need a friend. I asked him particulars, but he said you would not talk to him and he thought I might be able to help."

"Oh, I see." Elise felt the heat rising in her cheeks. She removed her gloves and put them in her reticule. "That was very kind of him, but he should not have imposed—"

"Heavens! I have given you the wrong impression. This is not a favor for my brother. I had intended to invite you to tea ever since we met. I wanted to hear all about St. Claire. Men are so scant on the interesting details, you know. But before we come to that, I…oh, dear. I am going to seem quite the busybody to you."

Elise smiled. "You have led into it quite nicely. I am now prepared for nearly anything," she said.

"Well, I gather—not from anything Hunt has said, but from my own observation—that you have a great sadness. And, regrettably, I have concluded that your marriage is not precisely…happy?"

The understatement made Elise laugh. "You are correct on both counts."

"If there is anything I can do to help, I would be eager to do so."

"There is nothing that can be done."

"As to that, I would not be so certain. You might be astonished at what can be done. Where there is a will, they say. I know women—my friends, actually—who have overcome great odds to achieve their ends. If you could just bring yourself to trust me, perhaps we could find a solution."

Elise tamped out the faint glimmer of hope. How could she trust anyone when there was so much at risk?

"You have a son, do you not?"

She nodded.

"He must be a great comfort to you."

The sympathy undid her. She opened her reticule and retrieved her handkerchief. Oh, drat! She dabbed at her eyes and composed herself before she answered. "I have not seen William since my return."

"No? But where is he?"

Now she could barely speak for the lump in her throat. "I...Barrett has not told me. He has promised to bring William to see me tomorrow afternoon."

When there was no further comment, Elise glanced up to see an expression of speculation on Sarah's face. "I see," she said. "Yes, I see."

And, with a chill, Elise realized she did.

There was a commotion from the foyer and she stood with Sarah to greet the newcomers. Four young women joined them, and Sarah began the introductions.

"Lady Barrett, may I present my friends, Lady Auberville, Mrs. Hawthorne, Lady MacGregor and Lady Morgan. Ladies, please be seated. I believe Elise is in need of assistance."

Hunt woke in a cold sweat. The dream, the same one he'd had nearly every night since his return, had come again. He was standing on the cliffs overlooking Blackpool cove. From the inky blackness below, Layton's face emerged like a reproach to Hunt for his stupidity. How had he missed all the clues—the arrival of the new ship, the conversation at the tap, the way the men had surrounded Layton as they'd gone outside? But he had, and Layton had paid the price. It should have been him, damn it. It should have been him.

He'd been at this job too long. He'd been too lucky. Odds favored a failure and it was time to get out before someone else paid for his misstep. This assignment had been a disaster from the beginning, and he'd have no peace until he could put it behind him.

The mantel clock chimed midnight and he threw off his covers and stumbled out of bed. It had been a mistake to think he could sleep before dawn these days.

He tied his robe around his waist and went to his fireplace to stir the flames. The night chill crept beneath window sashes and across thresholds to invade even the coziest corner and, for a moment, he wished himself back on St. Claire. He could not seem to drag his mind away from there.

The brandy bottle on his bureau beckoned him. Perhaps that would drug him enough to sleep. He poured himself a measure and went to his window. A halo of yellowish light surrounded the streetlamps in the gently falling snow—beautiful tonight, but dirty slush in the light of day.

He turned back to his room, to the empty bed, and envisioned Elise there, her sun-kissed hair spread across his pillow, the dark fans of her lashes lying like crescents on cheeks flushed from making love. He grew hard with desire and a longing so strong it nearly doubled him over.

He stopped at his writing desk, swallowed the remains of the brandy and placed the glass on the blotter. For a perturbing moment, he stared at the conch shell, remembering that long-ago night.

Can you let yourself dream, Daphne?

He had let himself dream that night. Dream that he could

build an ordinary life. That a woman could love him, despite the dark things he'd done in the name of God and Country. That he had something of value to offer. That— No. Such thinking could drive him insane. He would be better served to learn to live without hope.

But he could not help himself when he lifted the conch shell and carried it back to his bed. As he placed it on his nightstand, a withered wild orchid fell out of the curve. Faint but distinct, the scent wafted to him, conjuring the hiss of waves, the flash of lightning and the roll of thunder over the vast expanse of ocean.

He stroked the sleek pink inner curve of the shell and closed his eyes as he lay back against his pillows. It was Elise he stroked. Elise who lay open to him. It might be torture to think of her when he knew he could not have her, but it was the only thing that kept him sane.

Elise wrapped the pocket puzzle in brightly colored paper and put it in a small velvet pouch with candied plums and marzipan figures. There would be no time to watch him open it, or to see his smile as he savored the sweets, but he could take it with him and enjoy it later.

She glanced at the tall case clock and schooled herself to patience. Traffic could have delayed their coach. Or perhaps Barrett had misjudged the distance. He'd still come. Surely he'd come. Wouldn't he? Oh, pray this was not another of his tricks to raise her hopes and then dash them for his amusement.

Or perhaps he was punishing her. He'd been almost angry yesterday when she'd told him that tea with Lady Sarah had been just that—tea. She'd sworn that there had been no secret motives or nefarious purposes. And she prayed she'd been convincing.

Indeed, she was still not entirely certain what Sarah and

her friends thought they could do. They hadn't told her, nor had they made any promises. But they had listened and had given her hope. More than that, she was grateful for their friendship. There was, she discovered, great strength to be found in friendship.

She pulled a Windsor chair in front of the fireplace and sat to warm her hands and feet while she thought. There had to be something she could do to make Barrett relent. Perhaps, if she stopped baiting him, she could persuade him to allow weekly visits with William. And if she could manage to give the appearance of even mild affection for her husband, perhaps he would let William stay longer.

As for granting Barrett access to her bed, she did not know if she could bend that far. Just the memory of it made her stomach gurgle and her heart constrict. She would have to be very drunk, indeed, or unconscious, to endure his touch.

The sound of a coach stopping outside sent Elise running to the window. Yes! Barrett stepped down onto the pavement and turned to reach up to someone still in the shadows.

Small, touchingly thin, a dark-haired lad emerged. Elise held her breath. William's eyes were sunken and he looked as if he would refuse Barrett's helping hand. He was clearly frightened as they climbed the front steps.

She turned from the window and went to sit on the sofa and compose herself. She couldn't let William see her distress. And she knew she dare not give Barrett any reason to refuse future visits. But, if her plan worked, perhaps she would not need Barrett's permission soon.

"Mama? Mama!"

She stood and took a few steps before the parlor door flew open and William burst though. A lump formed in her throat and she could not speak. Instead, she held her arms out to him.

William ran to her and landed against her, his thin arms

wrapping around her waist. "Oh, Mama. Where have you been? I thought you gave me away."

She glared at Barrett over William's head. Her heart was breaking to think of William, alone and believing she had deserted him. Is that what Barrett had told him to make him leave Charleston with him? "Never! Never think that, William. I would never give you away." She knelt and held him away from her to give him a steady look. "I love you, darling. And I came to you as soon as I could. I have been so worried about you. Are you well? Have you been eating? Are you keeping up with your studies?"

William looked over his shoulder at Barrett. "Papa says I mustn't talk about such things. That I will only worry you."

She lowered her voice. It was a risk, but one she had to take. "Is...is Uncle Alfred being good to you, William?"

Her son looked confused, as if he had not understood the question. Was it possible she was wrong? That William was not being held by Barrett's brother?

Barrett sneered as he came forward. "I warned you not to pry, Elise. I told you what would happen if you did."

She widened her eyes in innocence. "How is that prying, Barrett? I told you I would ask after his welfare." She turned back to the boy. "Are you getting enough to eat? You look so thin."

"That's enough, Elise," Barrett warned.

She could feel William trembling beneath his thin wool jacket. His fear of Barrett was obvious. She handed him the pouch and drew him into her arms again. "Be strong and brave, William," she whispered in his ear. "Remember that I love you and I will find a way for us to be together soon."

Huge tears swam in William's green eyes as Barrett pulled him away, still clutching his velvet pouch.

The moment they left the room, Elise removed her dark hooded cloak from the window seat and drew it around her, and the moment the coach pulled away from the curb, she flew out the door and followed at a distance. Thank heavens city traffic was slow, at best. Alfred's house was not far, and if William were being held there, she would know it soon. If not, she would lose sight of the coach.

Chapter Seventeen

Once again, Hunt found himself across the room from Elise. That was happening far too often these days. How could he forget her when she was constantly in front of him? Constantly beautiful. Constantly alluring. Tonight was no different. Her cream gown was cut to advantage, revealing the tempting swell of her breasts over the lace ruching at the neckline. The long sleeves did nothing to mask the blatant sexuality of the gown—especially with a sapphire pendant falling between those glorious swells. He glanced around and caught sight of Barrett in hushed conversation with two other men. Looking to drum up a game of whist, no doubt.

Hunt had left Charlie in Horace Thayer's library, attempting to convince Thayer to allow Charlie access to his banking records and accounts. Charlie was close, he said, to narrowing his lists of investors and insurers to a few excellent candidates. If he could match bank records with insurance and investment records, he insisted he could identify their culprit. As one of the most important bankers in London, Thayer was in a position to further their inquiry. Unfortunately, they had come in the middle of a musicale and were invited to stay. How could they refuse?

On a small dais at one end of the ballroom, Miss Hortense Thayer was playing the pianoforte while her sister, Miss Harriet, sang in a true, sweet voice. Afterward, another guest would play a piece by Mozart. Then another guest… and another…and another. Barrett's game was suddenly appealing.

As Hunt watched, Elise finished her wine, placed the glass on a sideboard and took another. Was the lady tippling? Oh, yes. She certainly was. Another glass was downed and then she took a third with her to her position in a shadowed corner in the back of the ballroom. God only knew how many she had consumed before he arrived.

Curious, Hunt edged closer, keeping an eye on Barrett. It would never do to be interrupted. Then one of Barrett's companions produced cigars from an inside pocket of his jacket and the men slipped out the French windows to the terrace—but not before Barrett fixed his wife's position. Hunt knew Elise would be the first thing Barrett looked for when he returned.

Hunt reached her as the applause for the Misses Thayer began—a convenient cover for his movements. He placed his own empty wineglass on the sideboard and came up behind Elise. She had not noticed him and he waited patiently for the next performer to begin.

When the slow measured strains of Pachelbel's *Canon in D* filled the room, she closed her eyes. A tiny glimmer at the corners made him wonder if she was crying. Her shoulders relaxed as she gave herself over to the melody. She tilted her head slightly to one side, as if she were straining to hear the nuances of the music. He noted a discoloring at the base of her throat and wondered at its cause.

He slipped his arm around her midriff, barely touching her.

She did not jump or protest, and she was all the more beguiling for that, as if they were the only two people in the room. Her warm wine-scented breath rose to him as she whispered, "Good evening, Lord Lockwood." Her words were not slurred, just a little soft around the edges.

"How did you know it was me?"

"Who else would dare?"

He smiled, taking a quiet satisfaction in her answer. And he believed her. In fact, he had never seen Barrett touch her in anything resembling a kind manner. "You could have been mine, Elise," he sighed in her ear.

"No. I never could have been yours. Barrett…"

"That is not a marriage. It is a mockery." He splayed his hand over her midriff and pressed her back against him. The soft curve of her buttocks jutted against his crotch and, by her tiny gasp, he knew she could feel it, too. "Evidence of my devotion," he muttered.

She still had not turned to look at him, and did not move or betray anger or disgust in any way. Instead she lifted her glass and drank deeply. "My marriage will not be a mockery after tonight, Lockwood."

"Why?" he asked, caught up in the feel of her against him, the scent of her perfume, the slight tilt of her head exposing the sweet curve of her throat.

"I have decided to…pay Barrett's price. T-tonight I am going to…open my bedroom door."

Everything inside him stilled. There could be no question what she'd meant. Ah, but the hidden news was that she had *not* shared intimacies with Barrett since her return. "Is that why you are trying to get drunk, madam?"

"Easier that way," she confirmed.

"Then why? If it is so loathsome, why?"

"Contrition. Penance for my sins. And mostly, for William.

Couldn't find him. And I'm tired of waiting. Tired of not knowing when…" She finished her wine and he took the glass from her hand. "And perhaps, then, I will be able to forget you."

"You will never forget me, Elise."

"Is that a curse or a benediction?" She giggled and then covered her mouth. "Shh. Mustn't be indiscreet."

"God, no." He sighed, slipping his left hand up from her stomach to caress her breast. He watched, mesmerized, as her nipple hardened and pressed a perfect round dot against the light cream silk of her gown. How he longed to kiss it, to feel the firm bud against his tongue, but he contented himself with rubbing his thumb across it.

A quick glance around the room revealed that they hadn't drawn attention, but he knew that couldn't last. Sooner or later, someone would turn around or Barrett would return from his cigar. Mere days ago, he wouldn't have cared—might actually have relished the chance to embarrass her. But the sharp edge of his anger had dulled. Now taunting her had become secondary to wanting to be near her. Wanting to touch her.

Charlie entered the ballroom and looked around. Before he could shift his hand, Charlie saw him and smiled. Ah, yes. Charlie. He could count on his brother for what he needed done. And for discretion.

Charlie wiggled his eyebrows at Hunt. "So the lady accounts for your sudden interest in Barrett?"

Hunt scowled to squelch his brother's amusement. "Did Thayer consent to let you look through deposit and withdrawal records?"

"He did. But it's all on the hush. If anyone finds out, he says bank business will suffer for it. I'm to say I did it on my own and that no one gave me permission. I swear, Hunt, I'm beginning to feel like a common workaday clerk. I pore over ledgers all day, compare records, enter names and dates." He heaved a dramatic sigh. "Not quite what I had in mind when I asked the home secretary for a position."

"If you want something a little more interesting, I could give it to you."

Charlie's eyes lit up. "Well? Do not cheat me of it now, brother. I crave excitement."

Hunt glanced back at Elise. She stood in almost the same position as when he'd left her, but with a fresh glass of wine. "Barrett is outside with a cheroot. When he comes in, I want you to approach him. Pretend you are jolly old friends and that nothing will do but that you go whoring tonight. Gamble with him—"

"Good Lord! The man is beginning to think I am his bosom companion. He's got the damnedest luck, Hunt. He'll fleece me seven ways from Sunday."

"—and I will reimburse your losses," Hunt continued. "Buy him whiskey. Take him to Alice's. There's no act, no perversion, that woman will not accommodate. Just make damn sure Barrett doesn't make it home until after dawn."

"You wouldn't—"

"No, Charlie. I wouldn't. But Barrett won't, either. The lady is vulnerable at the moment and not thinking straight."

"I'll try, but I'm not sure I am up to the task."

"Find Andrew. He will help. Hell, he'll outpace you all."

Charlie laughed. "And what about the lady?"

"Insist that you take Barrett's coach, and offer *ours* to take the lady home."

"And you, dear brother?"

He shrugged. "I'll be making certain the lady arrives home safely."

* * *

Hunt waited across the street from the Thayers' until Elise was handed into his coach and the driver pulled into the stream of traffic. Next, Charlie and Barrett entered a coach that headed in the opposite direction. Then Hunt rounded the corner where, on his previous instructions, *his* coach had pulled over to wait. He swung up to the passenger step.

"Circle Hyde Park until I tell you to change direction, Anderson," he called to his driver before entering the darkened coach. He realized with wry amusement that, for a man who had spent his life avoiding social indiscretions, he was becoming expert at them.

Elise's eyes widened and then she laughed. "Oh, thank heavens! I thought for a moment I would get home safe."

He took the backward facing seat so that he could watch her. "Just what do you think I am going to do to you, madam?"

"I have no idea, but I know it cannot mean anything good. I usually cannot sleep after one of our encounters."

"You've had enough wine to sleep quite well."

"Oh, not nearly enough yet." She looked into a door pocket. "D'you carry any with you? I am thirsty."

He crossed his arms over his chest and gave her a sardonic smile. If he was any judge, and he was, she had consumed just the right amount—sufficient to be reckless enough to tell the truth, and not enough to lose all sense of herself. "I've never been so desperate for strong drink that I couldn't wait. But now you mention it, would you like me to have Anderson stop and fetch some from a tavern?"

She heaved a melodramatic sigh. "Please do not inconvenience him. I believe it is a short drive home."

"Not so very short as you would imagine," he said.

"Then, yes. I would like some wine. 'Twill never do to sober up."

"Is this a new habit, madam? Or one of long-standing?"

"Recent, my lord. But one I think I am going to thoroughly enjoy. Certainly one that is necessary to my entire future."

"About that, madam. Could we clarify, please? Am I correct in assuming that you have not resumed marital relations with your husband?"

She wagged a finger at him. "Tch-tch, Lockwood. That's rather personal, wouldn't you agree?"

"Oh, I would, indeed. Am I?"

"Correct, you mean? Why, yes. But that cannot be a surprise to you, given that Barrett is a disgusting specimen."

He laughed. "Actually, it *was* a surprise to me. I had assumed that, since you had returned to him, you must bear him some affection."

She shuddered as if he had held smelling salts under her nose. "Where is that wine? I believe the effects are beginning to wear off."

"And I think you've had exactly enough."

"Not nearly enough," she contradicted.

"You will not need it tonight, Elise."

She was silent for a moment, looking out the window. In one of those mercurial changes of mood that sots are prone to, her smile disappeared. "What I need, Lockwood, is to be completely unconscious tonight."

"Then why are you doing it?"

"Every night he forces my door a little more. Soon, he will lose all pretense at subtlety and simply break it down. I cannot stop him, and we both know it. But, if I can stomach it, and before he can simply force it from me, I intend to use my…favors…as a…trade."

Good God. Elise was living in terror. But—then the other hints she'd dropped since he'd returned began to make sense. "He is holding something over you, is he not?"

She closed her eyes and leaned her head back against the squabs. "Where is that wine?"

"But you came back, believing that you'd go to jail. You wouldn't come back for me, Elise. So what convinced you?"

"Please…"

He moved to the seat beside her and took her hand so she couldn't look away. "No, Elise. If you are about to whore yourself, I want to know why."

She opened her eyes, and he thought he'd never seen such hopelessness and despair. "Whore…" she repeated. "Yes, the very thing I feared I would become."

He hated seeing her this way and wished he could spare her any further agony. But not yet. Not before he got to the truth. He cupped her face and smoothed her hair back with his thumbs. The scars caught his attention. He knew about the more recent one, but she'd never told him about the faded one. He looked downward, to the discoloration at her throat. And suddenly it all came clear in his mind. He touched the faded scar at her temple. "It was Barrett who did this to you, wasn't it, Elise?"

She sighed and nodded.

"Why?"

"He was going to hurt William and I tried to stop him."

Rage tightened his breathing and churned in his gut. "Leave him. I will find you a town house until you can divorce him."

"On what grounds, my lord? He has a lawful right to beat me. I am in the wrong. I tried to kill him, you know. I stole the Barrett jewels. I kidnapped William, and I disappeared. Any one of those things could see me hanged. Oh, and you mustn't forget that I'm an adulteress. I certainly shan't, with you to remind me of it constantly."

"Elise, you didn't know he was alive."

"And that is not the worst of it. The worst is…" She lifted her chin and looked up at him, her eyes pleading with him to understand. "The worst is that I would do it all again and may yet. But I will be certain he is dead next time. So you see, my lord? I *am* a whore. And a murderess, and a kidnapper, and a thief."

Dear God. He recognized the despair in her eyes, the hollow look of someone who'd forfeit her soul. He wouldn't let her do that. He could not allow her to live with the weight of that on her conscience. He'd kill Barrett himself first. When it came to Elise, it would seem *he* had no conscience.

"Give me a few days, Elise. I will take care of it. Take care of you. I will find a way."

"No!" She stiffened and pushed his hands away. "You mustn't. Swear you will not." She tugged frantically at his cravat. "If anything happens to Barrett, William…"

William. She had said that she couldn't find him. "Is he using William against you?"

"He found him at school in Charleston and brought him back to London. He knew I would come if he had William. It was a trap, and it worked. It is still working. And how can I divorce him when the courts would grant him custody of William?"

Hunt knew he'd lost the argument. But at least all the pieces of the puzzle finally fit. He knew why she'd come back, and why she stayed with Barrett. There was nothing else she could have done until her son was safe. But there was something he could do.

Before he realized what he was doing, he was kissing her, drawing her close against him, lost in the feel of her in his arms again, her heat, her yielding softness. Her throaty moan was all the encouragement he needed.

He untied the cord of her cloak and pushed it open. He hated the sight of Barrett's jewels lying so intimately against her flesh and he unfastened the sapphire pendant and dropped it on the floor, leaving the ivory expanse of her flesh pristine.

He kissed the sweet perfumed spot beneath her ear, then trailed his tongue to the dip of her collarbone. She shivered, and he was instantly hard. How he longed to feel her close around him, her inner muscles gripping him, as greedy for him as he was for her. She reached for him, and he let her fumble with his cravat, though that was not where he wanted her hand.

"Hunt," she pleaded.

He cherished the hollow of her throat, wanting to leave his mark there but knowing she would suffer for it. Instead he hovered, barely touching, feeling the beat of her heart against his lips. Her heart, the one thing he most wanted in this world.

And then he could not wait any longer. He pushed the lace ruching down and dipped his head to take the firm peak between his teeth, gently teasing until she arched and tangled her fingers in his hair.

"Hunt…Hunt," she crooned.

At last he took her fully into his mouth, sucking and rolling the tight button with his tongue. And now she was nearly frantic with longing. He swept her skirts up her leg, pushed his hand past her smallclothes and found her center, hot and wet with arousal. He stroked her there, too, as he stroked her breast with his tongue, and he felt the first faint tremors pass through her.

He ached. He pulsed. He needed her, and yet… And yet he could go no further than this. She was another man's wife.

She reached for him, and he knew he'd be lost if she touched him. He brushed her hand aside and increased his pressure. She moaned and wept at the same time, rising to his hand and falling back again, sated.

The storm passed, and he eased his hand away. She pulled him back up to her mouth and he noted the flush of passion on her cheeks. "Think of me," he whispered against her lips.

He lifted the hood of her cloak and tucked it around her

face, then traced her lips with his index finger and hovered there for a long moment, cherishing their softness. Then he retrieved the pendant and pressed it into her palm. "Hold on," he whispered. "Sleep well, and do not do anything you'll regret. Be resolute, Elise. I will find a way to help you."

The clink of silverware against porcelain plates made Elise wince. But, down the lunch table from her, Barrett was in much worse condition. His eyes were bleary and he merely stared at the food, pushing it around his plate with his fork. Finally, he dropped his fork and knife and took a deep drink from his wineglass.

"A little hair of the dog, Barrett?" she could not resist taunting.

"Hold your tongue, woman. Men are free to do as they please. But you, I understand, were making a spectacle of yourself last night. You were well in your cups before I put you in the coach for home."

"At least I arrived home and climbed the stairs without assistance. Good heavens! Where were you until this morning?"

Barrett frowned and pressed his temples with his fingertips. "Cannot recall. I remember going to Thackery's, and then to Alice's…" He looked up and shot her a reproachful glare. "I would not have gone to that old whore if you were doing your duty by me."

"If I recall correctly, you were frequently at Alice's even before I left you." She forced another bite of meat down and laid her fork across her plate. In truth, it did not bother her in the least that her husband was blaming her for his whoring. Better Alice's bawdy house than her. She shuddered, remembering how close she'd come to surrendering. Oh, but William! How would she find William?

Misreading her shudder, Barrett snickered. "Best get something into your belly, madam. We are going to Travis's extravaganza at the Argyle Rooms tonight. I committed us to Travis."

"Lady Sarah's husband?"

"One and the same. I was carousing with the entire family last night. Good God! The Hunter brothers are bloody unnatural. They never stop!"

"All of them?" she asked.

"To a man," he confirmed. "Charlie and James are good enough company, but Andrew's debauchery is truly stunning. I doubt Satan himself could keep up. And Lockwood…well, he paced me drink for drink after he joined us. The man has an inhuman capacity."

Lockwood had gone looking for them after he left her? "Which of them brought you home?"

"Don't know. Had to be Lockwood or Andrew, though. I recall someone pulling me up by my breeches and tossing me into the coach. Damn." He paused to press a spot between his eyes. "I wish I could remember what he said. Something about how I damn well better go straight to bed?"

Heavens! Lockwood had tried to save her from herself.

"Pay attention, damn it!" Barrett roared, then cringed at his own voice.

"What…what sort of extravaganza are the Travises hosting?" she asked. "Is it a masquerade? Does it have a theme?"

"Damnation," he muttered. "I've forgot. Most likely something to do with the holiday. I think I'd remember if costumes were required. Foolish to have grown men and women sporting about looking like idiots."

"No costumes," she agreed.

She stood and dropped her napkin on her chair. She wanted to lie down with a cold compress over her eyes. She prayed that would be enough to banish her reddened eyes.

"Oh, and Elise?" Barrett called when she was halfway to the

stairs. "Try to be gracious and engaging, will you? I am tired of you standing around like you are too good for the rest of us."

She bit her tongue before she could remind him whose idea that had been.

Chapter Eighteen

The sheer opulence of the Argyle Rooms was astonishing. Elise felt gauche as she handed her cloak to a footman and looked around. Grecian columns, gilt frescoes, more alcoves than she'd seen at Belmonde's, plush carpets, polished paneling and glittering crystal chandeliers dazzled her eyes. Though the rooms had opened in 1806, she'd never been to an event here. Judging by Barrett's familiarity, though, he was quite at home. Was this not the place the Cyprians' Ball was held annually?

He led her up another wide set of stairs and handed their invitation to an officious looking individual who nodded them in. She sighed with relief when she saw not a single costume. It was a simple holiday gala, if galas could be called simple. To be sure, everyone was dressed elegantly.

She patted her hair self-consciously. Anne had swept it up to the crown and then let curls fall from a clasp to which she'd fastened a sprig of holly. Barrett had made her wear the rubies tonight to complement the little red berries still attached to the holly. The short train of her deep green velvet gown swept the carpet as she followed Barrett to find their host.

Lord Ethan and Lady Sarah stood to the side of the double doors in an attempt to avoid clogging the entrance with well-wishers. When they approached, Lady Sarah stepped forward and kissed Elise's cheek.

"I am glad you could attend our holiday gala on such short notice," she said. "I did not even know you when the invitations went out, but I am so glad we were not deprived of your company."

Elise smiled. She actually believed the woman meant what she said. Then Sarah's husband took her hand and bowed. "Lady Barrett. So nice to see you again."

"And you, sir." He looked remarkably fit for a man who'd been carousing with her husband last night. Could it be that not everyone had been as drunk as Barrett?

"I shall look for you later," Sarah said. "I would so love to have a little chat."

"And I always insist upon at least one dance from our female guests," Lord Ethan said. "So do not try to hide."

Elise's heart warmed. She did not doubt their sincerity, even though she wondered at the cause of it.

Barrett took her arm, led her toward the punch bowl and filled a cup of eggnog for himself. "Ah, there's Charlie Hunter," he said. "I believe he owes me money. I shall be back presently."

She exhaled deeply as he walked away. She was always relieved when Barrett was not close by. She was still chilled from the winter night and went looking for something warm to drink. When she arrived at a wassail bowl, she stopped. There was a faint smell of alcohol, but nothing as strong as she'd had last night. She did not think she could stomach another such night so soon.

Hunt leaned forward in his chair at the round table in the small retiring room adjacent to the ballroom, watching his companions as Charlie gave them his preliminary report. Eastman looked nonplussed, Charlie exhibited moderate enthusiasm, Auberville's eyes were narrowed as if he were calculating the information and Ethan stood and went to gaze out the window.

"So this is how we are going to catch our traitor?" Eastman asked when Charlie was finished. "Money?"

Charlie nodded and looked at Hunt for confirmation.

"Money will give us a list of suspects. We will narrow it to those names with opportunity, then find which of them has a motive."

"Damn clever, lad," Eastman said with a smile in Charlie's direction. "It never occurred to me that our traitor might never have left the country."

Hunt shrugged. "That remains to be seen. I think it would depend upon how many people are involved. There has to be a connection between London and St. Claire. We are still trying to determine how the information is passed. But we're a damn sight closer than we were."

"What's next?"

"I plan to appear as slightly down on my luck. Charlie, here, is helping me by losing prodigious amounts of cash to Barrett. I shall let it be known that I am looking for a high yield investment to recoup my losses and do not care if it is high risk or slightly shady, as long as it pays a high return. It should be interesting to see who, if anyone, approaches me. I am hoping that, by the time Charlie has finished his ledgers and accounts, I will have narrowed the list of suspects. And, if my ploy pays off, perhaps I will be given the opportunity to invest in a ship or two."

"Be careful, Lockwood. You do not want society to think you are a wastrel, do you?"

Frankly, he did not care in the least. He was well aware that he had already risked his reputation when he'd begun deviling

Elise. "What I need from you, Lord Eastman, is for you to 'confide' to a few men at the Foreign Office that I am desperate. We shall see if that draws anyone out. You, too, Auberville, and you, Ethan. And, by the way, Ethan, I shall be transferring a large sum into your account tomorrow. I want to look like a pauper in the event anyone should inquire."

Ethan nodded.

Sarah linked her arm through Elise's and led her toward a small grouping of chairs, vacant for the moment. "I am so glad you came, Elise. I was afraid…there might be some reason you would not be able to make it."

Elise laughed. "Barrett, you mean?"

"Well…" Sarah paused while they sat and settled themselves. "I gather he is not always easily led. Ah, but enough about husbands. I wanted to talk to you about your current situation regarding your son."

Elise glanced about, wanting to make certain Barrett was not in a position to overhear. He was standing across the room in deep conversation with Charles Hunter. She released a long breath and nodded. "Pray, continue, Sarah."

"After you left us the other afternoon, the ladies and I discussed your current dilemma. Though you did not ask our help, we decided to look into the matter to see if anything could be done. We appreciate the delicacy of the situation, given that Barrett is a peer."

"Thank you for your concern," Elise began, feeling her cheeks grow warm. How embarrassing to know that her new friends were discussing her private business. It had been a tremendous relief to tell someone about William, but she really hadn't expected them to help her.

"Not at all, dear. This is not the first time we have looked into matters for friends."

"Oh?"

"Well, enough times that we have begun to understand the intricacies of investigation. We hired a Bow Street runner to follow Barrett's coach when he left with the lad yesterday afternoon."

Elise groaned. What if Barrett had caught on? She felt sick to her stomach. Her husband did not need to raise a hand to her to strike her down. All he need do was punish William for her errors. But she had followed the coach and lost it in traffic after a few streets, and she had not seen anyone else following. "Please, Sarah. If you find him, you must leave him where he is until I can make arrangements to hide him. If I do not have everything ready, Barrett will find out and stop me."

Sarah leaned close and placed her warm hand over Elise's. "Barrett is watching. Please smile so he will not suspect we are discussing anything of import."

Resisting the urge to look across the room, Elise forced a smile and even managed a small laugh. "If Barrett caught on that he was being followed—"

"He did not, Elise. And he will not. However, our runner, Mr. Renquist, was unable to follow. The coach headed out of the city on the Oxford Road. Mr. Renquist did, however, ascertain that William was not being kept at Barrett's brother's home."

Elise kept her anxiety under control with great difficulty. "So I am no further ahead than I was yesterday?"

"A bit further, dear. We know where William is not. Now, shall we make another attempt?"

"How?"

"If you will convince Lord Barrett to bring little William for another visit, Mr. Renquist could be waiting on horseback."

Convince Barrett? To convince Barrett, she would have to trade favors. She glanced over at him and felt the bile rise in her throat. And once again she asked herself whether she could do that. William's face, pale and sunken, as she'd last seen it, rose to her mind. Could she not?

She looked back at Sarah. "Yes, I will convince him. I shall send you the date and time of William's visit. If your Mr. Renquist can determine where they are holding him, please inform me at once. In person, or verbally by messenger. Please do not send a written message, which could be intercepted."

Sarah nodded. "I understand. And please be assured that we are looking into making arrangements for you, as well. We simply must find a way to deal with your husband in a manner that will ensure your safety."

"I…I do not know how to thank you and your friends, Sarah. You barely know me. How will I ever repay you?"

"We shall think of something." She turned to watch her husband and brother come toward them.

Lockwood met Elise's gaze and grinned, and she knew he was thinking of last night. *Think of me.* Dear Lord, how could she ever forget?

"I have never seen Lockwood in such a state," Sarah said under her breath. "Every time he looks at you, his heart is in his eyes. I have put two and two together and have come up with…well, two. You two, to be precise. I gather you knew each other fairly well on St. Claire."

Fairly well? That was an embarrassing understatement. "Did Lockwood ask you to help me?"

"Heavens, no! He asked me to invite you to tea. He has no idea what the ladies and I are up to. You know men. They would think they had to put a stop to it, then take over in their typically heavy-handed way."

Hunt stood on the street outside the Argyle Rooms and watched as Andrew pulled away with Barrett in the Lockwood coach and as Elise, in Barrett's coach, pulled away in the opposite direction. Not surprisingly, Andrew had embraced the challenge of keeping Barrett from his bed. His brother's wicked smile and his wicked ways were coming in useful after all.

"I hear you are looking for investments, eh, Lockwood?" Gavin Doyle asked over his shoulder.

Hunt turned. "Why, yes, I am. Do you have something for me?"

"Might. I will look into it. You're not averse to shipping ventures?"

"Not averse at all. In fact, I'd be willing to risk a considerable sum on them."

"The greatest return is on the uninsured ships, you know. But the risk is greatest, as well."

Hunt shrugged. Was it going to be this easy? "I do not mind a risk. In fact, I find that the more hungry I am for funds, the greater the risk I am willing to take."

"Excellent. Where shall I find you?"

"At my club," Hunt instructed. "Or send 'round to my house. I must say, I am surprised. I hadn't any idea that you were an investor."

Doyle gave him a sharp glance. "What? Because of my humble beginnings, you mean? All the more reason. If one is to rise, one must have the wherewithal."

"Ah, a self-made man," Hunt replied in a soothing tone. "Admirable. I hear there are fortunes to be made in India, as well."

"So it is said. Alas, I begin to doubt that I will ever make it there."

"Surely you are not turning down the posting?"

"No. But another opportunity may be arising."

"Something closer to home, I would hope."

A smile curved the corners of Doyle's mouth. "One can always hope, eh, Lockwood?"

* * *

The sky was nearly the same color as the soot-darkened snow as Elise hurried up the church stairs. She'd never been to a funeral before. She'd been considered too young when her father had passed away, and the remainder of her years had been lived in happy isolation.

She was surprised to see so few people in attendance, but then she recalled that Captain Gilbert had been a seafaring man and, after his wife's death years ago, had lost touch with many of their former friends. But she was a little dismayed by the fact that she was the only woman.

Elise took a seat in the back. An ebony coffin stood before the pulpit and she could not reconcile her mind to the fact that Captain Gilbert, or what was left of him, was enclosed in it. A lump clogged her throat and she withdrew a handkerchief from her reticule.

Though the minister's voice droned on and the congregation made appropriate responses, Elise did not participate. She could only look at the coffin and remember Captain Gilbert patting her on the shoulder and walking away without a goodbye. Even the day they had docked, he had waved to her from the deck but had not called a farewell. How she wished she could see him now, and laugh at his teasing as he hid the newspapers from her.

She lifted a corner of her veil to dab at her eyes. How impossibly sad it was that good men like the captain could fall victim to murderers and thieves, while men like her husband could commit all manner of villainy against the innocent and go unpunished.

She said her own prayers for Captain Gilbert's peace and repose as the others read from the Book of Common Prayer. Somehow that seemed more personal.

And then it was over. No burial would follow immediately,

the minister announced, since it had been Captain Gilbert's wish to be buried beside his wife in Dover. At the mention of his wife, Elise's eyes flooded with tears. Oh, how she prayed he was with her now, after so many faithful and lonely years.

She stood and hurried out to the street, anxious to be away before anyone could talk to her. Alas, that was not to be.

"Lady Barrett!"

She stopped but did not turn.

Mr. Doyle caught up with her and bowed. "Had I known you would want to be here, madam, I would have fetched you myself."

Elise removed her veil and wiped at her eyes with resolute strength. All the while, she heard Barrett in the back of her mind, haranguing her that any display of emotion was unseemly. She cleared her throat. "I only learned of the funeral this morning, Mr. Doyle. I read the notice in the *Times*."

He took her gloved hand and bowed over it. "Nevertheless, I am very sorry. If you will come with me, my coach is waiting and I will convey you home."

"Thank you, sir, but no. I believe I will find the walk restorative."

Doyle looked uncertain. "If you insist."

"I do, sir. At times such as these, I find I prefer to be alone with my thoughts."

"We shall have to have a talk very soon, madam." He tipped his hat, bowed and walked to his waiting coach.

Elise sighed with relief. She pushed Mr. Doyle's odd goodbye from her mind and began walking, looking down at the street. She did not want to meet the eyes of strangers and see their pity at her tears, nor did she want to call attention to herself by wearing the veil.

She had walked several blocks before she realized that sleet had begun to fall and that someone was following her.

She registered footsteps measuring hers pace for pace. She stopped and turned.

Lockwood halted behind her and gave her a slight bow. "Madam. Are you well?"

"Have you been following me, Lockwood?"

He nodded, seemingly not the least sheepish to have been caught.

"Why?"

"I was concerned. I heard you say that you wanted to walk, so I did not want to disturb you."

She looked around him and saw his coach halt behind him. She tried to hide her smile at what an odd lot they must have looked—the coach following Hunt, Hunt following her and she with her head down in her own world.

"Were you going to follow me all the way home?"

"Or until you tired."

She lifted the hem of her dark gown to display her wet slippers. "My feet are cold, Lockwood. If you are still of a mind, I could use a ride home."

He waved his coach forward and opened the door. Rather than offer his hand to help her up, he lifted her in by her waist and followed quickly. She settled against the soft leather seat and sighed, trying to wiggle her toes.

He sat beside her and rapped on the roof. "Hertford Street, Anderson. No rush," he called, then turned his attention to her. "Lady Barrett, is there anything I can do to make you more comfortable?"

"So courtly, Lockwood? Have I ever seen you so solicitous?" She began to doubt the wisdom of accepting his ride. What would Barrett say if he saw her getting out of a coach with the Lockwood crest?

"I doubt it, madam. It is the tears, you see. We men are notorious for not liking women's tears."

"Some do not mind in the least."

Lockwood looked thunderous. His fists clenched and unclenched as though he longed to hit something. She hadn't meant to elicit a response, and certainly not this one, but she did not know how to undo the damage.

"I pray you do not judge all men by your husband, madam. We deserve better."

Lockwood did, and perhaps Captain Gilbert had, but they were the exception in her experience. Her father, her brother and now her husband had been indifferent at best. Abusive at worst. She looked down at her gloved hands, folded in her lap.

"Have you nothing to say to that, madam?"

"Please, Lockwood, I haven't the heart for a battle today. Speak plainly."

He raked his fingers through his dark hair and shook his head. "Do you remember what you said to me in the coach night before last?"

"Vaguely." Oh, she hoped he was not going to remind her of her surrender to him. Of her wanton response.

"You told me everything, Elise. I do not think you meant to, but now I know why you came running back here, how Barrett makes you stay with him and what he holds over your head. I thought I would feel better if I knew those things, but I do not. You see, in the end, you were right. It makes no difference. You still belong to Barrett—just like his horse, his house and his jewels."

She turned the narrow gold band on her finger beneath the glove and nodded. "I am painfully aware of that, my lord."

He tilted her chin upward and looked into her eyes. "But I cannot bear seeing you with him, knowing he is the father of your child, imagining him in your bed doing the things we did."

Her laugh was harsh as it echoed in the confines of the

coach. "Believe me, Lockwood, if it is any comfort at all, he and I do nothing that you and I did."

He lowered his mouth to hers and left the hint of a kiss on her lips—a bittersweet farewell. She slipped her arms around him, demanding another and he returned to her lips with a strangled moan. How could she ever let him go?

She wasn't aware of the coach stopping until his driver opened the door and cleared his throat.

Chapter Nineteen

Charlie was the last man to arrive and he closed the door behind him. Hunt, Ethan and Auberville were already seated. He slid his ledgers across the desk to Hunt and took the last remaining chair. "Sorry I am late," he said.

Hunt flipped the top book open and looked at the pages. "Save us some time, Charlie, and tell us what you've found."

"Would if I knew for certain," he said with youthful good cheer. "But have a look." He opened another ledger and laid it beside the first. "There are some obvious patterns. I think I know what it means, but I want you to decide."

Glancing at the legends, Hunt read them aloud for the others. "The first is a compilation of losses due to piracy, and the second is payoffs to investors of insured vessels." He ran his finger down the first list and then the second. Charlie was right. There was a pattern. Two names jumped immediately to the fore. Langford and Doyle.

On closer inspection, a few other names were also prominent. Two were underwriters from Lloyd's. Eastman made the list to a lesser degree, but who was Langford? Hunt tried to place the name. He knew he'd heard it, but where?

"Five men," he mused aloud. "By comparing the lists, these are the men who profited both when a ship arrived safely and when it was pirated. But which of them were in a position to know beforehand? Charlie, have you looked at the bank records yet?"

"Haven't had time. Now that we have names, that is next. I will check the ledgers against withdrawals and deposits. They should match, but…"

Auberville leaned back in his chair. "And who do you favor, Charlie?"

"Hard to say. Lord Eastman's position in the Foreign Office would suggest he is trustworthy, eh? The Lloyd's underwriters appear a bit suspicious, but I still cannot figure how they—indeed, *any* of them—could know in advance which ships would arrive at their destinations safely, and which would fall prey to pirates. Would that not require access to shipping schedules and knowledge of the cargo? And would that also not require communications with the pirates, alerting them to which ships were worth the risk and which to allow safe passage?"

"Exactly," Hunt confirmed. He turned to Ethan and Auberville. "I told you the lad was bright."

Charlie laughed. "But how will we ever prove such a thing?"

"There will be a trace of it somewhere. The trick is in knowing where to look. And now we know where to look." He pointed to the names in the ledgers.

"Of all the names on that list, I think Doyle is most likely to be involved," Ethan said.

Hunt silently agreed, but his opinion was more rooted in instinct than evidence. "Why do you say that?"

Ethan shrugged. "I studied him when we were debauching with Barrett. He pretends to drink and carouse, but he is always watching everyone else. I think he calculates his every move and his every word. Only a man with something to hide would be that deliberate."

Auberville shot Hunt an amused glance. "He might not necessarily join in, but he would try to make us feel at ease in doing so ourselves—perhaps to catch us unguarded. And speaking of that, Hunt, why *are* we debauching with Barrett?"

"I…want Barrett to be home as little as possible."

"Especially at night," Charlie guessed.

Hunt gave him a chilling glance and, by Charlie's faint nod, knew he would not mention what he'd seen at the musicale.

Ethan was the first to speak. "Sarah confided that she believes Barrett may be committing violence against his wife."

Bloody hell! The bruise at the base of Elise's throat rose to his mind like a reproach. He'd known that Barrett was a bully, but he hadn't quite believed the man was stupid enough to abuse his wife right under the nose of society. And yet…

This morning when he'd left her at her house, he'd have sworn he saw a curtain move in the window. Someone had been waiting for Elise. Pray it was not Barrett, and pray he had not seen that last kiss. There wouldn't be another. Hunt hated that he was an interloper and had no rights where she was concerned. He could not keep torturing himself that way.

Or he could kill the son-of-a-bitch. He'd killed men for less.

Auberville's quiet voice cut through the awkward silence. "Easy, Hunt. By the look on your face, I can guess what you are thinking. But consider carefully before you do anything rash. It is one thing to love the lady, and another entirely to compromise her by challenging her husband."

Was it so obvious, then? If his friends had recognized it, was all of the ton whispering behind closed doors? "Compromise be damned," he growled. "She is married and there is not a damn thing I can do about that, but you cannot expect me to stand idly by while he abuses her at will?"

"You must," Ethan muttered with a lack of conviction.

Even Charlie nodded.

But, judging by the looks on their faces, it was clear that none of them believed he would.

Elise glanced at her reflection in the looking glass over the foyer side table. She secured the remaining emerald earbob and then shifted her gaze to Barrett's reflection behind her. "Will the emeralds do, or have you brought something else?"

His eyes swept her with the hint of insult. "You think I've been ostentatious, do you not? But I think there is no harm in showing the ton that you and the jewels are mine again." He flicked the earbob with his finger. "You *are* mine again, are you not, Elise?"

There was something nasty in his voice and she turned to him. "I am here, am I not?"

"I give you a little rope and watch whilst you hang yourself, m'dear. I saw Lockwood's coach bring you home, and the little pause before you emerged. Then I realized what has been bothering me. You knew him in St. Claire."

She nodded and pushed a handkerchief into her reticule, praying that he hadn't seen them kiss.

"How well did you know him?"

"He only arrived on St. Claire a week before I left."

"Not an answer, wife." He circled her, looking her up and down as if inspecting her before allowing her out of the house. "At first, I thought he disliked you. Now I am wondering if there is more to it than that. Something—" he bent close to her ear and placed his hands on her bare shoulders "—*intimate*. Did you spread your legs for him, madam?"

She fought her rising panic. Surely he couldn't know such a thing? She lifted her chin. "Your vulgarity astonishes me, Barrett."

"Or perhaps it is Doyle I should worry about. Was he not assigned to St. Claire for two or three years?"

"I believe so. But we did not mingle in the same circles. I only got to know him shortly before my return."

"How very coincidental that you should return at the same time, and on the same ship. Did you share a cabin?"

"Why are you so obsessed with my virtue or lack of it, Barrett? It is not as if you are in love with me. I should rather think you would be anxious for me to take a lover so that I would not care about your own carousing."

"Do you care, my sweet?" His upper lip curled in a sarcastic sneer. "Perhaps my carousing has been a mistake. Perhaps I should stay home more and give attention to my love-starved wife."

"Not if you value your life."

"Interesting. I notice how you refuse to answer my questions regarding Lockwood and Doyle. If I should find out, madam, that you have made me a cuckold, I shall kill you with my bare hands." He circled his fingers around her throat and applied pressure.

Elise stood very still. This was Barrett's favorite way to provoke her fear, but she would not give him what he wanted. That would only feed his sadistic appetite. She waited until he eased his grip and then asked, "Are you finished, Barrett? I believe the coach is waiting."

He slipped his fingers over her shoulders and squeezed her upper arms before dropping his hands to his sides. "You think I am a fool, madam? We shall see who the fool is. You do not care for yourself? Well, that makes two of us. But I know what you do care about. Your sniveling little cub."

She feigned a weary indifference. "You would not kill your heir, Barrett, no matter what you tell me. There would be too many questions. Too much gossip. As a peer, you would have to answer to the king himself. And I am tired of listening to your absurd threats."

Barrett narrowed his eyes. "We shall see about that, madam. Perhaps I will bring him here to live. Then you would see what I dare."

It had never occurred to her that William might be safer as a hostage than he would be in his own house. The thought was sobering. And terrifying.

"But then you would leave, eh? Once you had him back, there'd be no further inducement for you to stay."

She swirled her fur-trimmed cloak around her shoulders and tried her own ploy. "Do warn me when you next intend to bring William to visit, Barrett. I shall be very busy in the future. I am joining Lady Sarah's Wednesday afternoon reading group, and I have decided to volunteer at the foundling hospital."

"Anything that will keep you away from home? Very clever, m'dear. And what if I brought William every day?"

She laughed as she opened the door to the street. "You *would* do something like that just to spite me."

"I shall bring him tomorrow, madam. See that you are here, or it will be his last visit."

Elise said a tiny prayer of gratitude as Barrett entered the coach ahead of her and waited for the driver to hand her up. She would send a note to Sarah the moment she arrived home.

Hunt gave his coat to the footman in Thackery's lobby and waited for Andrew to follow suit. They'd been looking for Doyle all night. Now that the investigation had narrowed to a scant few men, he wanted to keep a close watch on them. Eastman was content at home most evenings, Charlie was off trying to find out who the devil the Langford person was and Hunt had assigned runners to watch the two underwriters.

That left Doyle. And Hunt planned to ask about the investment Doyle had dangled in front of him.

Andrew straightened his jacket sleeves as he joined Hunt. "Too bad Ethan and Auberville decided to stay home with their wives tonight. I must say, they haven't been nearly as entertaining as they were when they were unshackled."

Amused by Andrew's assessment, Hunt laughed. As the second-born son, there hadn't been much that Andrew hadn't indulged in. As he was quick to point out, he did not have to uphold the family name or reputation, and he took his career as the black sheep very seriously. Someone had to do it, he said.

Hunt scanned the crowds at the tables and then glanced up at the mezzanine to see who might be watching from above. "Busy tonight," he observed.

Andrew nodded. "Brisk. I've seen two and three men deep at the tables and the management opening the private rooms upstairs to accommodate the overflow." He snagged a glass of wine from a passing footman and asked, "Doyle, eh? What happened to Barrett? I thought that little maggot was our game. Amusing in his own way, but tiresome after a few hours. Keeps up, though. I have to give him that."

"Tonight, I am after Doyle. You take Barrett, if we should come across him."

"Oh, we will. I saw his coach in the queue outside." Andrew narrowed his eyes as if that would help him see through the perpetual gloom of half-light. Where Belmonde's was all glitter and light, Thackery's was dim and secretive.

Hunt could not curb his curiosity. "What does Barrett talk about? What occupies his mind?"

"Mind? He has a mind?" Andrew gave him a lopsided grin. "I thought all he had was a toothsome wife."

"Drew…"

He held one hand up. "Aye. I'm not slow-witted enough to

have missed your interest, Hunt. But I must say I am surprised. Not your usual sport, to fish in the married pond. I do not mind keeping him out of the way for you whilst you dally, but one day you will have to repay me in kind."

"I have not…" Not entirely true, Hunt realized. He *had* dallied. "It is not to keep him out of my way, but hers."

Andrew returned to the original question. "What occupies his mind? Hmm. Not much beyond the next debauchery. He is somewhat creative there. I gather the *filles de joie* draw lots to see who must accommodate him. One is left to conclude that he is a bit rough on them."

Hunt remembered Elise's soft question in the middle of the storm. *Will you hurt me?* He wished, again, that he could thrash Barrett soundly. "So when I see the ladies flock to you, Drew, what should I assume?"

Another lopsided grin. "That I pay well, perform well or am at least amusing?"

"Must be the money."

Andrew chuckled. "I shall remember you said that when I am occupying Barrett. And speak of the devil…"

Hunt followed his glance. Standing at a *rouge et noir* table, Barrett was laying a wager while Elise seemed in her own world, stroking the line of a necklace that lay against her chest, a large tear-shaped emerald at the center. And suddenly, Hunt understood why Barrett made her wear the jewels. They branded her as his property.

He started toward them but had taken no more than two steps before Andrew stopped him. "Let Barrett come to us. 'Twill give him something to think about, eh?"

"And if he doesn't come?"

"He will. He fancies he can beat me at my own game. He will not pass up an opportunity to try."

"Your game, Andrew? Dare I ask?"

"That might not be wise, Hunt. Come. Shall we go upstairs? Barrett has just spotted us and will follow presently."

Hunt suspected he would. The rooms off the mezzanine were given over to very private and high-stakes games, and the salon at the head of the stairs was the exclusive purview of the crème de la crème of the demimonde. Undoubtedly Barrett would not be able to resist the lure.

A voice called to them as they reached the foot of the stairs. "Lockwood! Drew!"

They turned and found Gavin Doyle coming toward them. Just the man he was hunting. "'Lo, Doyle. Care to join us? We were just going upstairs."

Doyle glanced upward and smiled. "Hold that thought, Lockwood. Must find Barrett first. I was supposed to meet him here an hour ago, but I got caught up elsewhere."

Hunt followed Andrew up the stairs. The multitude of private rooms opening off the mezzanine were all closed for serious play and they were able to make a circuit of the balcony overlooking the main salon before joining the boisterous laughter and general hilarity of the demimonde's salon.

From his vantage beside one of the potted palms placed at intervals along the railing, Hunt could see Barrett and Elise quite clearly. He watched while Doyle joined them and saw, as well, the way Barrett's fingers dug into Elise's arm as she moved slightly away from him. Her eyelashes fluttered, but her expression did not betray pain or annoyance. God! Barrett was draining the life from her!

When Barrett turned back to the play, Elise looked upward and met his gaze. For the briefest moment, he caught a hint of fire behind the cold exterior, then the mask dropped over her features again. He nodded, feeling awkward with the formal gesture, and she nodded back—as one would do to any passing acquaintance.

Andrew sighed heavily. "Do not do this to yourself, Hunt. She's lovely, but there are dozens of women more suited to the role of Lady Lockwood. I know you, and I know that you will never be satisfied to settle for seconds from any man. And, not inconsequentially, she is married."

"Only if one could call Barrett a husband."

"Nevertheless…" Andrew chortled.

"I am seconds." Hunt turned his back and walked away. It was true, but he did not like to hear it.

The air in the mezzanine salon was thick with perfume, smoke and sex. The demireps were spilling out of their gowns and behaving boldly. A titian-haired beauty caught sight of them and smiled widely.

"Lockwood!" she called in a husky voice.

"Betty brings a man's blood up, does she not?" Andrew asked over Hunt's groan.

The woman in question came forward and linked her arm through Hunt's. "Have you come to play, sirs? Or have you come to *play?*"

Andrew looked around the room with bored indifference. "We shall see, Betty."

"You know where to find me, gents." She leaned toward Andrew and shrugged to give him a generous view of her equally generous breasts before moving off.

"This was a bad idea," Hunt said. "Barrett will not leave his wife to come up here."

Andrew raised an eyebrow. "Then do not turn around, brother."

Chapter Twenty

"Lockwood! Here you are!"

Hunt turned at Doyle's greeting to find Barrett beside the chargé. "Ah, glad you could join us. You, too, Barrett." He made a show of looking over Barrett's shoulder. "And where's your lovely wife this evening? I thought the two of you were inseparable."

"Thank you for always being so solicitous of my wife, Lockwood. She told me of your…friendship on St. Claire. But she has come home now and does not need you looking after her."

"As long as someone does," he said evenly. He wanted to wipe that bloody smug look off Barrett's face, but Andrew's hand on his shoulder reminded him that he could ill afford a scene.

Barrett's mouth twisted but he said nothing. Instead, he turned to Andrew. "What have you got planned for us tonight, Mr. Hunter?"

"There's always the ladybirds," Andrew ventured with a nod in their direction. "And there's a cockfight in Whitechapel. But, if you're in a mood for something more exotic, I hear there's a Black Sabbath at the burial ground in Clerkenwell. Your choice, gentlemen, depending upon your interests this evening."

Hunt looked at his brother in surprise. Though he knew their tastes were different, he had not suspected Andrew of being quite such a rogue.

"Here," Doyle said, eyeing Betty across the room.

Barrett disagreed. "Clerkenwell," he said, his voice betraying something dark and lustful.

Andrew looked at Hunt for his opinion. "Clerkenwell," he said. That should keep Barrett occupied until dawn.

It was Andrew's turn to look surprised. "Bless me, Hunt, I did not know you had that in you."

"Desperate times…" Hunt knew from Andrew's grin that his brother understood exactly what he was thinking.

Andrew stepped between Doyle and Barrett and hooked his arms over their shoulders. "Come along, my eager disciples. Shall we slake our thirst for more mundane fare before hieing off to Clerkenwell? We have time. Those satanic things never get underway until well after midnight."

Hunt edged toward the salon door. There was no end to the trouble Elise could get into alone. Thackery's was not like Belmonde's, where a woman could go from table to table unmolested. It was far more likely that she was trying to fend off some obnoxious would-be beau while her husband sported upstairs.

And that is exactly how he found her. He came up behind her and took her arm. "Here you are, madam. Sorry to have left you alone so long." He cast a cold stare at her companion, a green youth who looked fresh from the country. He would not be long for London if he did not learn to avoid places like Thackery's.

Wisely, the youth backed away, bowed to Elise and nearly ran back to his companions.

Her eyes were wide and very green when she looked up at him. "He thought I was a…a…"

"Demirep? Yes, that is the sort who frequent Thackery's. Barrett shouldn't have left you alone." Ah, but he'd been wise not to bring her upstairs. Someone would have had her in a private room before she could have called for help.

Elise blanched. "I suppose I should have guessed as much when he asked me how much I ask for my services."

Hunt chuckled. "I doubt he will make that mistake again, madam."

Some of the tension drained from her and she sighed. "I doubt it, also. You looked quite fearsome."

"I *am* quite fearsome." He took her by the arm and led her away from the tables. "Barrett tells me you informed him that we were friends in St. Claire. I gather he was not pleased with this news?"

Her lips twitched in a smile. "Why do you say that?"

"He has warned me away from you."

"And yet, here you are."

"Here I am," he confirmed. "Your husband was stupid enough to leave you alone. I thought you might need help."

He had led her close to the middle of the room, where a chandelier provided direct light. As he turned to face her, he noted another bruise at the hollow of her throat. Fury built inside him and he looked at the slope of her shoulders where they disappeared into her sleeves. Livid blue marked the spots where Barrett's fingers had been.

"Wait for me in the foyer, Elise."

"No…" Her eyes were enormous. "Please, Lockwood…"

But it was too late and Barrett had gone too far. He took the stairs two at a time, entered the salon and spotted his quarry in the far corner.

Andrew saw him first and recognized his mood. He moved

away from Barrett with a curious lift of his eyebrows. A ladybird turned at Andrew's move, exposing a clear path to Barrett.

"Here, now…"

Hunt seized a handful of cravat and slammed Barrett against the wall. An inch from his face, he ground out his warning between clenched teeth. "Touch her again and you'll answer to me. Do you understand, Barrett? All I need is an excuse."

Barrett pushed him back a foot. "You might outrank me in the peerage, Lockwood, but you don't outrank me in my bedroom. Elise is mine, and there's not a damn thing you can do about it."

"Brave words coming from a coward who abuses women. And there *is* something I can do about it. I can kill you, and I'd need damn little reason to do it."

"Hunt," Andrew said, a hand on his shoulder. "Easy. You're drawing attention."

Hunt released Barrett's cravat reluctantly. "Remember what I said, Barrett. There will be no place that you will be safe from me."

Barrett began straightening his cravat, his complexion florid, but he did not speak again. When Hunt turned, he nearly groaned to find that the entire room had fallen silent and that he and Barrett were the focus of attention.

Then a piercing scream followed by a loud shattering noise rent the awkward silence.

Unwilling to cause more trouble with Barrett, Elise had moved to the perimeter of the main salon. She did not want to wait for Lockwood in the foyer, because she could not leave with him or William would pay for it. She would have to make Lockwood understand when he came back downstairs.

An unnatural hush fell in the rooms above. Oh, heavens! Everyone would soon know what Barrett had done, and how

Lockwood had responded. In the silence, she heard a light scrape above her. When she looked up, it was to see a potted palm hurtling toward her. She screamed and lunged for the protective cover of the columns supporting the mezzanine balcony. A cold rush of air brushed her cheek and the edge of the delftware pot knocked her left elbow as she fell. Soil and shards of pottery burst outward as the container shattered on the floor.

She lay still for a moment to be certain there was not more to follow, and then pushed herself up into a sitting position. The shocked silence gave way to sudden pandemonium as questions were shouted and men rushed forward.

She was lifted by her elbows from behind. She turned to find Lockwood, his expression a mixture of anger and concern. "Are you injured, Elise?"

"N-no." She did not have time to think before she was surrounded by Mr. Doyle, Barrett and Andrew Hunter, all talking at once, but it was Barrett's voice she heard.

"What have you done now, madam?"

"Nothing. I—"

"If anything—anything—happens to Elise, I will hold you responsible," Lockwood snarled at Barrett.

Heat swept through her. How humiliating to have her husband treat her with so little regard in public, and how bittersweet that Lockwood had taken that position. "Please, I am fine. Really," she pleaded.

Lockwood released her and scanned the crowd. "What happened?" he asked.

"I...I heard a scrape and the palm fell. I jumped out of the way."

He looked down at her and she was startled by the cold calculation in his eyes. "Pots do not crawl over railings, madam. Someone helped."

Heavens! He was right. But who would do such a thing? Obviously Barrett had been with Lockwood at the time, and who else would wish her harm?

"I shall have a footman fetch your coach," Lockwood told her. "You should go home at once. We shall look into this."

"*I* will take her home," Barrett interjected.

"You—"

"I am her husband, Lockwood. Best you remember that."

The crowd was growing silent again and she could not bear to have her sins exposed to strangers. "I will go with Barrett," she said in what she hoped would be a reassuring tone.

She could see that Lockwood was struggling to control his anger, and that Barrett was bent on provoking it. Although she did not want to be alone with Barrett, she knew she needed to separate them before the awkward situation could deteriorate further. Even Lockwood's brother looked concerned.

"I shall send you word of our findings, madam," he finally said.

She nodded and Barrett took her elbow to lead her away.

Hunt found marks on the railing where the pot had been pushed over. The falling plant could easily have killed Elise, had she not gotten out of the way. The palm itself had been as tall as a man and would have provided cover for anyone behind it.

Andrew questioned the men in the private rooms, asking if they had seen or heard anything unusual, but received only negative responses. Doyle questioned the footmen and other servants, and all denied any knowledge of the deed.

"Could it have been an accident?" Andrew asked.

Hunt gave him a cold stare.

"Not that the pot fell by accident, but that Lady Barrett was the intended victim."

"It would be damn difficult to mistake her for anyone else."

"But who would want to harm her? Barrett was with us when we heard her scream. How many enemies could the lady have?"

That was precisely what was troubling Hunt. Unless Elise was keeping even more secrets, she was not likely to have angered anyone enough to provoke this response. Unless...

Unless the incident was somehow connected to St. Claire and the activities there. God, pray he was not somehow responsible for this. Bitter though it was, he could bear Layton's death because Layton had known the risks and taken the job anyway. But Elise? She was innocent in all of this. How would he ever live with her death on his hands?

"Leave it alone, Lockwood," Doyle advised. "Perhaps we are making more of it than it deserves—especially if she was not the intended victim. Surely the more we persist, the more this will be discussed over breakfast. She has had enough notoriety, do you not agree?"

Yes, he did. He searched the crowd a final time, certain the would-be killer was among them.

"Who's for Clerkenwell?" Andrew asked, rubbing his hands together.

"Not I." Doyle straightened his jacket. "Think I'll go see Betty and then make an early night of it."

"Hunt?"

He shook his head. In truth, he had never intended to go— just to see Barrett out of Elise's way.

"If you haven't any further need of me, I am off, then," Andrew said. "I believe I shall go dig up James or Charlie. They're always game for a new amusement."

Andrew departed and Doyle excused himself to go back upstairs in search of buxom Betty. Hunt, however, claimed another glass of wine and went to stand opposite the spot where the pot had crashed. Uniformed servants were still quietly cleaning up the mess with dustpans and whisk brooms. Hunt measured the distance from the balcony to the floor below with a critical eye.

Lifting the planter would have taken a strong man and hefting it over the railing would have required even greater strength. Hunt had to believe it had been deadly deliberate and that Elise was, indeed, the target.

Rigo was dead, as was his henchman, Lowe, but the man named Saldon was not. He could easily have passed information to a contact in San Marco. But…why Elise? He remembered the incident at the picnic, where she'd been felled by a rock. Could someone have been trying to kill her even then?

A shriek of laughter called his attention back to the balcony. Betty was leading Doyle along the balcony by the hand. They were headed for one of the very private salons reserved for trysts.

Doyle, who had been elsewhere when Hunt confronted Barrett.

Doyle? But again, why Elise?

Hunt had been aware that someone was following him ever since he left Thackery's. It was not unusual for footpads to lie in wait for a lone gambler to take to the streets. Late at night, senses dulled by drinking and women, most were easy targets for a spry pickpocket or more forceful robber. He'd turned a quick corner, pressed himself against the cold bricks of a building, slipped his dagger from his boot and laid his own trap.

A wiry man dressed in black, with a soft cap pulled over his hair, came around the corner and attempted to press himself into the same shadows. He landed right against Hunt's chest. Hunt seized him with one arm around his neck. The other pressed his dagger against the man's heart.

"Your business with me, sir?"

"'Ere now, gov'nor. I ain't got business wi' ye."

"Then why are you following me?"

"An 'oo says I'm followin'?"

Hunt pressed his dagger through the cloth of the man's coat and shirt beneath until he squealed like a pig at market. "I said. And I am never wrong."

"Easy! Easy, gov'nor. Some bloke just gave me a quid an' tol' me to follow ye."

A quid. Is that what his life was worth now? That was probably generous. "Just follow, eh?" Still holding the man around the neck, Hunt turned, pushed him up against the wall and held the dagger beneath his ear to keep him immobile. He ran his other hand down his assailant's side and pulled a cudgel from beneath his coat. He slammed the cudgel into the small of the man's back before dropping it on the ground. "And this was just supposed to be a friendly 'hello'?"

"That don't mean anything!"

Hunt nearly cut himself on the long bladed knife he pulled from a sheath fastened to the man's waist. "And this? You just use it to pick your teeth, I gather."

"You can't prove nothin'."

With not so much as a twinge of conscience, Hunt flicked his dagger and the man's earlobe dropped to the shoulder of his dirty coat. He'd have screamed if Hunt had allowed him enough air. "I am not looking to prove anything, my good man. I just want answers. Think you can manage that?"

He nodded, unable to speak for his whimpering.

"Who hired you to kill me?"

"Dunno. Gent like you. Didn't give a name."

Hunt traced his dagger in a line across the back of the man's neck toward his other ear. "What a pity that I am not satisfied with that answer, but at least now your ears will match."

"Wait! Wait, gov'nor... I swear 'e didn't give me no name. But 'e said 'e'd 'ave more work for me if I did this. 'E said 'e'd find me if 'e needed me."

Hunt was inclined to believe the man. Still, "Describe him to me."

"Tall-like. Not so tall as you, gov'nor, but tall. Built like you, too, 'e was. I didn't get a good look at 'is face. 'E wore 'is cap real low an' 'twere dark."

That, too, was probably the truth. Only an idiot would allow himself to be seen, lest his hireling be found out and give a description. "A quid, eh? You came cheap. Will he want his money back?"

"Dunno 'ow, gov'nor. 'E won't be findin' me."

Hunt pulled the man away from the wall and pushed him around the corner toward the lamppost. He'd turn the street rat over to the night watch and have him followed when he was released. If he was released.

Barrett had sulked all through the coach ride, casting her dark looks. His silence was more unsettling than anything he might have yelled at her. His escort home portended unpleasantness. Not only had she made him an object of ridicule by prompting Lockwood's confrontation, but she'd spoiled his evening.

Although she had been planning to grant him access to her bed for William's sake—she couldn't think of it as making love—she would not do so tonight. In his current mood, he was likely to take his anger and frustration out on her. He was brutish at the best of times, and this was not the best of times.

Her life had just grown more complicated. Had someone really meant to kill her tonight? Or had it been a case of mistaken identity? Lockwood had seemed so certain…

At home she tied her light wrapper around her, slipped the pins from her coiffeur, sat at her dressing table and began brushing her hair. Her gaze flicked over the bruises on her arms and throat. She could not look closely because her reflection had become a reproach. To look in the mirror every day and see what she'd become—Barrett's scapegoat—was more painful than it had been before she'd left him years ago. She hadn't tasted freedom then, or self-respect or dignity. Despite that, she was willing—nay, eager—to forfeit those things for William's safety.

She glanced at her bed in the mirror and noted that the covers had been turned down for the night. Anne, for all that she was Barrett's spy, took her job as Elise's maid seriously. Rather than finding that thought comforting, Elise was annoyed that she wouldn't be able to depend upon Anne in a conflict with Barrett.

She dropped her brush and stood again, longing for the cool sheets and warm blanket, and for the chance to escape into dreams where there was no Barrett. Only Lockwood. Only William.

The sound of a knob turning drew her attention. She spun to the door and saw it give slightly. She froze and held her breath. The chair was not snugly wedged beneath the knob and began to slide on the wood floor. Barefoot, she padded to the door and held the chair in place.

Barrett's voice was muffled, as if he did not want anyone to hear. "Let me in, Elise. 'Tis your duty, damn you."

Evasion, recriminations or simple denial would only enflame his temper, so she said nothing. Perhaps he would believe she had already gone to bed and leave her alone.

"Do not force my hand, woman," he said, his words whispered against the crack he'd forced.

She shuddered, the fear rising in her breast to form a bubble in her throat. He pushed one last time, and then the pressure eased. Footsteps marked his passage down the hallway. She released her breath and let the tension drain from her muscles. She sat on the edge of her bed and rolled her shoulders.

The footsteps became slightly more distinct again. It sounded as though they came from a different direction. She frowned, cocking her head to one side to hear better.

Oh, dear God! He was coming through the nursery! Had she remembered to secure the dressing room door between the two rooms? She ran to the dressing room, but the door burst open before she could secure it.

And there was Barrett, leering and triumphant. She backed away as he advanced, wildly thinking of how to stop him. "I...I...it is the wrong time of the month, Barrett. I—"

"You lie, madam. Anne knows all your womanly secrets."

Please, God, no! She had thought she could do it, thought she could give him what he wanted, but she couldn't. Face to face with him now, just the thought of him touching her, of him forcing himself inside her body, caused a choking sensation. Her chest squeezed with fear and she could barely breathe.

"You think Lockwood is enough to protect you? I shall have him brought up on charges if he so much as touches me. I have witnesses to his temper. The man is unbalanced! But why not? He took *you* as a lover."

"Leave Lockwood out of this, Barrett. He is not unbalanced, only misguided."

"Come, madam, do not be naive. You know me well enough to know that I will use anyone or anything to achieve my aims. Lockwood. The brat you have been putting before me from the day he was born. They matter nothing to me. I want what I want. And tonight, madam, I want you."

Tears sprang to her eyes and she despised herself for that weakness. But she wouldn't be weak this time. For William. For Lockwood. She could bear it. Surely she could bear it. She halted her retreat and clenched her hands into tight fists at her sides.

Barrett recognized her surrender to the inevitable and grinned. "That's better, madam. Wish I could say it will be over before you know it, but it won't. I plan to take my time. It has been a long while, m'dear. A very long while. We have much to make up for."

She could stand still. She could remain expressionless. But she couldn't stop her tears. They rolled down her cheeks and dampened the front of her nightclothes as Barrett reached her, circled her, undid her sash and pulled her wrapper down her shoulders.

When it bunched around her feet, leaving her exposed in her thin nightgown, Barrett, still standing behind her, laughed. His breath was hot and foul in her ear. "Such a little puritan? Come, I know you've acted the slut for Lockwood. Show me what has so entranced him. For the life of me, madam, I cannot see it. Unless…"

He was baiting her. Trying to make her angry or hurt her. She ignored him until his next words caused a shudder to run through her. "Unless you do tricks, madam. Do you do tricks? Like Alice? Do all whores have the same tricks? Or do you know something special? Something that makes Lockwood come back for more? Show me that. Come, do your tricks for me, Elise. If you're good enough, I might let you see William."

His demand pulled her out of her self-imposed silence. "Bring William home. Bring him to me, Barrett, and I will do anything you ask."

"You will anyway, madam. Has it not occurred to you yet that you cannot say no to me? You will have what I choose to give you—nothing more, nothing less. And, my dear, how much I choose to give you depends entirely upon you."

A myriad of thoughts swept through her—the death of hope, the revelation that she'd never be able to bargain William's freedom, the knowledge that Barrett would eventually kill her outright, not just her spirit and soul. And worse—the startling realization that she'd been a victim her entire life. She'd been an undemanding daughter, a dutiful sister, an obedient wife—until she'd struck Barrett that long-ago night. And even then, she hadn't meant to put an end to her victimization, only to delay it. She had thought her strength was in submitting to Barrett. Oh, but that self-deceit was the real weakness.

Barrett released her shoulders and came around to face her. "So how much will you earn tonight, madam? Another brief visit? Perhaps half an hour? Down on your knees and perhaps you will earn an entire hour."

In that instant, she was finished with being a victim. She was done with Barrett's threats, false promises and lies. The sudden clarity was like the sun shining light into dark and forbidden corners. She had thought she was protecting William, but she'd only been prolonging his misery. And now she cared nothing for the scandal she would cause in making Barrett's cruelty public. Let him squirm, and let the ton look down their long aristocratic noses at her. Barrett would not dare harm William with all eyes upon him.

With great satisfaction and no thought to the consequence, she drew her hand back and slapped Barrett full across the face.

Stunned, he widened his eyes. Then an ugly sneer curled his upper lip. "Ah, you like it rough. As you know, I can manage that, m'dear." He seized a handful of her hair and forced her to her knees. Holding her there, he began to unfasten his breeches.

She raked her fingernails down his arm. He recoiled and she staggered to her feet. "I warned you, Barrett," she gasped as she backed toward the fireplace. She thought him mad to laugh until she found the poker had been removed. *Oh, Anne. How could you?*

Barrett seized her again, slammed her against the wall, held her by the throat and ripped her nightgown from neck to hem in one long pull. Her head spun and she groped for the mantel, seeking anything she could use as a weapon. And now she laughed, too—at the irony of ending back where she'd begun. Of being forced to defend herself.

Her hand found the miniature portrait of William, encased in a chased silver frame. She brought it down on his head, heedless of the sharp corner. He released her with a shocked expression, blood from a wound on his forehead spurting outward and spraying across her face before it slowed to a narrow stream. She flattened her hands against his chest and pushed as hard as she could.

Barrett staggered backward, his arms flailing, and knocked against her bedpost. He seemed suspended there for a moment, and then sank to the floor. She went to bend over him, careful to keep out of arm's reach. He was breathing. She could see the rise and fall of his chest and smell the alcohol on his breath.

Finish it this time, a demon voice whispered in her head. Her fingers twitched as they tightened on the frame again. She raised her arm. But she couldn't do it. She did not need to. Whatever power he'd had over her was gone. She'd taken it back.

She dropped the frame where she stood and went to her closet. She chose the first thing that came to hand and dressed quickly, giving more attention to speed than appearance. She did not bother to brush her hair or make herself presentable. Where she was going, it would not matter. It might never matter again.

Chapter Twenty-One

Hunt poured himself a glass of sherry while he waited for Ethan's valet to rouse his brother-in-law from his bed. He had thought the night could not have degenerated any further. From his confrontation with Barrett at Thackery's to his chase of Doyle through the warehouses and thieves rookeries along the Thames, to the street rat who'd tried to knife him, he'd had one crisis after another. Then he'd gone to his office and found the runner's report on Doyle, and the evening had gotten worse.

He was beginning to regret his insistence on seeing his brother-in-law without delay when the library door opened and Ethan appeared in a loosely belted robe. From the sight of the bare chest beneath, Hunt gathered his sister would not be pleased by his late visit.

"This had better be urgent," Ethan muttered as he sat at his desk.

Hunt suppressed his smile. "I thought it was, but now that I've had time to cool my anger, and a glass of your excellent sherry, it does not seem quite so imperative."

"Spill it, Hunt. I'll be damned if you got me down here for nothing."

"Doyle."

"What about him?"

"He may be the leak in the Foreign Office."

"Why?"

"I went to the office tonight and found the report on him on my desk. Did you read it?"

"No. Why don't you tell me what has you in a lather? And give it to me in order, please."

"Doyle was born in Southampton to a poor family. He was clever enough to ingratiate himself with a widowed aunt who had married well and who paid for his schooling. He was known for his charm and wit more than his grades. Early on, he demonstrated sudden bad tempers, which he learned to control—or at least to hide. He went on to Cambridge and played on a cricket team. His fellows thought well of him until he showed himself to have a ruthless streak. It was not beyond him to deliberately injure another player to win, they say."

"Interesting, but not necessarily devious."

Hunt took another drink and nodded. "True, but that is not what drove his friends away. It was his complete lack of remorse."

"Unapologetic?"

"No, quite apologetic, and all the while laughing up his sleeve. He knows what he ought to feel, but he is incapable of actually *feeling* it.

"And then there is the rumor of him being a deuced bad gambler. He was always owing his fellow students until they refused to lend him more. It was about this time that his aunt died suddenly, leaving him the bulk of her fortune. After that, he pulled himself up by his bootstraps and took a job in the diplomatic corps. Made himself indispensable. Worked his way up."

"So the past is behind him?"

"To all appearances. He has been assigned to India, but

something he said the other day makes me wonder if he is going to turn the assignment down."

"That would spell the end of his career, would it not? To refuse an appointment?"

Hunt nodded. "He hinted that something else might be in the wind for him. If so, Eastman has not mentioned it."

They were silent for a few moments and Hunt wondered if Ethan was thinking what he was thinking.

"A piece of good luck, was it not, that his widowed aunt died just in time to save him from social ruin?"

"Just what I was thinking." Hunt laughed without mirth. "You realize, of course, that this is just speculation?"

"For the moment," Ethan agreed.

Elise hardly knew where to begin. "I am so sorry, Sarah, to have dragged you from your sleep. I would have waited until morning, but…well, that wouldn't have been prudent."

Sarah tightened her dressing gown and sat beside her. "I had not gone to sleep yet. But what has happened? Are you all right?"

"Tea, my lady?" the stern man who had let her in asked.

Sarah turned to Elise with a critical eye. "No. Brandy, I think, unless we have something stronger. And could you wake Mrs. Grant and ask her to ready a guest room? And heat some water so that Lady Barrett can wash up."

Elise prayed that Sarah would still want to offer her hospitality when she knew what had happened. "Thank you," she said, trying to organize her thoughts to tell Sarah why she'd come.

"Do not mention it, Elise. Now, take a deep breath and tell me what has happened."

"I have come to beg you to help me find my son. I have done something that may put him at risk, and I must find him as quickly as possible."

"I see. Well, of course we shall press forward with all due speed. Shall I assume that you no longer want William left in place until you can make arrangements for him?"

"Yes. I must have him at once. I fear he may be in greater danger where he is, now that…now that I have left Barrett."

"Left?" Sarah nodded and breathed a sigh of relief. "Then you will need someone to deal with him on your behalf. I believe Ethan knows a good solicitor, and—"

"Good God!"

Lockwood appeared in the doorway, followed by Ethan, and Elise cringed. She had never thought to find him here at three o'clock in the morning. She wouldn't have come if she had. She looked down to the reticule in her lap as he and Ethan came to her side.

Lockwood knelt in front of her and took her hand. "Tell me you are all right, Elise."

"Y-yes. I am well." And then she remembered that she had come out without fixing her hair or so much as checking her appearance in the mirror.

"What has happened?"

His voice was more intense than she'd ever heard it. "Barrett and I had an argument. I have left him."

"Argument…" he repeated. He tilted her chin upward so that she was forced to look in his eyes. "Whose blood is this, Elise?"

Blood? She had a vague recollection of striking Barrett and feeling the fine spray of blood across her face and chest. She looked down at the skin exposed in the high *V* of her neckline. Droplets of blood were clearly visible. "Barrett's," she answered.

He sighed with relief and squeezed her hands as Ethan took a tray with two glasses and a bottle from the man who'd answered the door. Lockwood put a glass of something that did not look like brandy in her hand and ordered her to drink. The fiery liquid burned its way down her throat. She coughed and her eyes watered.

"Whiskey," Lockwood told her. "Let it settle, and then tell me what happened."

A sly heat seeped through her, relaxing her all the way to her toes and she began to breathe again. But Lockwood's eyes held her, wouldn't let her go, and his strength reached her. Whatever was wrong, Lockwood would fix it.

"Barrett," she began, but she glanced at Sarah and Ethan. What in the world would they think of her? "Barrett forced his way into my room. He was angry and made…threats. I realized he would never let me go. Never release William. I cannot remember exactly how it happened, but we struggled. I…I hit him with a picture. Then I came here."

Lockwood nodded. "Did the servants come? Did anyone hear you or see you?"

"I do not think so. The servants know better than to come in the middle of the night. And Barrett was stealthy tonight. He made little noise, and that is how he surprised me."

She was aware of Ethan and Sarah exchanging glances, but it was Hunt's face she watched. He nodded and gave her another glass of whiskey along with a reassuring smile.

"Go with Sarah, my dear. You will want to clean up. If you cannot sleep, have another whiskey. I shall come to you in the morning. For now, just know that we will work this out."

"But William—"

"Leave it to me, Elise."

Hunt pushed the front door open with one finger. Not only had Elise forgotten to lock it, she had not even bothered to close it. The utter silence of the house was unnerving and an uneasy feeling raised the hairs on the back of his neck. He did not call out. He did not want to raise an alarm to the servants or give himself away.

He followed a narrow wedge of light and found the library. Barrett was not there, but a half-finished glass of port was sitting on his desk, testament to his brooding and working up the courage to attack Elise.

Papers were strewn on the floor, as if he had been looking for something and simply dropped what he had not wanted. Or perhaps Elise had searched for the jewels before leaving the house. She'd done so once before.

Barrett, that maggot, had probably staggered off to bed—as if that would deter Hunt. He climbed the stairs and followed a dim light spilling into the corridor from a door left ajar.

He found Elise's room, not Barrett's. He knew that by the purely feminine touch of lace and the scent of perfume. He looked around, not surprised to find the place in a shambles. As he moved farther into the room, he noted a nightgown in shreds on the floor. His stomach turned to think of Elise at Barrett's mercy and he wondered how she had found the strength to fight him off.

With a sinking feeling, he noted a booted leg extending beyond the far side of the bed. He went closer. And there, with the corner of a silver picture frame embedded in his forehead, was Barrett. Hunt did not have to feel for a pulse to know the man was dead. Glazed eyes stared upward, steady and fixed.

He squatted by the body and examined the scene. That Elise had faced this horror sickened him and he made a silent promise that she would never endure this again. But he would have to live with the fact that he had failed her, too. He should have killed Barrett the first time he'd seen him squeeze her arm, or the first time he'd seen a bruise, or even the first time there'd been a mark on her throat. Hell, he should have killed Barrett on principle.

Regrettably, he hadn't, and now Elise would have to live with the stain of murder on her soul. But she wouldn't go to prison. She wouldn't hang. He could spare her that much, at least.

He snatched the shredded nightgown off the floor and stuffed it into his greatcoat pocket. He looked around, and wherever he saw signs of Elise's occupancy, he put them to rights. He picked her brush up and put it on the dressing table. He hung her robe on a peg in the dressing room. He righted the chairs she had used, unsuccessfully, to keep her husband out.

Lastly, he went back to Barrett's body. There were several wounds. One high on the forehead, a blow to the side of his face and the fatal wound in the center of his forehead. He had to tug the silver-framed miniature to dislodge it from the bone and he marveled that Elise had struck with such force. But he had seen instances of remarkable strength when one was threatened or excited.

He removed an edge of Elise's torn nightgown and carefully cleaned the frame and the portrait of her son within—a lad who looked so like her that he smiled—and put it on Elise's bed table. Now everything would look as if Elise had left before the struggle. The servants would know that she had come home, but he would swear that she had left by the time he arrived.

Then he would confess to Barrett's murder. Half the ton would know by morning that he'd threatened Barrett at Thackery's, and it would be no stretch to believe he'd killed the viscount. In fact, he had come to do it, but Elise had beaten him to it.

He stood and took one last look at the room before going down the stairs and silently back into the night.

Hunt watched Elise's pale face as Sarah excused herself, left her small sitting room and closed the door behind her.

Elise was wearing one of Sarah's gowns this morning, a fine bottle-green kerseymere that made her look so pale and fragile that he feared for her sanity. He wanted to hold her, comfort her and protect her, but he didn't dare touch her until they talked. He had to know, first, if he had destroyed whatever she had felt for him on the island with his behavior here. At times, to his shame, he'd been little better than Barrett. He had allowed that ugly hidden side of himself to control him.

Now that they were alone, he saw her anxiety rising. She looked bewildered by the announcement and her teacup rattled in the saucer. He knew she was fighting to maintain her composure. "Dead? But…I couldn't have…could I? Dead. Barrett is dead. He was breathing when I left. I…I am sure of it. And yet, he is dead. How can that be?"

He leaned forward and took the cup from her hand. "Peace, madam. Breathe. We shall discuss that in a moment." He prayed she would not argue with him.

"But who else? It was the middle of the night. Who could have…"

Had the trauma of the event blocked her memory? "You really do not know, do you?"

She shook her head, her eyes wide and bewildered. "Know what? Tell me, Hunt! There is something more than my husband's death going on here, is there not?"

He rose and went to stand by the fireplace, needing to put distance between them. He couldn't be so close to her without wanting to touch her. And when she heard his confession, she would want nothing further to do with him. He toyed with the idea of telling her the truth, but her lapse of memory was a blessing. If she knew the truth, her sense of honor would demand that she accept the blame. He couldn't let her do that.

She twisted her hands in her lap, her face registering shock mingled with anxiety. "What is wrong with me? Barrett is dead, and all I can think of is that the police will be coming for me soon. And William. I must find William at once." She looked up at him and her eyes were wide with disbelief. "And I keep thinking that I am unnatural because, you see, I am not sad for losing Barrett. I am sad for a little boy who will grow up without a father. And I keep thinking how it is—" She stood and shook her head, then pressed her fingers to her forehead as if she were about to make some awful confession. "How it is—*oh, for shame, Elise*—a relief that I will never have to wedge a chair beneath my door or wince when someone touches me, or cover bruises and scratches with rice paper and pretend that all is well." She stopped in front of him. "Am I some horrid monster that I cannot cry for my son's father?"

Unaware that he'd even been holding his breath, he exhaled in relief. Thank God she would not hate him. "You are not a monster, Elise, but there are complications," he admitted.

"Complications? Oh, dozens that I can think of, and not a single one pleasant. But what complications are you thinking? Tell me, Hunt. However unpleasant, I must know. It…it is not William, is it?"

"No, not William, though I have started a search for him. It is something else. Last night, after you came here, I went back to your house to talk to Barrett. To reason with him, but…"

"That is how you knew he was dead? But why have the police not come for me?"

"I did not report it. Your servants are likely just discovering Barrett's body. And the police will not come for you, Elise. They will come for me."

It took a moment for his words to sink in, and then her eyes widened in horror. "No. Lockwood, no. Say you did not—"

His silence was enough to convince her. The long overdue tears sprang to her eyes and she clutched his sleeve. "What have I done to you? I've made you a murderer!"

"Oh, I was that long ago, madam. And whatever I've done, I've done willingly. You have nothing to regret."

"You cannot take this upon yourself. I shall say that I murdered Barrett and fled here. If no one saw anything, no one can contradict me. And I *am* responsible, Lockwood. I am."

Dear Lord, how he loved her! That she would forfeit her future to save him was incredibly poignant. He slipped his arms around her and held her gently, still afraid she might have injuries he did not know about. "Hush, madam. I will hear no more of that. The blame is mine, and mine alone. And I shall gladly face whatever the future brings, knowing that you are free."

When Hunt returned to his office after a meeting with every official of the Home Office, he found a full complement of brothers awaiting him, with his brother-in-law and Auberville. He could scarcely get into the small room.

"Well?" Andrew asked.

He edged around them to get behind his desk. "No arrest will be made for several days."

Charlie smiled, his face clearing. "Then you recanted your confession."

"No. I did it. There's no way around that. I simply asked for a few days to put my affairs in order. As a courtesy, and in view of all I've done for my country, they have agreed to allow me time to conclude some outstanding business. Speaking of that, Charlie, how is your examination of bank records coming?"

"Interesting. Someone has been inquiring about your finances, you know. Gavin Doyle."

"I expected as much. He offered to find me an investment. We shall see if he takes the bait. When will you be done?"

"By tomorrow, but I can drag it out. If you need the time, I can delay a least a week."

Hunt laughed. "Thank you, but that will not be necessary. In fact, I need those results as quickly as possible."

"Bedamned!" James cursed. "How can you laugh when you are about to hang?"

"There will be a trial first," Auberville pointed out. "And if ever a man needed killing, Barrett did. You should have a sympathetic jury, Hunt. But I doubt you'll escape unscathed."

"Are the gossipmongers at work already?"

"Not a word about Barrett's death so far," Ethan said. "The Home Office will keep it hushed until you are in custody. But that will not last for long. Unfortunately, there is considerable gossip concerning your confrontation with Barrett at Thackery's last night. And it will be deuced difficult to hush a funeral, will it not?"

Hunt ignored the comment. It was far too late to be concerned with discretion. "Meantime, I want every resource at our disposal directed at finding Elise's son, William. I believe the matter is urgent. I put Harry Richardson on it yesterday, but he will need help."

"The boy is missing?" Auberville asked.

"Since his arrival back in England." He did not want to go into the sordid details of Barrett's cruelty and neglect. "Thank you all for coming. I appreciate your concern. But I need to have a private word with Andrew."

Andrew's eyebrows drew together and Hunt knew he suspected what was coming. He waited until the others filed out, opened his lower drawer, pulled out his bottle and two glasses and poured them both a generous glass.

"Andrew, should the worst happen, you will be the next Earl of Lockwood. I—"

"Stop right there," Andrew said, holding up one hand, palm outward. "I am not fit for this, and you know it. You are Lord

Lockwood and I am Lord Libertine. It was never in my plan to become your heir."

"I was not aware that you even had a plan. And, like it or not, you are my heir in the absence of a male child. The title may not rest easy on you, but it will be yours. I have charges for you, and I advise you to remember them well."

"Wait," Andrew said. He gulped his port as no mortal man should and placed his glass back on Hunt's desk. "Can you not plead self-defense? Say that Barrett attacked *you?*"

"For the love of God, Drew. We were in Barrett's house. In the lady's bedchamber. Not two hours earlier, half the patrons at Thackery's heard me threaten him. How should I explain that away?"

Andrew sat back in his chair and crossed his arms over his chest. "You're a bloody liar, Hunt. And I want to know why, although I suspect I already do."

"Liar? I do not know what you mean."

"Ye gods! I am not good at much, Hunt, but I know a lie when I hear one. It is my one talent in this life. If you want the others to believe you killed Barrett, well and good. And if you think we do not know the depth of your involvement with Lady Barrett, then I applaud your powers of self-delusion. But if you are going to ask this of me, you owe me the truth."

Hunt pushed his glass away. Perhaps Andrew was right. He should know the truth if he had any hope of protecting Elise. "He was dead when I arrived. Elise was in shock when she arrived at Sarah's. She does not remember killing him. I cannot say if Barrett was still breathing when she left, but he was damn near rigid by the time I arrived. She may have held the weapon, but Barrett's death *is* my fault. I set everything in motion. I enraged him further by publicly humiliating him, and I was foolish enough to think my threat would deter him from further abuse. Elise will not suffer for this, Drew."

"How did she do it?"

"A silver framed miniature was stabbed in his forehead. I found…signs that he had attacked her and that she was only defending herself."

"Then let *her* plead self-defense."

"Drew, the law does not give her the right to refuse him. And remember that she has done him violence before and only just returned to England. No one will believe her."

Andrew nodded for him to continue.

"And that is what I must ask you. Look after them, will you? Elise will do well enough, but the guilt will weigh her down. The boy will need someone to look up to. I fear there is no one to teach him how to be a gentleman."

Andrew coughed. "Gentleman? You cannot seriously tap me for that task?"

"You're a better man than you think, Drew. Whether you act the part or not, you know what is required. But there is more. If I haven't been able to conclude the matter before I must turn myself over, you will have to finish a job for me."

"Aye?"

"Someone is trying to kill Elise. That potted palm last night was not the first attack on her. There was one in St. Claire, and that would mean…"

"Doyle," Andrew finished.

"I have a strong suspicion that the attacks on her are somehow linked to my investigation. Without someone looking out for her, they might succeed."

He watched the emotions play across Andrew's face and wondered if he would accept the charge. It wasn't surrender he saw there, but anger. Drew was furious. He had a conscience after all.

Chapter Twenty-Two

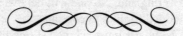

"I must say, madam, it was not easy to find you. When I heard the news, I went straightaway to your house, only to discover that you were not there, and the servants could not tell me where you might be found."

Elise closed the sitting room door and went to the tea table. Her head ached and she wished now that she had declined to receive him. "How *did* you find me, Mr. Doyle?"

"Why, I ran into Charlie Hunter, who told me you were staying with his sister. Excellent idea, that. Not good to be alone at times like these. Do they know who did it?"

He did not know? Well, she was still bewildered enough by the events of last night that she could not make much sense of it either. But she would not be the one to explain any of it to Mr. Doyle. "I have not heard."

"Oh? Well, you have my sympathy, madam. Though…"

"Yes?"

He gave her a sly look, as if inviting her confidence. "Perhaps there is not excessive reason to mourn?"

His frankness startled her. What could she say to such a veiled question? She poured out tea for them both without making any comment.

"Now, Master William—begging your pardon, *Viscount* Barrett—will, no doubt, miss his father."

"No…doubt," she responded, wondering when she had gone from enjoying Mr. Doyle's company to being unnerved in his presence.

"And I gather Lockwood will step into the breach."

She looked at him in wonder. Did he realize how dreadful he was making everything sound?

"Beg pardon," he said when he saw her expression. "I noted on St. Claire how you two had formed a tendresse. I assume there will be no impediment to your liaison now. As long as his business does not interfere, that is."

"Business?" Whatever was Mr. Doyle talking about?

"The business that took him to St. Claire in the first place, madam. All on the hush, of course."

Elise felt as if she'd walked in on the middle of a conversation. How had they come to talk about her and Lockwood? "I have no notion of what you mean, sir. And I think it would be better if we did not discuss Lockwood."

"Ah, I've done it again, have I not? Won't breathe a word of it to anyone. I swear. Why, that might actually give Lockwood the best motive ever for…oh, sorry."

Her head was still spinning when he touched her on the shoulder and asked, "Do you have everything you need, madam? These are difficult times, and if there is anything I can do to ease your mourning, I hope you know I would consider it an honor."

Puzzled, she turned back to him, wondering what in the world he thought he could do for her. Money? Favors? Heavens! Was he trying to ingratiate himself with her? Did he plan to woo her when her mourning was over? If, indeed, she mourned?

"You must have come here suddenly," he said. "Not much time to pack. If you would make me a list, I should be happy to fetch your things. Whatever you may need."

She put her teacup down, stood and crossed the room to look out the window at the passing carriages. "Sarah has been kind enough to lend me some of her things. We are of a size, and…" suddenly she was tired of explaining herself to Mr. Doyle. "No, sir. I have no needs, and if that situation should change, I shall inform you of it or take care of it myself."

He gave her a shamefaced grin. "I've overstepped. I have a tendency to do that, you know. It is only because I care. And when I thought of you with nothing but evening gowns and your light island cottons, I thought you might need something warmer. Or have you had winter gowns made and put your island things away until the summer?"

In truth, she did need a few things. Personal items—comb, brush, toothbrush, a nightgown and robe. Perhaps Barrett had a cash box. She would be needing money for incidentals and to pay the Bow Street runner who was searching for William. And she would need her writing box. She did not relish the task of sending the news of Barrett's death to her brother. And Barrett's. And yet she could not bring herself to ask Mr. Doyle to assist her in fetching her things. For some inexplicable reason, she did not want to be in his debt. Perhaps it would be easier if she just returned home.

"Thank you, sir. If I should think of something…"

Sarah bustled into the parlor, met Elise's pleading gaze and assumed an air of efficiency. "There you are, my dear. Mr. Doyle, I do hope you will excuse us. The vicar has come and wishes to discuss…arrangements. Are you up to it, Elise?"

"Yes, of course," she said gratefully. She turned to Mr. Doyle and offered her hand. "Thank you so much for coming, sir. It is times like these when we learn who our true friends are."

"Not at all, madam. Not at all. I shall call again very soon to see how you fare."

* * *

Hunt saw Doyle cross the foyer and exit by the front door as he was coming in the back from the mews where he'd left his horse. What business did Doyle have here? Elise? After the incident at Thackery's last night, he'd be damned if he let Doyle anywhere near her. "Sarah?" he called.

"In the sitting room, Hunt," she called.

He found both Sarah and Elise standing at the window, watching Doyle's coach draw away down the street. Sarah looked concerned as she turned to him. "Shall I pour you a cup of tea?"

"No, I…"

"Elise was just telling me that she thinks she should go home. I have asked her to stay, but she is reluctant."

He looked back at Elise. "I think she should stay right here. In fact, I insist upon it."

"But—" Elise began.

"Sarah, will you excuse us, please? There are some matters Lady Barrett and I must discuss."

His sister gave him a somber nod and left the room.

He went to Elise and took her hand. "There are compelling reasons why you need to stay here, Elise. The incident last night, most notably."

"Barrett? But he cannot hurt me now."

"Thackery's, madam. That pot dropping at that precise moment was chillingly deliberate. Do you have any idea who might wish you harm?"

She shook her head, sinking back onto the sofa. "Only Barrett, and he was with you, was he not? I…I think it must have been a mistake."

He struggled with his conscience. He did not want to burden her with further worries, but neither did he want her wandering into disaster.

As he sat beside her, he took her hands in his. "I would rather that you trust no one for the time being. Most especially not Mr. Doyle."

"Mr. Doyle? But he has been a good friend to me. He has come to pay his respects, and also asked if he could bring me anything from Barrett's house."

"Whatever you need, madam, I will fetch it for you. I cannot account for Doyle's whereabouts last night when that pot was dropped over the railing. And we had just left him at the Grahams' picnic when you were hit with a rock. The coincidence is sufficient to warrant caution."

Her eyes widened. "Why?"

He took a deep breath. "I went to St. Claire to look into rumors of a pirate base there. Our friendship may have endangered you. Perhaps someone thought you were helping me or that they could stop or distract me by injuring you. I cannot say, but I believe there is a connection between my business and your accidents."

"So that is the business that Mr. Doyle hinted at. But I have brought danger to *you*," she said with a flash of anger in her eyes. "Have you not already killed for me?"

"Elise—"

She squeezed his hands and leaned toward him. "You must be careful, Lockwood. Do not take any more risks for me, nor intercede on my behalf. Should you come to harm, how would I live with myself?"

God. He had been trying to keep his distance, trying to allow her time to catch her breath and for the shock to wear off—trying desperately not to take advantage of her vulnerability. But how could he keep his hands off her when she was pleading with him for his own good? He might be going to prison, or even the gibbet, but he couldn't go without a proper farewell. Still holding her hands, he leaned forward and kissed her. He was about to apologize when she released his hands and slipped her arms around his neck with a breathless little moan.

He'd never known her to be so desperate. Her tongue met his with a demand he could not mistake, but the middle of the day in his sister's sitting room was neither the time nor the place. "Softly, Elise," he whispered, breaking her kiss and her embrace before he cast caution to the winds.

She looked embarrassed and a delicate color seeped up her cheeks. "I…I did not mean to impose myself…."

He laughed—his most genuine laugh since he had made love to her those long-ago nights on St. Claire. "Patience," he said. "Now make me a list of what you need from Barrett's house."

Hunt had made all the necessary arrangements for Elise's things to be sent to her by the time he returned to his office just before dark and found Sir Henry Richardson waiting for him. Sir Harry, as he was known, was currently without an assignment from the Foreign Office and had leaped at the chance to escape boredom by agreeing to take on the task of finding young William, now Viscount Barrett.

"Ah, well met, Lockwood. I was just going to leave you a note and go on to my evening engagements."

Hunt grinned. He knew what sort of engagements Harry planned, and they rarely included formal dress. Or any clothes at all. "Do you have something for me?" he asked.

"I believe I've found your missing child. A waifish little thing. Dark hair and green eyes?"

He remembered the miniature portrait he'd found in Elise's bedroom and nodded. Yes, that would be William. He was impressed. "So soon? I expected this to take longer."

Sir Harry laughed and shrugged. "Wasn't much of a challenge, and no great mystery. The obvious tends to be obvious for a reason."

"Barrett's brother," he guessed.

Sir Harry shook his head as he leaned against the doorjamb, looking like he couldn't wait to get on to his "engage-ments." "Nearly as obvious. Franklin Clarke. *Her* brother."

"Elise's…Lady Barrett's own brother was hiding her son from her?"

"Aye. A dull-witted gentleman, that. Looks as if he is in the depths of his cups most of the day, or has found an opium den local to his village."

Money. He remembered Elise telling him that Barrett bought people, and that he had bought her. Her brother had been so heavily indebted to Barrett that he'd consented to the wedding. And now his addiction had led him to deceive his sister. He would deal with this man personally.

"You spoke with him?"

"He answered the door. I gather the servants were let go some time back, or at least it looks that way. The house is barely better than a sty. The lad was behind him, looking nearly as bad as his uncle. I concluded that he has not been abused so much as completely overlooked."

"What story did you use?"

"None. There was no need. I told Clarke that Barrett was dead. He looked relieved but did not seem to realize that I'd come looking for the lad. When I told him, he seemed indif-ferent, then offered to be his guardian for a stipend."

"Was he serious?"

"Seems so. When I told him the boy's mother wanted him back, he laughed and accused her of wanting the money for herself. She had abandoned the boy in a foreign country, he said. 'Twould appear Barrett was good at fabricating stories.'"

"Where is William now? Did you bring him back to London?"

Sir Harry rolled his eyes. "Clarke would not release him to me. He thinks the lad is as good as cash. And not an insig-nificant sum. He said if he gives the boy back to Lady Barrett she will profit by it, and why should he not profit as well? After all, according to him, he has been loving and nurturing to his nephew."

"How much does he want?"

"Ten thousand pounds."

Hunt could have that tomorrow morning when the banks opened. "I'll pay it."

"Not like you at all, Lockwood. I've never known you to pay extortion. Informants, yes, but blackmailers are an ugly business."

What could he do? Clarke was Elise's brother. Hunt could not have him gaoled. There'd been enough scandal already.

"You see the problem, eh?" Sir Harry continued. "Lady Barrett can go through the courts, with the gossip that would entail, or she can pay her brother off. Neither of them is a good choice."

"I will pay it," he said again. "And I will see to it that the leech never asks for anything again. Believe me, Richardson, this is not blackmail. It is a once and final offer. Impress that upon him."

"Your choice," he said. "How shall I proceed?"

"Meet me here in the morning. I will have the money. When you fetch him, have one hand on the boy before you hand over the cash. Make Clarke give you a receipt that clearly states the purpose of the payment. And then bring William to me here."

"Not to his mother?"

"I need to be certain he is well, and indeed William. I do not want Lady Barrett subjected to another disappointment. Aside from that, I wish to have him examined by a physician so that I may assure his mother of his health and well-being."

"Sounds as if you've thought of everything, Lockwood," Sir

Harry said as he pushed off from the doorjamb. "If Lord Barrett can ride behind me, I should be back by dark tomorrow."

Hunt hoped so. He did not have much time left before he would have to turn himself over for Barrett's murder.

Chapter Twenty-Three

Even in death, Barrett was spiting her!

Elise knocked louder on Lockwood's door. The brisk walk to his house in the winter night had not cooled her anger. The very thought of Lockwood languishing in prison or hanging from a gibbet infuriated her. Barrett's life had not been worth so steep a price, and she would not let Lockwood pay it.

An expressionless butler answered her third knock and gave her a clipped bow. "Madam?"

"I would like to see Lord Lockwood, please."

He looked her up and down. "I shall see if his lordship is in," he said, beginning to close the door on her.

"He is in."

Elise looked around the butler to see Lockwood standing by a door opening off the foyer. He was in his shirtsleeves and holding a sheaf of papers. The butler stepped aside and held the door for her.

"Thank you, Mott. That will be all."

The man bowed, closed the door behind her and disappeared down a corridor leading to the back of the house.

Hunt swept his arm toward the room and stood aside as she

passed him. It was a library or an office, she wasn't certain which. Books lined the walls and stacks of them were piled on a low table in front of a sofa that faced the fireplace. A lamp illuminated a desk buried in papers and littered with pens, inkwells, blotters and ledgers.

"I've interrupted you," she said.

"Just putting my affairs in order. Would you care to have a seat? Can I get you anything? Port? Sherry? Have you had supper?"

Putting his affairs in order? She turned back to him and braced herself. "Nothing, thank you. But you are wasting your time. I have no intention of letting you take the blame for Barrett's death."

A flicker of regret passed across his face. "You have remembered something?"

"Remembered? What do you mean?"

"Never mind." He dropped the papers on his desk, laid her cloak over the back of a chair and took her elbow to lead her to the sofa. "I was going to come by my sister's a little later, madam. I wanted to go over some details with you."

"That's just it, you see. I do not want to go over details unless they are the details regarding William."

He sat beside her and frowned. "William? But what has he to do with any of this?"

"Lockwood, I cannot let you take the blame for Barrett's death. Regardless of who actually did it, you are not to blame. I am. And I intend to go to Bow Street in the morning and make a confession. The only business I must put in order is that of William's custody. I do not think Barrett's brother or my own would be suitable. So I must ask you to petition the court on his behalf to appoint a neutral guardian. And if it will not, to petition the king."

"That will not be necessary, madam."

"You do not know Barrett's brother Alfred or you would not say that. I know my request places you in an awkward situation, and you will be asked why you are interceding, but I cannot think of anyone else I trust with William's future."

"It will not be necessary because you are not confessing. Now suppose you tell me what has you in such a state."

Her frustration was growing with his refusal to take her seriously. "I have been fretting over your confession from the first. I have never liked the idea of you taking the blame. Had you not come to St. Claire, had I not lied about who I am, you would never have been involved in any of this. Barrett merely reaped what he sowed. And, had he lived another few days, 'tis likely I *would* have killed him."

He shook his head to deny her words. "I never would have let you. Killing…leaves a stain on your soul. I am so tarnished now, Elise, that Barrett's death scarcely added a speck of dust. But you? No, I could never let you live with that."

"But you would let me live with *this?*" She opened her clenched fist to show him the single white orchid that had been delivered with his calling card, bearing the words *Think of me…* on the back. "Think of you? I think of nothing else! Can you not see that I would rather die than live with the guilt of *your* death on my soul?"

Lockwood's face hardened. "Bedamned, madam! Do not do this to me! Are things not painful enough already?"

She started to rise but he pulled her back down beside him. "I have confessed. Leave it alone. Swear it."

"Never. I will shout my guilt from the gallery at Old Bailey, if I must. You cannot stop me."

"I bloody well can!" He pulled her against him, cupped the back of her head with one hand and kissed her until she stopped struggling.

"Let me do this, Elise," he whispered, his breath hot in her ear. "Let me redeem my ruined life by freeing you. This may be the only thing that can save my soul."

How could she deny him? But how could she let him go? If he would not listen to reason… She fumbled with the knots and folds of his cravat.

"What are you doing, Elise?"

"I will not let you go without—"

He tightened his arms around her and stood. "God help me, I know I should send you away, but I am not that strong." He grappled with the fastenings of her gown as she clung to him, so dizzy with passion that she could not stand steadily.

When the black silk slid to the floor with a soft hiss, her heartbeat sped. He unfastened the tapes of her chemise next, and then the drawstring of her pantalettes and they pooled around her ankles. He stood back to appraise her and waves of heat washed through her lower abdomen at the admiration in his gaze. Her knees nearly buckled.

She reached out to him, wanting to have his skin next to hers, and he helped her, as anxious as she. With each new expanse of flesh exposed to her, her pulse rate quickened. She wanted him with an intensity she could scarcely contain. She wanted to know every inch of his skin, every muscle, every scar, everything that made him who he was.

And then they were lying tangled on the sofa, his teeth tugging her earlobe, his hands cupping her bottom as he drew her up to him. She burned to have him inside her, but she could not make him hurry. He would not let her.

He bent to nibble at her aroused breasts and she arched to him. He ignored that invitation, and slid lower still. She wanted to be shocked by the things he did to her then, wanted to deny him or to be repulsed. But he was making her frantic with longing, begging her to surrender, praising her beauty and urging her to breathe and relax. How could she relax when her every nerve was stretched to the snapping point?

When she could not bear the tension any longer, she dragged him upward by his hair and tumbled him over. If he would not give her what she needed, she would take it. She straddled him and he moaned when she lowered herself on him. He held her waist, guiding her, holding her gaze, his handsome face a study in strain. She found his rhythm and matched him, building, soaring until something inside her burst and bloomed, leaving her shattered.

"Think of *me*…" she whispered as he poured his passion into her.

Charlie burst into Hunt's office, his face split by a grin. "I've got it, Hunt! The list is done. You will not believe what I've found."

Hunt looked up. "Sit down, Charlie."

His brother took the chair across from him and dropped an armload of ledgers on the desk. He opened one on top of another until they covered every available inch. "Look through those and see how I figured it out. I thought you were crazy and just trying to keep me out of the way when you told me to trace money, but you were right. It's all there."

"I'll look through it later. I have a meeting with Lord Eastman in an hour."

"But I thought this was urgent."

"It is. Summarize, then, and I will look at the ledgers when I return." He sat back in his chair and sighed. Charlie was going to relish every moment of telling his tale. Hunt stifled a yawn, almost wishing he'd gotten some sleep last night, but he wouldn't have missed Elise's passion for anything. Still, he needed a cup of coffee to wake him up.

"I've got the names you wanted."

"Doyle," he guessed.

Charlie nodded. "And a few others. And one surprise. Well, it was a surprise to me, but perhaps not to you."

"Oh, for God's sake, Charlie! Just tell me."

"Everything started to come clear when I compared the insurance and investment records with the bank records. I could eliminate most names as coincidence. Auberville is one of those."

Hunt had never considered Auberville a viable suspect. He nodded for Charlie to continue.

"I also eliminated the two Lloyd's names. That left us with Gavin Doyle, Lord Eastman and Edward Langford."

Not possible. Eastman? He had wondered, but he always came back to one inescapable fact—why would Eastman request an outside agent to investigate this matter if he was involved? He had known they were looking at bank records, and thus he had to know they'd find those deposits. Had Hunt been too hasty in assigning Doyle the blame of hiring someone to kill him? Had it been— "Eastman? Are you sure, Charlie?"

"Positive. You see, according to the bank, deposits were recorded after insurance payoffs, investments returned, and one more thing."

"Out with it, Charlie," Hunt groaned.

"From the Lloyd's list of dates that ships were pirated, I made one last comparison. Only the men on that list recorded deposits every single time a ship was pirated—even if they hadn't invested in *or* insured it. Every single time, Hunt. But Eastman's participation only dates to this past September."

"Too much for coincidence," he conceded. He closed the top ledger and tapped it with his finger. "Does anyone else know about this?"

"Just us."

"You can tell Auberville and Ethan, but no one else until I've verified the facts. If anyone asks, you're still working on the problem. Understand?"

It was Charlie's turn to nod as he stood and headed for the door. "Are you still going to meet with Lord Eastman?"

"Wouldn't miss it," Hunt muttered before the door closed.

Something about Charlie's findings troubled him and he pulled the ledgers toward him, running his finger down columns. Yes, Charlie was right. There were far too many deposits for these men than could be accounted for by coincidence. The one thing Charlie hadn't mentioned was that Doyle's accounts were diminishing. He had withdrawn large sums of money intermittently ever since his return to London. Blackmail payments? Gambling debts?

He looked at the column with dates and noted that Eastman's deposits had begun almost the same day Hunt had left for St. Claire. But he was still troubled by the Langford name. Where had he heard it?

He unlocked his middle drawer and withdrew his file on the case. Nothing was in order and he'd scribbled a few notes on miscellaneous scraps of paper before he'd departed for St. Claire. Names, addresses and directions along with leads, impressions and conclusions were jumbled together, but he found the notes from his first meeting with Eastman.

And there it was. Langford. Eastman's clerk. He recalled now that Eastman had told him he could go through Langford if he had anything urgent. He closed the file, returned it to the drawer and turned the lock. If Eastman was the leak, the whole secrecy issue had been a pretense. And why would he order an investigation of himself?

Hunt stood and retrieved his greatcoat from a peg. He had one final question.

* * *

Back in the same lounge where his assignment had begun nearly four months ago, Hunt put his newspaper aside and took a drink from his stout cup of coffee. The clock in the foyer struck half eleven. Eastman was late.

He was about to leave when the undersecretary rushed in, looking harried. He dropped into the chair facing Hunt and leaned forward, looking over both shoulders before he spoke.

"Have you heard the news? Good God! When will it end?"

"When will what end?"

"It's Bascombe. He's dead."

Of all the things that might have put Eastman in a dither, Hunt had not expected that. The governor had appeared well when he'd last seen him, but if Eastman had heard the news so quickly, Bascombe must have died shortly after Hunt left the island. He remembered the man's florid complexion and asked, "Apoplexy?"

"Murder."

Murder. Had Bascombe betrayed his partners? Then why was Eastman nearly stricken by the news? "Do you know how it happened?"

"No one knows. His clerk reported that he found Bas-combe in the foyer of his mansion. He'd been knifed in the middle of the night. No one heard anything. They think he must have come in late and the murderer was waiting. Or that he answered a late caller himself instead of waking the servants."

"Is that all you were told?"

Eastman shook his head and waved one arm dismissively. "Some rubbish about a black-sailed ship making port after dark and leaving before dawn. Twaddle. An outrageous excuse by the local constabulary to cover their incompetence."

Hunt met Eastman's glance. "I've seen that ship, Eastman. It is not the first time it's made port in San Marco. Previously,

I believe the locals were paid to look the other way while it took on supplies. That was the schooner I saw in Blackpool."

"Pirates? Bascombe was killed by pirates?"

"Just a guess," he said. But it was a good guess and gave rise to another question. What had the governor done to enrage the pirates enough to take the great risk of sailing into San Marco and sending someone to the governor's mansion to kill him? And who was issuing orders, with Rodrigo gone? "When will you get another report?"

"The next packet due from those parts should arrive a fortnight hence."

Hunt leaned forward and lowered his voice. "When you asked me to take this job, you told me that no one in the Foreign Office knew about it, because you feared a leak. But you told me that in case of an emergency, I should contact you through your clerk. A Mr. Langford?"

Eastman nodded. "That's right."

"So Langford knows about my investigation? And he knows everything else that passes through your hands?"

"Well…" Eastman hedged. "Not everything."

Hunt stopped right there. One way or another, both Langford and Eastman were involved. But to what extent? Until he could unravel this knot, he could not trust anyone.

Eastman braced himself by taking a glass of sherry from a footman and then waving him away. "One more thing," he whispered. "Doyle is being appointed governor and being sent back to St. Claire."

"When does he leave?"

"Day after tomorrow."

Blast! He would have to work fast.

Elise folded a nightgown and put it away in a bureau. A trunk containing the items on the list she'd given Lockwood had been delivered earlier in the morning. Sarah's maid was pressing her black bombazine mourning gown and a few other items.

She felt a little silly, though. With Barrett dead, she should have gone back to the house. Surely Lockwood was wrong. How could she still be in danger when the greatest threat to her life and sanity was now lying in a coffin?

Oh, but at a price she never would have paid!

Hunt. Surely she was entitled to think of him as "Hunt" after last night? Her limbs weakened with the memory. What could she do? He'd already confessed to a murder that was, in fact, her fault. Had she not come to Sarah for help after Barrett's last attack, had she not told Hunt what had happened… Then it would have happened again. And again. Hunt had paid the price for her freedom.

Tears welled in her eyes and she blinked them away. Now was not the time for weakness. No matter what Hunt said, the moment William was safe and she had petitioned the court to appoint a suitable guardian, she would confess to the murder. She would insist that he had accepted the blame in a mistaken act of chivalry and she would claim responsibility.

And William would be raised without a mother or a father.

There were no good decisions for her but to preserve her honor. And to free Hunt.

A soft knock at her door pulled her from her introspection. "Come in," she called.

A maid curtsied. "My lady, Lord Lockwood is below and requests your company."

Her heartbeat tripped, as it always did when she thought of seeing Hunt. She patted her hair into place and smoothed her gown before hurrying down to the sitting room.

He turned from the fireplace as she entered the room and smiled. She felt a telltale heat sweep up from her middle all the way to the roots of her hair. He was remembering last night. And so was she. And if he did not stop looking at her that way, it would happen again. "Lord Lockwood," she said, dropping a quick curtsy.

He laughed. "The maid is gone, madam, and so is my sister. 'Tis I who should give the bow." He came to her and pulled her into his arms, and his heat seeped into her. How would she ever live without him?

When she looked up at him, he dropped a tender kiss on her lips and then held her away with a sigh. "None of that at the moment, my dear. I fear I might disgrace us in my sister's sitting room. How would we ever live *that* down?"

Elise could only imagine the teasing he would endure in such a case. She smiled as she sat on the sofa. "I think we have much more to live down than a tiny indiscretion in your sister's sitting room, Hunt. But why have you come in the middle of the day?"

Hunt sat beside her and took her hands. Oh, dear. Nothing good came of it when he did that. She braced herself and waited.

"I met with Lord Eastman of the Foreign Office this morning and he informed me that Governor Bascombe has been murdered."

She took a moment to comprehend the news. She hadn't known him well, but the governor had been kind to her. "Who would do such a thing?"

"We have reason to believe it was someone from Blackpool. And we believe it was on someone else's orders."

"Who?"

"Elise, I know you have a fondness for him, but—"

"Mr. Doyle," she guessed.

He nodded.

"Surely you are mistaken. Why would Mr. Doyle order such a thing? I never heard him say anything derogatory about the governor and never saw the slightest enmity."

"I would stake my life on the fact that he is involved in the surge of piracy in the eastern Caribbean. Doyle killed Bascombe to gain the governorship, and now that he has it, there will be no impediment to him doing as he pleases on the island."

"Governor? I wonder if that is what he meant when he hinted that he might not be going to India after all. That he had other possibilities."

"When did he tell you that, Elise?"

She frowned, trying to remember. So much had happened in the last few days that she could not recall exactly when. "A few days ago. Three? Four?"

"The news only just arrived in London this morning," Hunt said.

"Mr. Doyle? But that is preposterous." But was it? "Hunt, there was a man from Blackpool who used to buy pastries when he came for supplies. His name was Mr. Lowe, and he said the 'charge man' liked sweets. But he always laughed when he said those words, and I recall thinking he meant something else entirely. Could he have meant chargé?"

"I wish I had known this, Elise. Yes, he could have meant just that. What else do you remember?"

She remembered Governor Bascombe sitting behind his desk and agreeing to oversee the transfer of titles. "He was a good man. I wish I could have done more…." The letter! Heavens! She had forgotten entirely about it. The shock of finding Barrett alive and of not finding William had completely erased any memory of it. "A moment, please," she told Hunt as she stood and ran from the sitting room.

Upstairs in her bedroom, Elise found her writing box sitting where she'd unpacked it. She had not had time to remove the dust it had accumulated during its storage in the attic, but it appeared entirely undisturbed. Barrett would have had no interest in anything she would have written previous to her return. She opened it and lifted the pen tray to find the sealed oilskin pouch. She stared at it for a moment, wondering what to do, then moaned with the fear that it could contain something that might have saved the governor's life, had she only delivered it in time.

Back in the sitting room, she placed the packet in Hunt's hands. He looked at the address, then back at her. "How did you get this, Elise?"

"Governor Bascombe asked me to deliver it upon my arrival here. I…forgot. And now it is too late."

"Why did he give it to you and not put it in the courier's pouch?"

"He said it was personal and did not want it sitting on a clerk's desk waiting to be delivered. I swore I would deliver it to Lord Eastman at once—to put it in his hands only. I failed him, Hunt." She sank onto the sofa beside him. "What if there is something in there that could have saved him?"

"Nothing could have saved him, Elise. Doyle must have given the order for Bascombe's murder before he got on that ship. Perhaps before Bascombe even gave you the letter."

She hoped that were true. She could not bear to have another death on her conscience.

"And I think it may be best that you never delivered this." With an apologetic glance, he broke the seal, opened the packet and withdrew a single sheet of paper.

"But, Lord Eastman—"

He read the letter, then read it a second time. His face was less troubled when he looked back at her. "I will take it to him, Elise. He will need to see this. Is there anything else?"

"I…from the day I saw him skating on the canal, Mr. Doyle has been asking about anything I might have brought from St. Claire. Any souvenir or keepsake. I thought it was because Captain Gilbert had died…."

Hunt cursed and stood, going to look out the window. "Doyle killed Gilbert for this letter. He thought the governor had given it to him. He has been searching for it since."

The robbery! Barrett's papers riffled. And it had been Mr. Doyle looking for that little packet safely tucked in the attic? "When he came to pay his respects yesterday, he asked me if there was anything he could fetch me from my house. And he asked again about the things I'd brought from the island."

Hunt turned back to her. "Listen to me, Elise. If he thinks you have the letter, he will not hesitate to kill you for it. Do not be alone with him, whatever you do. Turn him away if he calls again. This is the last piece," he held up the letter. "I think we have everything we need to make a case for treason, now. But it will take a day or two to put it together. I'll go to Eastman now and put it in his lap. Then I will be back this evening. Meantime…"

Elise stood as he came toward her. "Yes?"

He slipped his arms around her and kissed her deeply, as he'd done last night, until she was weak and senseless. "Think of me."

Chapter Twenty-Four

Hunt had not thought it possible to crowd even more people into his tiny office, but somehow they fit. Auberville, Travis, Charlie, Eastman and Andrew stood lounging against bookshelves, walls and cabinets, listening in rapt attention as he finished his story.

Eastman reached out for the letter Hunt had just read aloud. "So Bascombe suspected Doyle all along? Why the hell didn't he tell me?"

"He couldn't trust the courier pouch. He knew Doyle, as the chargé d'affaires, also had access to that pouch. The only thing he could think to do was request that he be re-assigned. I suppose he thought if Doyle was in some other part of the world, he would forget about piracy. And without him on the island to pass the information to Rodrigo, the whole operation would fall apart, thus solving the problem."

"So Langford, as my clerk, could copy shipping schedules, routes, bills of lading, and any other useful particulars—thus from Langford to Doyle to Rodrigo. The men be damned!"

"It is worse than that. I believe Doyle planned the whole

thing years ago, just after his first assignment on St. Claire. He saw the potential and seized the opportunity.

"And they were ready to blackmail you," Hunt added with a grin. "I nearly believed it. When Charlie showed me the deposits into your account, I could think of no other reason. Then I noted that the deposits were all recent. You see, from the time Doyle knew he was going to be sent home, he was planning to return. He arranged for Bascombe to be killed, and should anything happen to Rodrigo, Sieyes would take over. And all with scarcely an interruption in their scheme."

Eastman looked thunderstruck. "Is that what those deposits were for? I thought it was an error and would be corrected."

Hunt took the letter back. "I'd like to keep this for the time being. I have reason to believe that Doyle killed Captain Gilbert looking for this. And I think he made more than one attack on Lady Barrett—one on St. Claire, and one just two nights ago at Thackery's. He would be the one who told Rodrigo that Layton was a spy, and that we were coming to Blackpool. And he hired a killer here in London to put me out of his way. He wants this letter, gentlemen, and he is going to have to come to me to get it."

"Good work, Lockwood," Eastman said. "I am off to arrest Langford."

"Not yet, if you please. Keep your eye on him. Have him followed. But do not let him know we have discovered his game. I do not want anything alerting Doyle that we are on to him. Once I've found him, we'll arrest Langford."

"Be careful," Auberville warned. "Seems to me you are painting a target on your chest by keeping that letter."

Hunt nodded. "That is my plan."

There was a knock and Andrew, closest to the door, opened it. Harry Richardson was standing there, a handsome young boy at his side. His dark hair and wide green eyes were so like Elise's that Hunt felt a tug at his heart.

Harry grinned. "See, lad? I told you there'd be a party."

"We had him," Sarah said, a scowl marring her pretty face. "We knew exactly where he was. And then, when Mr. Renquist went back to fetch him, *poof!* He was gone."

Elise took a deep breath and braced herself, all Barrett's threats coming back to haunt her. *My brother knows where he is, and he knows what to do if anything happens to me.* "Where was he, Sarah?"

"Just out of town, with…your brother."

Her brother? Oh, how could he? But she knew quite well how he could. Money. Everything had always come down to that for Franklin Clarke. But would he actually harm William? That would be stooping low, even for Franklin.

"Do you have any idea where he might have hidden him? Any place he would feel safe in leaving him?"

Elise shook her head. "Did he say anything?"

Sarah wouldn't meet her eyes. "He said, 'Good riddance to the boy.'"

She wished she could tear at her hair, scream her frustration to the heavens or raise Barrett from the dead and make him tell her what he'd done with William. Instead, she stood up from her dressing table and went to look out her window at the sound of a coach arriving. Pray it was Hunt! She needed him now—his solid strength, his undaunted determination, his calm reassurance that everything would come aright.

Though night had fallen, the streetlamp was bright enough for her to see the Lockwood crest. She was about to turn and go downstairs to greet him when she saw him reach back into the coach and lift something out.

And there, beneath the streetlamp, Hunt knelt in front of a

little boy, straightened the lapels of his jacket and smoothed his unruly brown hair. She covered her mouth to silence her sob of joy. Then Hunt held the boy's shoulders as he spoke, and the boy nodded and threw his arms around Hunt's neck.

Elise's heart swelled and she nearly burst with love for both these men.

Beside her, Sarah gave her a quick hug. "Thank heavens! Go to them, Elise."

She raced down the stairs just as the butler opened the door and Hunt walked in.

"Mama!" William cried and ran into her arms. "I missed you so much!"

"William!" she sobbed. She looked into Hunt's eyes, unable to speak for utter joy. He smiled at her and nodded.

"Mama, Hunt says I am to stay with you now. May I?"

"Yes. Forever, Will."

Hunt slipped one arm around her and the other around William, ushering them toward the small private parlor in the back of the house, Sarah trailing behind with a beaming smile.

"And he says that I am Lord Barrett now."

"Yes, that is so," she said, wondering what else Hunt had told him. She did not have to wait long to find out.

"And that Papa is with God now?"

She hesitated, then nodded. "Yes, William. Does that make you sad?"

William regarded her somberly, looking much too old for his eight years. "I think we will be better without him. He was not very nice to us."

She coughed to hide her laugh of relief.

"And Hunt says we will not be going back to St. Claire?"

She shook her head.

"And he says that, if I go wash up, I can have tarts, but not as good as the ones you used to make."

She met Hunt's amused gaze. "He told you a great many things, it would seem."

"Yes, but I am not supposed to tell." William smiled at Hunt. "It's a surprise."

"Shh." Hunt placed a finger over his lips. "Later." He turned and indicated Sarah with a sweep of his hand. "This is my sister, Sarah. If you will follow her, she will show you where to wash up and then take you to the kitchen. Are you hungry?"

"Oh, yes! Very. I have not eaten since this morning. Where will you be, Mama?"

"Right here, Will." She watched as Sarah led him out the door and closed it quietly behind her.

Then she turned and threw her arms around Hunt, releasing all the emotion she'd held in check. "Thank you, thank you," she cried. "How will I ever repay you?"

"I can think of dozens of ways, madam. Dozens. And they all start with this." He kissed her very thoroughly and then held her at arm's length. "Now sit, so I can think."

She sat in a dainty chair and folded her hands in her lap, thinking how completely she would thank him later.

"You and William should go to Barrett's funeral tomorrow."

"But—"

"He is not too young, and you are not too delicate. It is important that society sees you grieving. After talking with William, I believe he needs to know that it is over. He needs to say goodbye to his father in a very real manner."

Of course he did. Why had she not thought of that? "And do you really think it appropriate that I be there?"

"Given that you are escorting your son, I think society will understand that, however distraught you may be, your duty to your son comes first. My brothers will all be there to support you, as will I."

"You do not have to do that, Hunt. I have faced censure before, you know."

"Unfairly, madam. And never again, if I have anything to say about it. But I must know if there is anything I can do, any detail I can manage for you in the next two days."

"Two days?" Oh! He was going to surrender himself to the authorities! She shook her head. "I…I was going to ask you to bring the miniature of William, but you have brought the real thing. I want for nothing." Nothing but him.

A furrow formed between his eyebrows. "Miniature? You mean the portrait you…"

"Hit Barrett with? Yes. That is the one."

He gave her an odd look, was silent a long moment and then asked, "Where was it when you last saw it, Elise?"

"I…dropped it on the floor. I was standing near the fireplace, I think. Did you see it?"

"You did not leave it…with Barrett?"

"After he fell, I dropped it and went to my dressing room. I was afraid he would wake before I could leave. He would have killed me, I think."

He let out a long breath and shook his head. "Bloody hell! This changes everything, Elise. I thought…never mind what I thought. Mr. Doyle owed Barrett money, did he not?"

"Yes. I believe he had paid most of his debts, but a few might have been outstanding. I warned him not to gamble with Barrett. I have never known my husband to forgive a debt."

"If you please, Elise, could you stop referring to him as your husband?"

"My late husband?"

"Better." He gave her a rueful smile. "Much better. I did not kill him, my dear."

A sick feeling followed relief. "Oh, then I—"

"And neither did you." He dropped a kiss on the top of her head and went to the door. "I have urgent business. I will see you tomorrow."

Elise could read William's fidgeting and inattention quite well. He found his father's funeral boring. He kept turning in his seat to look at Hunt and his brothers, several pews back. At one point, he had leaned toward her and whispered, "Hunt is going to take me fishing on his estate when spring comes."

"Shh," she told him and squeezed his hand.

Outside in the frost-laden air, William endured a few pats on the head and then excused himself to go into the graveyard to wait for the coffin. She hoped he would use the interim to run off some of his pent-up energy, then said a silent prayer of gratitude for the resilience of youth.

And now, as she stood near the churchyard gate, men came forward one by one to offer their condolences. And such strange condolences! The usual, "He will be missed" was absent, as was, "Such a great loss." Instead, they would take her hand and offer a weak, "I hope you are getting on well, madam."

Though Barrett had had a great many acquaintances, he'd had few, if any, real friends, it seemed. His habit of buying people and ruthlessly stripping his gambling victims of their possessions had garnered him no genuine affection.

Still standing on the church steps, the Hunter brothers watched her closely lest Mr. Doyle accost her in public—an unnecessary precaution, she was certain. Hunt, more intent than the others, hovered nearby. She was certain that his less-than-subtle presence would be remarked upon tonight over dinner tables.

Led by the minister, hired pallbearers carried the coffin down the stairs and toward the churchyard gate. A solemn hush fell. Elise followed the pallbearers, and was in turn followed by the others. As they drew close to the open grave, she looked around for William. He should be at her side for this last ritual, but she did not see him.

A glance at Hunt told her that he was thinking the same thing. He separated himself from his brothers and disappeared as the minister began the readings. Within a few minutes, her anxiety was rising alarmingly, and when Hunt reappeared alone, she was near to panic.

"Amen," the minister intoned.

"Amen," those gathered behind her answered.

She turned to see if William had come from that direction, but still did not spot him. The men tipped their hats and turned to go. Ignoring the minister who offered his hand in comfort, she hurried to Hunt.

"Where is he?" she asked, hating the edge of hysteria in her voice.

Hunt gripped her arms as his brothers surrounded them. "He will not hurt William, Elise. He would not dare."

"M-Mr. Doyle?" she guessed.

He nodded and put a folded paper in her hand.

My dear Lady Barrett,

Please excuse my lack of protocol, but simplicity seems best. I want the packet Governor Bascombe gave you. You want your son. I suggest a trade. Meet me at Black Friars Bridge tonight at midnight. Come alone and do not think to cross me, or the lad goes over the bridge. Does he swim, madam? Do you?

The note was not signed, but she could not mistake the sender. Mr. Doyle. She looked up at Hunt, her hand trembling so badly that the single page fluttered in the still air.

"Hold fast, Elise. And have no doubt we will win out."

"We? But I am going alone."

"We shall see about that."

Elise could not see the middle of Black Friars Bridge as she started across, keeping to the footway. By midnight the temperature had dropped well below freezing. The fog rolling off the Thames mingled with smoke from coal fires, muffling sounds and obscuring her vision. The air was so thick that she could barely hear her own footsteps.

The utter silence and isolation were unnerving. Late at night, in weather this foul, people did not venture abroad, and Mr. Doyle would be able to do as he pleased without fear of discovery. Pray that he would let William go. She felt for the oilskin packet again, snugly stuffed in her bodice.

Hunt had argued with her, warning her of the folly of meeting a murderer alone, but she had been adamant. She would not risk William's life. He had scowled at her, dropped the packet on her lap and departed Sarah's house without another word. She had never seen him so angry.

There was a scuffling sound ahead of her. Her heart leaped into her throat and she stopped in fear. Had she reached the middle? "William?" she called.

Another muffled sound, and then a laugh.

"W-William?" she asked again.

"Did you bring it, madam?" a disembodied voice asked.

She shivered. "Did you bring William?"

A dark form materialized in the fog and then grew larger, though not yet distinct. Fear, never very far from her since she'd set out tonight, grew and became a palpable thing.

"He is here, madam," the voice replied.

She recognized the voice as Mr. Doyle's now, but it carried a note of repressed fury that she'd never heard before. The tone made her painfully aware of how vulnerable she was and she realized that Hunt had been right. She should have let him come with her. Too late now.

The single figure emerged from the fog and became two. Mr. Doyle was pushing William ahead of him on the footway as a shield. They were mere feet away by the time they became distinct. He had gagged William so he could not call out, and bound his hands in front of him. His eyes were terrified and every instinct told Elise to kill Mr. Doyle. Alas, she had nothing to use against him but the oilskin packet.

"Let him go," she demanded.

"The letter?"

She pulled her cloak open, withdrew the packet from her bodice and held it up for him to see. "I have it. Now let him go."

Mr. Doyle moved next to the stone balustrade. "Let us not play games, madam. Bring me the letter or say goodbye to the little viscount, eh?"

He was mad. She could hear it in his voice.

She held the packet out to him, trying to draw him away from the edge. "Here it is. Bring William to me."

He began to lift William toward the edge. "I warned you, madam. No games."

"No!" she screamed. "Put him down, Mr. Doyle. Here! Here it is."

Hunt heard Elise's voice, muffled through the dense fog. She was pleading with someone, entreating him. Blast! Too late to intercept her. She'd already met Doyle.

He proceeded cautiously, determined to give Doyle no reason to bolt. And, please God, no reason to throw William over the side. Of all his cases, of all the ugly things he'd seen and done, this was the only situation in which a child's life had been at stake.

Doyle was a conscienceless killer, and he'd begun to lose

his grip on sanity. God alone knew what he was capable of. William, Elise, Hunt himself—all were mere inconveniences to him. He truly did not realize that, even without the letter, he had been found out. Perhaps the other evidence was circumstantial and could not prove his guilt in a court of law without Bascombe's letter, but—

He turned and held one hand out, palm first, to stop Auberville and Travis. "Stay back, out of sight," he whispered. "If Doyle sees you, the game is over."

They nodded, their faces somber and anxious.

He went forward again until Elise's back appeared out of the fog. She was pleading with Doyle, a note of panic in her voice. He could not trust his instincts. Elise was too important to him. If he lost her as he'd lost Layton, he couldn't live with it. Nor could he sacrifice William.

He touched her shoulder and she whirled to him, then spun back to see what Doyle would do.

And what he did shocked them both. He placed William on the edge of the balustrade. Bound and gagged, William had no possible way to keep his own balance. Only Doyle's hand on his shoulder kept him safe. He would sink like a rock in the frigid water below.

"Hold a moment, Doyle. Think, man. We already know everything—about what you've done. You cannot get away with any of this. It will only make you look like a villain if you let young William go over the side."

Doyle glanced at William, one hand still clamped over his shoulder. "You know nothing, Lockwood. But you've just condemned young William here."

"I *do* know," Hunt said quickly, keeping Doyle's attention. "I know that you are behind the piracy on St. Claire. I know that you had Bascombe killed so that you could return there and continue your operation. I know that Langford was your contact in the Foreign Office. He is in custody now, Doyle. It's over."

Doyle's eyes took on a mad look and William teetered on the edge as he pulled a pistol from his greatcoat pocket. "You don't know the half of what I've done."

Hunt stepped in front of Elise and held his hand up in a conciliatory gesture as he took one guarded step forward. "I know that it was you who threw the rock at Elise when she appealed for a patent for Gilbert, because she interfered with your access to the courier's pouch. How else were you to get the information you needed? Then you sent word to Rodrigo that Layton was a spy. They killed him first and were coming for me when I escaped."

Behind him, Elise gasped. He could not let her interfere now. Doyle had almost forgotten her. He pressed forward another step. A few more and he'd be within reach of William. "And 'twas you who tipped that pot onto Elise at Thackery's to get her out of the way before she found Bascombe's letter, and hired a thug to kill me when I got too close."

"You are too clever by half, Lockwood. Seems as if you do know almost everything. But I still have a few secrets. And if I cannot have the governorship, I shall at least escape with enough to make me comfortable on the continent."

Hunt ignored Doyle's comment to keep his attention. "But the most ingenious thing you did was to kill Barrett after I was seen threatening him. Damn clever, that—have me arrested for murder, search Barrett's house for Bascombe's letter and reclaim your debts, all in one bold stroke. Should have worked. Too bad it did not."

"I got my vowels back, Lockwood, and the infamous Barrett jewels. I couldn't believe my luck when I found that bastard lying on the floor. He was just coming around, but he never will again." Doyle laughed and the crazed sound sent chills down Hunt's back.

He could see the desperation in the dilated eyes and knew instinctively what Doyle planned to do. But he was not close enough yet.

"I even know that you killed your aunt for your inheritance." That, more than anything else he'd said, disconcerted Doyle. Knowing it would be his last chance, he lunged for William.

Too late. The little boy tumbled into the fog.

A shot echoed in the night and Elise screamed. Fire ripped along Hunt's left arm, tearing a hole through his greatcoat and jacket. He heard running and knew Travis and Auberville were close. He went down on one knee and withdrew his dagger from his boot as Doyle turned to run, supremely confident that Hunt and Elise would be distracted.

Elise. My God! Had the ball hit her, too? A blind rage filled him and he lunged for Doyle. They tumbled together and Hunt twisted behind him, knowing his left arm would fail him soon. He'd get one chance, and then be at Doyle's mercy. With the last of his strength, he drew the blade across Doyle's neck.

Panting, he looked up to see Elise climbing over the balustrade. "Elise! No!"

Her pause was enough for him to get to her, seize her around the waist and drag her back. Sobbing, she struggled until he leaned over the edge and shouted.

"Charlie? Drew?"

"We've got him!" Charlie's voice came to them. "Drew is wrapping him in blankets now. Meet us at the embankment."

"A boat?" She looked up at him in wonder. "You planned all this?"

He grinned. "You did not think I would leave anything to chance, did you?"

Then she saw the blood-soaked rip in his jacket. Her face paled. "Hunt…"

"A scratch. I'll have it seen to once we're home."

Auberville stood from his examination of Doyle. "Dead," he confirmed.

Hunt nodded. Doyle would never kill again. And neither would he. He was finished. Tomorrow, he'd tender his resignation—this time, for good. "Get the coach, pick up Charlie, Andrew and William and come back for us," he told them. "Then, if you wouldn't mind, could one of you stay with the body until the night watch arrives?"

When they were alone, Hunt slipped his good arm around her and kissed the top of her head. "Thank God Doyle did not harm you. When I formed this plan, that was the one thing I couldn't plan for."

She tightened her arms around his waist and came up on her toes to fit her lips against his. "But you are sure of my love? Because I love you to total distraction."

He sighed, relishing those amazing words and the heat of her body against his in the freezing night. He couldn't let her go again. Not for a single minute. "What say you, Elise? Shall we throw caution and propriety to the winds and risk one last indiscretion? To hell with banns and mourning. Marry me. Tomorrow. And devil take the consequences."

Elise laughed, then gave him her answer and a promise for the future in the most delectable way.

Epilogue

∞◦◦∞

April 3, 1821

The baby's cries echoed through the long corridors, piercing the silence with shrillness. Elise lifted the hem of her gown, ran up the third flight of stairs and turned toward the nursery. A baby's cry always terrified her.

A lump formed in her throat as she followed the sound, hoping, praying, that she could calm her niece before she disturbed the entire house. Sarah had warned her that Violette was a colicky baby, but nothing had prepared her for the reality.

The sound suddenly stopped and the eerie silence returned. Elise halted and caught her breath, listening. What had happened to stop Violette's cries? Oh! She had not stopped breathing, had she? This time she did not stop running until she burst through the nursery door.

Panic nearly clogged her throat as she saw a man bending over the crib. And then he turned around.

Hunt was cradling Violette in his left arm and letting her chew on his right knuckle as he made soothing sounds. He looked up from the baby and met her gaze.

"Shh," he whispered. "She's almost asleep again. She just needed a little comforting."

Elise nodded and went to look down at the peaceful little girl. Her face screwed up into a grimace, working into another cry.

She held her breath as she looked into Hunt's face. He was smiling as he shifted the bundle to his shoulder. Actually smiling. He winked at her as if he suspected what she'd been afraid of. And then it occurred to her that she'd never have to be afraid of a baby's cry again. Never.

"Good practice for us, wouldn't you say?" he asked as he dropped his gaze to the small swell just becoming apparent at her waistline.

She nodded again, marveling that a man like Hunt—a man who had brought an end to a murderous pirate scheme, who had found the strength to do the dreadful jobs that other men shirked from, who had nearly sacrificed his own soul—could be so patient and tender. Her eyes filled with tears at the wonder of it.

He eased Violette back into the crib, pulled the blanket over her and then bent to lift Elise in his arms to carry her back to their bed.

She could not help but think how far she had come in the past few months. From isolation and fear to friends and acceptance. From uncertainty to security. But most importantly, from loneliness to love.

No more hesitation, no more doubts and, please, God, no more indiscretions....

* * * * *

On sale 1st June 2007

ROGUE'S SALUTE
by Jennifer Blake

They are the most dangerous men in New Orleans,
skilled swordsmen who play by no rules but their
own – heroes to some, wicked to many, irresistible
to the women they love…

At ease making life-and-death decisions between breaths,
maître d'armes Nicholas Pasquale proposes marriage to a
beautiful and desperate stranger. She's a challenge
he can't resist.

Though pledged to the church since infancy,
Juliette Armant must save her family in the only way
possible…by marriage.

A practical arrangement, which someone is desperate to
prevent. But practical turns to heady desire when a rogue's
kiss unleashes the sensual woman within…

MILLS & BOON

Historical

On sale 1st June 2007

Regency

THE RAKE'S PROPOSAL
by Sarah Elliott

Katherine Sutcliff would bring a scandalous secret to the
marriage bed. She needed a suitable match – so why was
she distracted by her most unsuitable attraction to the
disreputable Lord Benjamin Sinclair?

THE KING'S CHAMPION
by Catherine March

With Eleanor's reputation compromised, the King
commands her to marry. Ellie is overjoyed to be tied to her
perfect knight. But Troye is desperate to resist the emotions
she is reawakening in him…

THE HIRED HUSBAND
by Judith Stacy

Rachel Branford is intent on saving her family's name.
And handsome Mitch Kincaid may be the answer! Abandoned
in an orphanage, Mitch has struggled to gain wealth and power.
Until he finds himself tempted by Rachel's money…
then Rachel herself!

THE STEEPWOOD

Scandals

Regency drama, intrigue, mischief...
and marriage

VOLUME SEVEN

Mr Rushford's Honour by Meg Alexander

Gina, Lady Whitelaw left Steepwood as plain Gina
Westcott. Now, years later, she's returned home
– and has to face the man who stole her heart...

An Unlikely Suitor by Nicola Cornick

At three-and-twenty and a bluestocking to boot,
Miss Lavender Brabant feels her chance of marriage
has passed. But now she's met Barnabas Hammond,
a shopkeeper's son!

On sale 4th May 2007

M&B

A young woman disappears.
A husband is suspected of murder.
Stirring times for all the neighbourhood in

THE STEEPWOOD
Scandals

Volume 5 – March 2007
Counterfeit Earl by Anne Herries
The Captain's Return by Elizabeth Bailey

Volume 6 – April 2007
The Guardian's Dilemma by Gail Whitiker
Lord Exmouth's Intentions by Anne Ashley

Volume 7 – May 2007
Mr Rushford's Honour by Meg Alexander
An Unlikely Suitor by Nicola Cornick

Volume 8 – June 2007
An Inescapable Match by Sylvia Andrew
The Missing Marchioness by Paula Marshall

FREE

2 BOOKS AND A SURPRISE GIFT!

We would like to take this opportunity to thank you for reading this Mills & Boon® book by offering you the chance to take TWO more specially selected titles from the Historical Romance™ series absolutely FREE! We're also making this offer to introduce you to the benefits of the Mills & Boon® Reader Service™—

- ★ **FREE home delivery**
- ★ **FREE gifts and competitions**
- ★ **FREE monthly Newsletter**
- ★ **Books available before they're in the shops**
- ★ **Exclusive Reader Service offers**

Accepting these FREE books and gift places you under no obligation to buy; you may cancel at any time, even after receiving your free shipment. Simply complete your details below and return the entire page to the address below. You don't even need a stamp!

YES! Please send me 2 free Historical Romance books and a surprise gift. I understand that unless you hear from me, I will receive 4 superb new titles every month for just £3.69 each, postage and packing free. I am under no obligation to purchase any books and may cancel my subscription at any time. The free books and gift will be mine to keep in any case.

H7ZEE

Ms/Mrs/Miss/Mr..........................Initials ....
BLOCK CAPITALS PLEASE

Surname ....

Address ....

....

....Postcode ....

Send this whole page to:
The Reader Service, FREEPOST CN81, Croydon, CR9 3WZ